The Unicorn Confessions
An Unconventional Romantic Fiction Novel
Cheryl Terra

Bang It Out Writing

Content Warnings

Please note this book is written in Canadian English, which has aspects of spelling from both American and UK English.

I have tried to address potential triggers here without spoiling the story, however if you have concerns about any of the items listed and wish to know more, please reach out to me via email at info@cherylterra.com

This book is intended for mature adults. There are multiple explicit scenes and profanity. This book is categorized as "why choose" and discusses non-traditional relationship structures, including discussions of "unicorn hunting," polyamory, ethical non-monogamy, unethical non-monogamy, and casual sex.

This book deals contains major themes, discussions, or plot points surrounding cheating (not by the main characters and not presented in a positive light), age gap relationships, toxic family situations, lying/deception, and divorces/breakups.

There are moderate mentions of alcohol use, anxiety, pressure to have children, and misogynistic opinions.

There are brief mentions of sexual situations that could be considered by some readers to be dubious consent or traumatizing (involving a situation where a character desires to revoke consent but doesn't). Brief mentions of implied slut-shaming, queerphobia, and racial stereotyping also occur.

Body image and fat positivity are main themes of this book. There are brief mentions of fatphobic situations or comments, but that is not a primary focus of the series and is not internalized by the main character. If you are triggered by fat people celebrating their bodies and viewing themselves as hot, my books are not for you.

Part 1

Confession: Two's a commitment. Three's a good time.

Chapter One

A MAN AND A woman walked into the bar and I immediately knew that I was going to fuck them.

Mostly because they were there to meet me so we could fuck.

But that first meeting could go either way. Sure, I vetted my potential hook ups before even suggesting we meet, and I'd been talking to these two for a week already, but there was always that *risk*. I might have missed something, or they were catfishing, or one of them was trying to cover up their lack of basic hygiene by bathing themselves in some kind of manly fragrance with a name like *Ocean Power Strong Bear Killer Manly Men's Cologne for Men Who Are MEN*.

Though in fairness, that had only happened one time.

But I had a good feeling about these two. Good enough that, as many times as I'd done this, I got that instant spark of excitement, that moment of knowing the high I was chasing was about to be *real*.

I leaned back against the booth, sipping my beer until her eyes danced over the rest of the patrons in the bar and landed on me. Smirking slightly, I lifted my pint glass to her. Her eyebrows raised in recognition and she grinned, then grabbed her boyfriend's arm and tugged him through the bar to the empty seats across from me.

"Tessa?" she asked when she was close enough.

"You caught me," I said, putting my beer down.

The air around her seemed to vibrate with a nervous energy as she extended one hand. "Wow. Hi. I'm... wow. I'm Eva. I'm so, so excited to *finally* meet you. And this is Landon, obviously. We, um, have been chatting with you. So you know. Our names. Already."

Landon, to his credit, seemed less skittish than Eva, though there was still an air of nerves around him as he extended his hand as well. "Hi. I'm... what she said."

I tried not to laugh as I shook each of their hands. "Nice to meet you."

"It is," Landon said. "Nice, I mean. To meet you."

"So," I said once the bullshit pleasantries were completed and they'd slid into the booth across from me. "How did this whole threesome thing come up for you?"

Landon laughed nervously. "Just jumping in right away, eh?"

"Mm-hmm." I sipped my beer. "I'm not super into beating around the bush, but if that's your thing, I'm open to discussing it."

Eva giggled, then ran a hand through her hair. "Well, we like... we like sex. And we like to try new things."

Landon nodded, but didn't say anything. I waited again, my excited spark dimming even further.

"What kinds of things?" I pressed.

Eva looked at Landon again, then nudged him in the ribs. "You tell her."

"Um, like... restraints," he said. "And we've introduced some... toys."

"What kind of toys?" I asked.

He frowned. "What?"

"What kind?" I repeated impatiently. "I need to know what you're into before I agree to this. Like, if you tell me you can't get off without using a giant horse-cock shaped dildo on me, I might have a slight problem with that."

"Uh, no," he said. "Just like... vibrators. Um, butt... butt plugs."

Just as Landon stuttered the last bit of his sentence, the server approached the table. I didn't know the server's name, but he was one of the main reasons I went to Bar One instead of one of the other bars in the area. Short blond hair, a pleasant smile, and a butt that looked so good in dark grey dress pants that it was probably why the bar hadn't changed their staff uniform in as long as I'd been coming here.

I figured that, on the off chance that a couple didn't show, weren't who I thought they were, or simply didn't want to fuck, blowing him in the alley or something would be my backup plan.

You know, so my night wasn't a total waste. But I'd yet to have a need for Plan B, so I still didn't even know his name.

The slightest raising of his eyebrows was the only hint that he'd overheard what Landon had said. That was another reason I always picked this particular booth at this particular bar; this man had developed *quite* the poker face after seeing me in his section every couple of weeks or so over the past few years.

"Okay," I said after the server took their drink orders and left. "So butt plugs. Nothing like... I dunno. Nipple clamps? Anal beads? Ball gags, whips, chains, anything like that?"

Landon looked startled. "No. Is that a problem?"

"Not at all. I enjoy sex. I don't enjoy getting tied up and beaten. Like, you wanna put a butt plug in, go for it. I just don't want to be flogged."

"The... she uses the butt plug," he said.

"Landon!" Eva said.

For fuck's sake.

"I don't think this is going to work," I said.

Eva's jaw dropped. "But—"

"There aren't a lot of women who want to be in this position," I said. "There's a reason it's called being a 'unicorn.' I'm not here to waste my time. I'm here to meet couples, have sex with them, and move on with my life. If you can't even tell me you like to shove some silicone up your ass once in a while without looking completely scandalized, this will not work." I took a swig of my beer, then set the glass down. "So are we talking about this, or am I finally going to learn that server's name and see if he'll let me go down on him in the alley?"

"We haven't even had time to get our drinks yet!" Landon said, annoyance flashing across his face. "Let alone process the fact that you're actually *here*."

"Why wouldn't I be here? And why wouldn't I jump right in?"

He half-laughed, an incredulous look on his face. "This went from 'Hi, my name is Landon' to 'How do you use your *butt plug*' in the space of like, thirty seconds. Excuse me for having some conversational whiplash."

"Landon, stop," Eva finally said, her voice quiet but firm. She put a hand over his and looked up at me, her eyes apologetic. "I didn't expect you to be so... so..."

"What?" I asked flatly.

"Hot," she said in a small voice as her face turned red again.

Which was fair. I *was* hot.

And me knowing that would piss some people off. People don't like it when you admit you're hot. You're supposed to love yourself and be happy with your body and celebrate how beautiful everyone is, but the world only wants to *encourage* you to see yourself as beautiful. The moment you admit you are, they lose the ability to blow smoke up your ass and get something in return because you're just *so grateful* that someone thinks you're beautiful.

Especially when you're not hot in the way that people expected women to be hot. But that was their problem, not mine. My skin was on the pastier side of white, but it was clear and soft. My hair was a disaster combination of wavy with the occasional spiral curl, but it was soft and shiny and dark brown. Polite people would call me curvy. Honest people would call me chubby. I preferred the term "delightfully chunky" solely because the *unk* part of the word made me smile. Regardless of what word was used, I had thick thighs and wide hips and a flat ass and killer legs.

And I, along with all other people of good taste, liked it.

"I mean, your pictures were great, but in person you're... I just..." Eva sighed and let go of Landon's hand. "I didn't expect how flustered I'd get when I saw you. I haven't looked at anyone like *this* since Landon and I got together and it just... I got nervous."

Landon's hand shifted beneath the table and I assumed he'd put it on Eva's leg in a comforting gesture. He looked at me, annoyance giving way to a pleading look. "We didn't know what to expect, okay? We thought we'd have to beg you to consider going through with this."

"Even when my profile specifically said I'm looking for no-strings-attached threesomes?"

"We didn't want to be assholes. Yeah, this is primarily about sex, but we didn't... we didn't just like, pick you out of a catalog to meet our needs. So you caught us a little off-guard." He glanced at Eva, who bit her lip. "But I still want this. If you do."

She nodded. "I just... being with two people at once is new to me. And I don't talk about stuff like this very much. Except with Landon."

Now, they might not have been assholes, but I was.

That said, I wasn't completely heartless.

"Okay," I said. "You're right. I didn't see it that way. But I need you to communicate with me about this stuff. I am who I say I am, you are who you say you are, and I wouldn't have invited you out for a drink if I didn't think this could work. So let's get the rest of the cards on the table, okay?"

"Fine," Landon said. "We got talking about threesomes a few months ago. While we were, uh, doing it."

"Doing it?" I repeated, unimpressed.

I half-expected him to get annoyed again, but he surprised me by laughing and shaking his head. "While we were *fucking*. We were making out and talking dirty when I said I'd love to watch her eat out another woman. And then she blew my mind and said she wanted to watch me fuck another woman."

A grin spread across my face. "There we go. And then?"

"I couldn't stop thinking about it," Eva said. "Normally when guys say they want to watch two girls together, it's so…"

"Performative?" I said when she trailed off.

"Exactly!" she said, looking at me with a relieved camaraderie. "But the way Landon talked about it wasn't. We would go out for dinner or for a walk and see someone attractive and come up with all these scenarios for how we would approach them. Then we'd go home and tell each other all the things we'd do with this hypothetical third person." She looked at Landon. "We've always, like, checked out women together and stuff. But this was different. It started being something that we talked about more while we did it—"

"Fucked," Landon said, his lip twitching as he tried not to laugh, which nearly made me laugh.

Eva rolled her eyes. "We talked about it more while we *fucked*, and it started becoming more than just a fantasy. We wanted to *do* it."

"Have a threesome," Landon clarified. "Not just fuck again."

I had to laugh that time. Eva and Landon finally relaxed and smiled.

And that was when I decided I actually *was* going to fuck them.

I had a list of questions I liked to ask couples, but by the time I got to those questions, I already knew I was going through with it. Now came figuring out the details: limits and boundaries, wants and needs, and of course, my own personal list of rules for successful threesomes.

The only lull in the conversation was when the hot server came back with their drinks. He smiled reassuringly at Eva and gave me an amused look as Landon paid for his beer and then immediately took a long swig of it.

"Anything else for you at the moment?" the server asked in a quiet, polite voice.

Eva shook her head, since Landon was still drinking. "Thank you, though."

The server smiled at her, then Landon, who had finally put his glass down.

"Flag me down if you change your mind," he said. "Otherwise, you three have *fun*."

Eva blinked, I grinned, and Landon brought the pint glass back to his lips and took another giant swig as the server walked away.

"So why do you do this?" Eva asked.

"Have sex?" I asked. "Mostly because it feels good. I dunno. Why does anyone?"

She laughed. "I mean like, the whole... unicorn thing. You said on your profile that you're only interested in meeting couples."

"Less pressure," I said. "I don't have time for a full relationship, and I don't really want one right now. Also efficiency."

"Efficiency how?" Landon asked, putting his beer down.

"I don't have to fight against every other thirty-something looking for a one-night stand." I smiled at him. "And having sex with two people at once means half the effort for twice the orgasms, so..."

"What stops you from meeting people?" Eva asked.

"There's no one single red flag. I've had great threesomes with people who were like, 'Hey, it's my tenth wedding anniversary and I want to give my wife this fantasy she's had for ages.' But mostly, the people who think I'm the solution to their failing marriage or want to experiment with opening their relationship, but don't know if they can handle it."

"What, uh, was your first one like?" Landon asked.

The slight hoarseness of his voice and the half-hidden intrigue in his eyes betrayed him. We may have only just met, but I already knew enough about them to know that he wasn't just curious. After all, they'd just admitted to getting off by fantasizing about this exact situation for months.

No, it wasn't just a question. They'd decided they wanted to do this and now, this was foreplay. So in the interest of not completely ruining the mood, I lied.

Just a little.

"It was at a wedding," I said.

Eva's eyes widened.

"With the best man," I said. "And his wife."

She visibly relaxed.

"It was just one of those 'one thing led to another' things. You know how it is at weddings. I was sitting at the bar and we got chatting. They were both super hot and I hadn't gotten laid in a while, so I said I was up for it even though they were into some kinky shit. Like, who brings a strap-on to a wedding? But he seemed to enjoy getting fucked by her while he fucked me, so I can't complain too much."

Landon nearly spat out a mouthful of beer.

"It was just mind blowing," I said, and that was true. It was only when the rules got broken that it sucked. But my first time with Mel and Nathan... well.

There was a reason I was a unicorn now.

"I had no idea what to expect so she started by just pinning me to the bed and going to town on my entire body. Then after awhile she told me to get on my hands and knees so I could eat her out while he fucked me."

Landon's pint glass was halfway back to his lips, forgotten as he listened to me talk. Eva was fidgeting with her lip absentmindedly, raking her teeth back and forth across it as she looked into my eyes.

"And let me tell you, there's nothing quite like that," I said to her, my voice just low enough that she had to lean in a bit more. "You have a face full of pussy and you just know the guy fucking you can't take his eyes off what's going on. And you can hear him struggling to hold back because there's so much more he wants to experience. But he eventually loses it. And who can blame him?"

I glanced at Landon understandingly before looking back at her.

"But that's the great thing, right? 'Cause he can watch the two of you fool around until he's good and ready again, and by that point someone else has her ass in the air so he can just take that one instead. There are hands and bodies everywhere and half the time, you have no idea how you got to a certain position, just that you love it. You'll be on your back one moment, then suddenly you've both got your tits in his face and he's got his cock inside someone and his fingers inside someone else and he's not exactly sure who is who."

An electrified silence fell over the table before Eva released her lip from her teeth. "So, um, when do you think you'd... be available? To do... that?"

"There's a hotel down the street that's pretty nice. It's a little on the pricier side, though, so if you want something lower, we'd have to go to—"

Landon downed the rest of his beer and interrupted by putting his glass on the table firmly.

"Pricey place sounds great," he said. "Let's go."

Chapter Two

Howdy, TessTheUnicorn! You have 7 unread messages. Your last login was 10 hours ago.

pussydestroyer6969

Heyyy baby wanna choke on my fat dick while my gf eats your wet pussy?

Message successfully deleted.

HotNFitCouple

What the fuck, are you serious? You didn't even MEET us, how can you say you're not interested? Pretty bold of you to think you can do better than us when there are a hundred other sluts who—

User successfully blocked.

IWontMurderYou

Click to view photo message

7.5" uncut ready for you sexy

TessTheUnicorn

We're sorry you had trouble, TessTheUnicorn! User reported and successfully blocked.

"WHAT TIME IS IT, Tessa?"

I looked up from my phone. Standing in the doorway looking like she'd had something shoved up her ass and not in the fun way was all five-foot-seven inches of anxiety that was my boss, Dinah Sullivan.

"I'm not sure," I said, holding up my left arm. "Forgot my watch."

Her glare darkened. "You are holding your phone."

"Uh-huh."

"Which has a clock."

"Does it?"

"And there is a clock on the computer in front of you."

I glanced at it. "Huh. Would you look at that? Computers are amazing these days."

"Quite. Wanna tell me what it says?"

"The computer?"

"The *time*."

I looked at her innocently. "Not quite twenty after nine."

"And what time are you supposed to be at work?"

"I *am* at work."

"She was here at ten-to-nine, Dinah," Chuck said as he tapped at his computer. "Nice and early, even though it's Friday."

Dinah's nostrils flared. "So she's been here for half an hour and hasn't even *started* working yet?"

"I *am* working," I said, deleting another message on MatchMi. "Everyone on this app is a part of the community and since I work in community outreach…"

"Prostitution is not part of your job description."

"Maybe if it was, we'd actually work for a charity that has a budget."

"And maybe if you put your phone down and got some work done, we wouldn't waste so much money on your salary and you could get me that list of businesses who might donate to our auction at the Recycl-Ball," Dinah snapped.

"You should ask me for it, then," Chuck said.

"It's not your job to—"

"It is." He turned and rifled through a stack of papers on his desk before withdrawing a neatly highlighted stack and holding them out. "Seeing as you asked *me* to prepare said list. On Monday at the meeting. Remember?"

With a huff, Dinah snatched the papers from his hand and stormed away without another word.

Dinah was what would happen if the Devil's chihuahua had been bred by a particularly meticulous shrew driven by a desire to climb to the top of the trash pile. Without, of course, the self or spatial awareness to realize that being on top of the trash pile still meant she was on the fucking trash pile.

Literally.

CARE was the metaphorically-dropped-on-its-head brainchild of Loni Less, a woman with so much money, the phrase "she had more money than sense" would always be true because it was physically impossible to have more sense than she did money. The human brain simply wasn't capable of that level of intelligence.

Especially Loni's, because she was very stupid.

Stupid enough to pay and, for some reason, *like* me. Which absolutely infuriated Dinah, who would have fired me years ago if she'd had her way. And, considering she was the charity's director, she probably *should* have had her way, but as I said. Loni had absolutely no sense.

I mean, why else would she start a charity that used upcycled or donated "trash" to create art as part of a rich person's pissing contest?

It was a tale as old as time. Paige Martelle, eventual heir to the Martelle Makeup Group, had started a charity called ArtCycle. As her nemesis and the eventual heir to the LBD Fashion Group, Loni absolutely *had* to start a competing charity, which a pricey PR firm had branded as CARE: the Creative Artistic Recycling Endeavour, which was frankly, pretty clever.

Unfortunately, that was the last time CARE ever made a good decision. Loni was as flighty and capricious as she was demanding and the rest of us sort of just happened to work there. Which is how an out-of-work artist with no actual job experience got hired.

That is, me.

Dinah, as the only person who took the whole thing seriously, was personally offended by that.

She tried everything to get rid of me. One argument was that I didn't speak French, Mandarin, and Cantonese. Most of CARE's outreach stemmed from our office, which was just a few blocks away from Chinatown. When Chuck pointed out that the last person in my role had asked Jia, our high school intern-slash-receptionist, for help since she spoke fluent Cantonese, Dinah switched her argument to say that she needed someone more connected with businesses and people in Davie Village.

That argument fizzled out quite quickly when I asked what she meant by that and Dinah explained she thought someone better connected with the LGBTQ+ community should be in the role, and quicker still when I had to awkwardly tell her I was bisexual. After hearing that, Chuck took her aside for a quiet but firm conversation, and it was a while before she attempted to get me fired again.

So that was nice, her somewhat disgusting behaviour aside.

Chuck didn't know what I was supposed to be doing just as much as I didn't, but that didn't seem to matter. Despite being the sole thing that kept CARE running most days, he'd automated so much of his job that he had very little to do himself, so we spent most of our time chatting and gossiping.

Which was how we became friends so damn quickly.

Chuck and I were pretty similar: we liked the same type of music. We were night owls, not morning people. Both of us were queer and had come out the same way; that is to say, we hadn't really. Though in my case, my family still didn't officially know, whereas Chuck just brought a guy home one day and assumed his parents would understand he was pansexual.

"Dad was nonchalant about it," he said. "Mom was... well. Despite the fact that her parents moved across the ocean with her, she grew up and married a white man, and she talks to her grandmother no more than twice a year, she was *very* concerned about what her side of the family would say." He rolled his eyes. "The next time we went to Osaka, I let it slip that I had a boyfriend back home and the only reason my great-grandmother was disappointed was because I hadn't brought him with me. But you know how it is. Mom grew up with different expectations than I did. And we never want to disappoint our families."

"That's very true," I said, thinking about all the ways I disappointed my family.

The biggest difference between me and Chuck was that he was a way better person than I was. While we both had dry, cynical senses of humour and could spend half the day bantering off each other, he was a lot friendlier about it. People were in on the joke with Chuck, and I... well.

I was kind of an asshole.

"Did her eyes turn to slits this time?" I asked Chuck after Dinah had stormed away, my focus back on my phone as I opened yet another unsolicited dick pic.

"No. Ew," he said, leering across our tiny office to look at the image on my phone. "Is that..."

"Eight inches hard and ready for me to choke on, apparently. I'd love to see what ruler he's using."

I saved the picture before hitting the Reply button. Pulling up the last picture I'd received—Mr. Seven-Point-Five-Uncut who had creatively taken the photo from below so his balls were taking up half the picture—I attached it, typed my usual "I've seen better" message, and blocked him as soon as the message sent.

And sure, maybe it was an asshole move for me to send some guy's private pics to another guy without the first guy's permission. But it wasn't like either of them had asked my permission before making me look at their dicks, so I figured it all evened out.

"How did your meeting with what's-their-names go last night?"

"Eva and Landon." I deleted another message. "I fucked them."

Chuck looked at me with what might have been actual pride in his eyes. "You've come so far. Once upon a time, you wouldn't even consider a one-night stand, and now your hook up system is so optimized, you can go from hellos to hell-yeahs in a single evening."

"I'm the very model of efficiency," I said. "Believe it or not, this is what peak performance looks like."

He cackled and drained the rest of his coffee. "Okay, Ms. Model of Efficiency. Who's next on your fuck-it list?"

"Not sure yet. Most of the others have been duds."

"Hmm. Well, the day is still young. I'm sure you'll have a new prospect by noon and a date by seven."

"Oh, fuck," I said.

Chuck looked affronted. "What?"

I didn't respond. My phone had vibrated with not a message on MatchMi, but an email that made the coffee in my stomach churn.

Subject: RE: Miranda commission

Hi Tessa,

I'm sorry to do this again, but I brought the updated painting you did for the Mirandas to them last night and they weren't happy with the results. Their feedback on this version was that they were really hoping for something that captured the vibrancy of Paulo's hometown in Brazil and felt this was still on the muted side. You know I love your paintings and I hate critiquing your work, but it did come out a bit beige compared to the colour palettes I had sent.

Would you like to rework the painting? If not, I understand and can commission someone else. I won't ask for your share of the commission back either way. You did do the work and that's not fair to you. I would just hate for this to be something that caused any tension, so if it's a problem, then—

And on and on and *on* it went until:

—so please don't be upset, okay? And I'll bring back the canvas if you want to reuse it. Or maybe we could grab coffee? My treat? Or come over for dinner? Jackson would love to see you, too.

Let me know.

Lots of love,
Kira

"What is it?" Chuck pressed. "Did you get another dick pic?"

I shook my head.

"What's wrong?"

"Nothing."

"Tessa Delilah Lane." He set his eyes on me, the corners of his mouth turning up in that conspiratorial way that made people spill anything and everything to him.

"Nope. Nuh-uh." I turned my head away, folding my arms across my chest. "I'm not falling for that. Everything is *fine.*"

"Of *course* it is," he said, patting my leg again. "But just because things are fine doesn't mean there isn't something that's bothering you. Tell me what's going on. I'll keep it between you and me."

"No you won't. You're the biggest gossip I know."

"Just because I tell *you* everything I know doesn't mean I tell other people everything I know about you."

"Last month you spent a week telling literally everyone you came across that I thought you were supposed to pronounce the 'b' in 'subtle.'"

"Well, yeah, but you love me anyway," he said. "So what's wrong?"

I sighed. "Kira just emailed me because the Mirandas still don't like the painting I did for them."

"The Brazilian one?"

I nodded.

"Well, they clearly have no taste," he said. "Did she tell you why?"

I fidgeted with my empty coffee mug. "She said it was muted."

"*Muted*?!"

Sighing, I slid my legs off his lap. "Mm-hmm. As if I didn't know that my paintings suck right now."

"They don't suck. You're just going through... is painter's block a thing? Like writer's block? You'll get your inspiration back."

"It's been almost five years."

I swivelled my desk chair away and turned back to my desk, but Chuck wasn't having it. He scooted across the office, which didn't take long because the office was nowhere near big enough for two of us. With the backrest of his chair pressed against my desk, he took my hand and gave me a supportive but exasperated look.

"You will, Tess," he said. "Your paintings are nowhere near as bad as you seem to think they are. Or you could stop taking Kira's commissions for a while. I mean, that's not the kind of art you even enjoy doing."

"Yeah, but that's the kind of art that people pay for," I said. "And seeing as she's the *only* person who's sending any business my way…"

"Because she knows how talented you are."

"Because she's my former best friend and feels obligated to help me out."

Chuck sighed. "I don't think she feels obligated, Tess. I think she just misses you. But if you want my opinion—"

"—I don't."

He ignored me. "If you're going to keep doing these paintings, you just need to push past it. Find your inspiration somewhere else."

"Oh, of course. How simple."

"It is." He tapped a finger against his jaw. "What about an art class?"

"Brilliant. Almost like I didn't spend four years in art school."

"Don't be petty. One of the best ways to give yourself a little boost in *anything* is to take a class in it."

"What am I going to learn in a class that I haven't learned already?"

He shrugged. "Probably nothing, but it'll give you a chance to remind yourself how good you are compared to all the neophytes taking it."

I opened my mouth, then closed it. Chuck grinned.

"See? Brilliant."

"Purposely going to a class to see how much everyone else sucks isn't brilliant. It's an asshole move."

"And you're an asshole, Tessa Winifred Lane, so it's perfect for you."

"You're an asshole," I muttered.

"Exactly. So I'll go with you."

I burst out laughing. "You will?"

"Don't say I never do anything for you." He scooted his desk chair back to his desk. "I'll call Brenda McClane. She mentioned her studio does community classes. I bet she'll hook us up with a deal. Ooo, can we do one of the ones with nude models?"

"We..." I rolled my eyes, then sighed. "Sure. Why not?"

Chapter Three

"THAT BITCH IS TAUNTING me," I said.

My beer didn't respond.

The two of us sat there, staring at the blank canvas sitting on my easel. To the left, propped up against the wall, was the second painting I'd done for the Mirandas, which Kira had left leaning against the entrance to my garden suite while I was still at work the day before. To the right, I'd pinned up the mood board she'd printed for me, along with her original drawings for the Mirandas' new master bedroom and an aerial photo of Sorocaba, Paulo's hometown that I'd apparently failed to capture the vibrancy of.

The problem was Kira's design.

Not that I was blaming her. I mean, I was, but it wasn't like she'd done anything *wrong*. She was the interior designer and I was the semi-failed artist commissioned to create soulless works that complimented her high-end designs for her high-end clients that had high-end money to spend on things like artwork purchased for the sole purpose of matching their decor. Which meant that I was the one stuck painting semi-realistic landscape after landscape in styles that barely matched the kind of art I liked to make.

No, the problem was that creating a piece that *didn't* clash horribly with the colours she'd picked while still maintaining the "vibrancy" was going to be next to impossible.

That was obviously the entire problem, and it had nothing to do with the fact that the Mirandas were discovering what I'd known about myself for a few years now: I was completely inept as an artist.

"That was harsh," I said to my beer, even though I was the one who thought it.

My beer still didn't respond. Probably because it was a beer and I was a ridiculous artist sitting by herself in her garden suite on a Saturday night, fruitlessly trying to put brush to canvas to finish this goddamn commission.

Sighing, my beer and I leaned back, resting heavily against the wall. I took a sip, my eyes flicking back and forth between the blank canvas and the inspiration Kira had sent me, then sighed and took a longer swig.

"You are not helping at all," I muttered, then set the bottle down on the small table that held most of my paints and brushes as I stifled a small burp.

I'd thought the beer would help. Alcohol fuels creativity, right? But even after downing a bottle with lunch, I'd spent most of the afternoon staring at my easel, waiting for inspiration to strike. Then I'd grabbed another beer, which had also not helped, since I decided shortly after finishing that one that a nap was in order.

The nap didn't help. Nor did the long shower meant to help clear my mind, or the takeout sushi I'd ordered for dinner. And now this third beer was letting me down.

Just like I was going to let Kira down again.

Once upon a time, there weren't enough hours in the day for me to paint all the ideas I had. That had been way back when Kira and I first finished university; she'd gone on to start with an interior design firm right away and I'd been her go-to person for these kinds of commissions. Back then, I took them as a favour to her, not the other way around. And I'd never minded it. I still had the time and resources to work on the things that I wanted to make. It made me some money, but more importantly, it connected me with the kinds of people with the money to attend shows and galas and galleries, where they'd recognize me and my work and buy more of it.

But it had been a very long time since any of my work had been in a gallery, and even longer since I'd come up with anything visceral and exciting and passionate to paint myself.

Sighing, I put my hands on my temples, squeezing my eyes shut as I tried to rub some inspiration into my mind.

And, to my surprise, a sudden vibration rattled through me.

I jolted, my eyes flying wide open as a gasp got caught in my throat and my thigh bumped against the table next to me, making everything clatter and rattle. Even as the vibration faded, my whole body *tingled*, as if some kind of muse had heard my desperate frustration and shot down to possess me. Heart racing, I stared at the canvas, certain that the answer was about to show me itself—

—and then my phone buzzed in my pocket again.

Just my phone.

"I'm a fucking idiot," I said to my beer.

My beer responded by patting me comfortingly on the elbow, by which I mean that as I dug my phone out of my pocket, I elbowed the bottle and sent it flying onto the floor.

"Shit!" I said, then glanced down at my phone and groaned. "*Shit.*" Tapping the screen, I took a deep breath, then lifted the phone to my ear. "Hi, Mom. Give me one sec, I just spilled something and have to clean it up quick."

"Hi, Teacup!" Mom said. "I was just washing up the bedding for next weekend and I thought it'd be a good time to chat and—"

"Mom, just a sec. Let me wipe this up before it stains."

I put the phone down on the table, avoiding the puddle of beer, and grabbed a rag from the stack I kept on a shelf in the corner. Picking up the beer bottle, I set it next to the phone, then threw the rag down to absorb whatever was left on the ground while taking another to wipe up the spill on the table. Once I'd mopped up as much as I could and got the beer bottle out of the way, I grabbed my phone again.

"Sorry," I said. "What were you—"

"—Dr. Hameed, you know, Zain's dad?" Mom was saying, clearly in the same breath she'd taken before I'd put the phone down. "I *told* Nadia he was retiring too early, but they want to move to Kelowna to be closer to Rayan and Ashley and the grandkids. Not that I saw them at church, obviously, but I was chatting with her at the Women of Burnsley meeting last Wednesday. And let me tell you, Tessa, it took *everything* in me not to tell her I told her so. I mean, what is Zain *thinking*?"

"I couldn't tell you," I said.

She huffed. "Well, I certainly hope he reconsiders."

"Ah," I said. "Well, that sure is... something. So that's why you called? Or...?"

"Oh, no," she said. "I was calling to ask what time you're coming in on Thursday."

"Thursday?"

"For our anniversary party?"

I winced. "Right. Of course."

The only thing Mom was more of than talkative was dramatic, which is why she went dramatically silent for a moment.

"Don't tell me you forgot, Teacup," she finally said.

"Will you ever stop calling me that?" I asked.

She laughed. "Oh, you know I could never. You're my short and sweet little girl."

I tried as hard as I could not to grind my molars together—partially because of the reason for the nickname, but mostly because it was a friggin' tea*pot* that was short and not sweet, but *stout*—but failed miserably. "Lucky me."

"So Thursday?" she said, clearly ignoring me. "You said you were coming, Tess. You promised you'd help me set up the hall on Friday and—"

"I am," I said. "I just didn't realize that it was already this week."

Another dramatic moment of silence. "You didn't book a flight, did you?"

"I did. I'm coming in at... a time. On Thursday."

"A time."

"Yep. And when I'm off the phone with you, I can look up the specific time because it's in my email. Thursday night, I'm pretty sure. Or morning. Or... afternoon."

"Mm-hmm," she said, unconvinced. "And a hotel reservation? Dylan's staying in the guest room, but if you didn't make one, I can get your dad to dig out the air mattress for you and—"

"No," I said quickly. "It's fine. I have a hotel booked. And a rental car, so I can drive myself up from Kelowna."

"Just yourself?" she pressed.

Part of me very badly wanted to begin making staticky sounds as I pretended to go through a tunnel so I could just hang up on her. That part of me knew that wouldn't solve the problem, partly because I'd still have to face my mom on Thursday and mostly because it was Saturday night and Mom knew I didn't have a car. But it was the same part of me that was entirely in support of making that a problem for future Tessa instead of right-now Tessa.

But right-now Tessa also knew if she dealt with it now, her mom would hopefully have enough time to get over it before she had to see her face-to-face on Thursday.

"Probably," I said.

Mom almost wailed. "Teacup, I told you *months* ago and—"

"I can't control... his... work schedule," I said. "You know how, um, busy he gets. That real estate won't acquire itself, you know."

"It's our anniversary, Tessa," Mom said. "It would mean a lot to me to have *everyone* there."

I licked my lips, my throat suddenly tight. "I'll call him and ask."

"What?"

"What?" I asked.

"Why would you... why do you need to call him?" she asked.

Fuck.

"I meant in the morning," I said. "He's away on a business trip. That's why he, um, doesn't know if Thursday will work. He's hoping to be back by Wednesday but you know how it is."

"Of course," she said, even though she didn't know how it was because *I* didn't even know how it was since I'd made the whole fucking thing up. "But this is getting ridiculous, Tessa. Your brother is getting married in a few months and he... Tessa, he absolutely *has* to be at the wedding."

As much as I tried to stop it, the inherent need not to disappoint my parents began rising through me by way of extreme, heart crushing guilt.

"He will be," I said. "I promise."

"He has to." Her voice caught in her throat and the guilt surged even harder. "We lost all the photos in the fire and I told myself I'd never—"

"Mom, I know," I said. "You'll never miss an opportunity to take a family photo again."

I wasn't entirely sure if her silence just then was dramatics or legitimate grief, but a watery sniffle made me think it was actually real. I grimaced, not sure what to say.

The house I'd grown up in had burned down nearly five years earlier.

It had been a freak accident. A blown-out candle reignited. A window cracked open to let in a summer breeze. A sudden gust of wind caught by a gauzy curtain while my parents sat on the driveway with their neighbours, laughing and joking and enjoying a beer on a gorgeous summer evening. They'd smelled smoke, but there were plenty of people having backyard campfires, so it didn't raise any alarms. Except the smoke alarms, which they didn't realize were coming from their own house for far longer than was reasonable.

They'd lost everything. I could've sworn my dad missed his old set of golf clubs more than he did my grandma, who'd died before I was born. At least, he talked about those golf clubs more than he did my grandma. But for Mom, it was the mementos. The photos. The weird breakdown she had when I'd flown out to help them sort through the rubble and she'd realized all my and my brother's baby teeth she'd kept were gone.

"Why did you keep our baby teeth?" I'd asked, as bewildered as I was disgusted.

"Because I'm a *mom*!" she'd wailed, wiping soot-covered fingers beneath her eyes and leaving streaky black marks on her cheeks.

It hadn't answered the question, but I'd just hugged her until she stopped crying.

A lot of things were covered by insurance, of course, and they could've just bought a new house with the payout, but my parents were set on living in the same place they'd spent the previous thirty years. So they'd rebuilt, albeit with a smaller and much more modern floor plan and a bunch of upgrades they hadn't had in the original house. But that meant the former four-bedroom house was now just a three-bedroom house, and one of those bedrooms had been converted to a craft room for my mom's various hobbies.

Which had worked out in my favour, since it meant I didn't usually have to stay at their place whenever I went back to Burnsley. Which was as infrequently as I could possibly manage.

After reassuring my mom yet again that I would be there on Thursday and that I didn't need someone to drive the two hours from Burnsley to Kelowna to pick me up and that I'd talk to my "date" to see if he'd be able to make it, I hung up and sighed, the echoes of "See you Thursday, Teacup!" echoing in my ears.

Fucking *Teacup*.

I hated the nickname the moment I got it. I mean, who would really like having a nickname that stemmed from being four or five years old and being left at a carnival by their parents?

Not that they'd meant to. Just like everything from my childhood, it was a series of unfortunate events triggered by my brothers mattering more. Dad had stopped to chat with one of the other neighbourhood dads when Dylan, who was just a toddler at the time, blew out his diaper. Mom happened to see the Hameeds, who had only moved to our small town of Burnsley a short while earlier, but Josh and Zain knew each other from school, so Mom asked if he could stick with them for just a few minutes while she cleaned up Dylan.

By the time she finished, Josh and Zain had declared themselves best friends for life and Josh begged Mom to go to Zain's house for a sleepover. Zain's mom had looked at Mom, quietly pleading for her to say yes because Zain hadn't made a lot of friends yet, so she happily agreed and said she'd head home to get some clothes and pyjamas for Josh.

And while all this was happening, I was somewhere else.

I couldn't tell you where. I mean, I was four or five. I wasn't with Mom and for some reason she thought that meant I'd be with Dad. But I wasn't with Dad, who probably didn't think of me at all before inviting a gaggle of the neighbourhood dads over to our driveway to drink beers and talk about whatever it is dads talk about.

Thankfully, he was home when Mom arrived to collect Josh's things and she realized pretty quickly that I wasn't there, so rushed back to the fair to find me.

She'd found me sitting on one of those spinning teacup rides, completely calm and oblivious to the world as I spun around and around and around. When the ride stopped, she called my name and I'd gotten off, stumbled a few steps before falling dizzily to the ground, then pulled myself back up just in time to puke all over my shoes.

"Someone tipped her over and poured her out," Dad had joked when we got home and Mom told him what happened, making all the rival dads laugh so hard that it earned me the childhood nickname of Teacup.

Tessa fucking *Teacup*.

My parents told that story over and over again throughout my life.

"She was on that ride for God knows how long," Dad would say to peals of laughter from whoever he was telling the story to. "They would've packed her up with the fair rides and she would've never noticed!"

The thing was, I would have noticed. I *had* noticed that my parents and brothers were nowhere to be seen. And since Mom had always said we shouldn't talk to strangers and Dad always chided us for crying or throwing fits in public, I'd lined up for the teacup ride. Plunking myself in one of the cups, I proceeded to sob as the ride spun and spun, assuming no one could see me cry because I was spinning too fast.

All I'd ever wanted was to make my parents happy. Even if it was at the cost of my own happiness. And the few times I *didn't* put their happiness over mine?

Well. I'd learned my lesson.

Chapter Four

Night is the best time to go for walks.

The quiet. The calm. The slightly spine-tingling aura of an empty street. Night time walks just *hit* differently.

Once upon a time, I might have found them inspiring, finding art in the way streetlights reflected off puddles on rain-soaked pavement or the starlight-like lights of the city twinkling from the buildings across English Bay. But I couldn't capture that kind of calm, that sensation of being alone and not.

Maybe a better artist could, but not me.

In any case, night time was when I walked, despite the safety concerns. I had a very specific route that was brightly lit and didn't take me past any hidden corners or darkness-drenched paths where someone might hide so they could snatch me, should someone want to snatch an exquisitely chunky thirty-year-old with an attitude problem. It led down to the beach, where I'd wander along the path without getting too close to the water.

Plus, it wasn't like I was alone or without protection. That protection just happened to be in the form of a small white dog that was more likely to push me towards any potential attacker so she could bolt.

But I still appreciated the company.

"Well, it's about time," my upstairs neighbour, an elderly Black woman with short, coiled grey hair named Dottie Price, had said when

I knocked on her door after hanging up with my mom. "Millie's been itching for a walk all day."

"Your old knee's acting up again, Mrs. Price?"

She scoffed and waved a dark brown hand at me, teetering slowly and resting on her cane as she turned to get the dog leash from the hook next to the door.

"It's Dottie, dear, as you damn well know," she grumbled. "Millie! Tessa's finally here to walk you."

The scritchy-scratch sound of nails tapping on laminate echoed through the house. Dottie shifted out of the way just before a white floofball barreled over her in its haste to pounce on my legs.

"Hey, Mills," I said, bending down to give the obligatory head pats and smooches to the little white dog. "Wanna go for a walk?"

"She's not gonna answer," Dottie said. "You gotta stop talking to things that don't talk back."

But Millie did answer. It was just by wiggling her butt and trying to ram her snout into my nose before I could stand up straight.

"Millie and I have our own language," I said, taking the leash from Dottie and clipping it onto Millie's collar. "We're besties like that."

Dottie snorted. "Sure you are, ya crazy bitch."

"You know it, you saggy old coot."

She burst out laughing, clapping a hand to her chest as a bright, musical laugh echoed through the air. "Damn. That's a good one, Tess. I'm tucking in bed with my book. Don't get murdered, dear."

"I won't," I said. "I'll let Mills in when we're back and lock the door."

And then we were off.

Dottie had owned the house for years, but I'd only been renting from her for the last four. Loving insults aside, she'd been good to me as long as I'd lived there. We'd gotten a lot closer after she'd injured her knee in a fall two years earlier, and while I didn't walk her sweet little dog Millie every single day, I tried to take her out a couple of times a week at least.

Although, that was using the word "walk" quite liberally.

"Come on, Millie," I muttered, tugging her leash as she stopped to sniff a discarded Tim Hortons cup sitting next to the sidewalk.

She, of course, ignored me, certain that *this* discarded Tim Hortons cup was completely different from the *last* discarded Tim Hortons cup she'd sniffed. Sighing, I stood there, waiting for her to get her fill of sniffs.

I mean, obviously I was annoyed she was taking her time. The longer this walk took, the longer it would be before I could back to my basement and work on the fucking painting for the Mirandas. Which I was absolutely not procrastinating doing.

When we got close to the beach, we wandered off the sidewalk and onto the grass like we always did. After Millie took some time to do her business, I loosened my grip on her leash a bit and grabbed my phone to amuse myself while she explored the same spots we visited nearly every night.

Which meant getting the dopamine hit that was seeing how many new messages I had on MatchMi.

There were only three new messages, which meant the dopamine hit was small but still effective. The first one was yet another single dude telling me he didn't have a girlfriend but he'd let me bring a third if I wanted to have a threesome with him, which I did not. Then I deleted the second one with barely more than an eye roll after sending him Mr. Totally-Not-Eight-Inches from the other day and saving the photo for the next degenerate asshole who thought sending me a photo of his penis was the perfect conversation starter.

And then there was the third message, which was possibly the longest message I'd ever received.

Finn&Julie

Hi TessTheUnicorn,

It's been three days since we found your profile and I've been sitting here trying to figure out how to start this message ever since. Like, do I want to stand out? Do I want to make you laugh? Is there some socio-cultural etiquette I'm supposed to follow when trying to initiate a threesome? Finn—my boyfriend—keeps giving me suggestions but they're… maybe a little TOO unique? He says I'm overthinking this, which I absolutely am, because that's just who I am as a person.

I'm also a list person, so I decided I'm going to make two lists for you: the list of reasons why I think you're probably not going to be interested in having a threesome with us and then the reasons I hope you'll consider it. Because your profile just really made me feel like you value people who are upfront and honest. So… yeah. Here are my lists.

Reasons TessTheUnicorn Probably Won't Want To Have A Threesome With Julie And Finn:

1. Julie has never been with a woman before
2. Finn has never been with more than one person at once before
3. Julie is a perfectionist overthinker who likes to thoroughly and excessively research things before doing them
4. Finn only has one penis (editor's note: this was Finn's contribution)
5. Julie is arguably more inexperienced sex-wise than Finn and likely TessTheUnicorn as well
6. Julie considered turning this list into a Powerpoint presentation but wasn't sure how to send that via MatchMi message

Reasons TessTheUnicorn Should Consider Having A Threesome With Julie And Finn:

1. Julie is 100% certain that while she has never been with a woman before, she is definitely bisexual and is not just looking to experiment with someone
2. Finn is a people-pleaser who would probably enjoy the challenge of pleasing multiple people at once
3. Julie's research tendencies mean she feels confident trying new things and exploring in a way that would be respectful and pleasurable to all involved
4. Finn has a tongue and multiple fingers to make up for his singular penis and is not opposed to nor jealous of potential inanimate penis-esque replacements (editor's note: again, Finn's contribution to the list)
5. Julie may be inexperienced, but she is a quick learner who is both eager and willing to gain more experience and, since she has no previous bias or bad habits, can be molded to be the exact kind of lover someone may want
6. Julie can vouch for the fact that Finn absolutely makes up for the things she's a bit less experienced at
7. Julie will happily convert this to Powerpoint if that is a more effective format to communicate the information
8. Julie and Finn both think TessTheUnicorn is pretty. Like, really pretty.

So those are my lists. I hope they weren't weird. Were they weird? If they were, I'm sorry. What I know is that you're gorgeous and I had to at least try shooting my (our?) shot because I'd never forgive myself if I didn't.

Hope to hear from you soon (list format not required),
Julie & Finn

"Jesus Christ," I said out loud.

Millie looked up from a patch of clover she was sniffing, but as she realized I was struggling not to laugh, let out a snorty huff and went back to what she was doing.

I'd never gotten a message like that before. And that was saying something.

I mean, it was practically a novel. So you'd think that at least parts of it would cross over with other messages that I'd received, but barely anything did.

My immediate reaction was to assume she was trying some bullshit reverse psychology thing. I mean, starting the message off with "Here's why you won't want to sleep with us" was a bold strategy. Sure, she said she thought I'd value upfront honesty, which I did, but I was cynical enough to know that she could easily just be *saying* that. There was a good chance she was saying what she did to be quirky and stand out. There was every chance she was just trying to say what she needed to say to trick me into responding.

And I didn't like being tricked into shit.

So I almost deleted it.

Almost.

But something stopped me before I hit the delete button. Maybe fate. Or the fact that it *was* kind of a cute message. Or maybe some hint of subconscious desire based on the miniscule thumbnail of their profile picture. Maybe the subtle whisper of the breeze reminding me that the more time I spent out with Millie, the more time I would have away from that stupid painting for the Mirandas.

Whatever it was, I didn't delete the message. Instead, I clicked on that tiny little picture, which brought their profile up on my screen, along with a much larger version of the photo.

And god*damn* was I glad I did that.

The profile itself didn't tell me much that I couldn't have guessed. Like everyone else on any dating app ever, they were a fun, open-minded couple looking for a new adventure. They both enjoyed movies, music, and other generic hobbies. Oh, and they hiked, because everyone always said they were into hiking.

Unlike most people, though, I actually believed the "we're into hiking and all sorts of other outdoorsy activities" thing about Julie and Finn. They just seemed like trustworthy people who had filled out their profile with genuine information.

And also the profile picture showed them on what appeared to be a hike.

And just... wow.

Everything about Finn could have easily added up to one of those total douche-bro types of guys. You know the type: the loud ones who think they're better than you and whose sex lives are more vanilla than their protein powder.

He was tall—it wasn't in their profile, but my guess was at least six feet, which was obviously very important information when dating, much like my weight or bra size—and had scored the genetic lottery when it came to that strong, chiselled bone structure. In the photo, he was wearing a sleeveless white t-shirt, showing off strong arms and tanned white skin, and baggy shorts that made it clear he never skipped leg day. Sunlight caught hair that looked like it could have belonged to a surfer: golden-blond and not quite long, but nowhere near short, just a shaggy carefree mass that he probably ran his hand through a thousand times a day.

But that was where the similarities between him and your typical gym-rat jock ended.

The smile in his photo was so genuine and so bright that I almost had to dim my screen, and considering I'd already dimmed it because it was dark and I was outside, that was saying something. Dimples pinched his cheeks on both sides as he grinned at the camera, his eyes full of blissful mindlessness and wholesome joy as he flashed his almost perfectly straight teeth.

It was the kind of smile I couldn't help returning, and it was a goddamn *photo*.

Guys like him weren't usually my type. Not that I had anything against them, but men who looked like Finn had the unfortunate tendency to get personally offended if someone so much as insinuated they were attracted to women who weren't thin, sporty, and perfectly coiffed. And yeah, that was a generalization on my part, but it wasn't like it *stopped* me from being attracted to them. Guys like that just weren't at the top of my fantasy list.

But Finn... somehow, I could just tell he wasn't like that.

Or maybe I was just projecting that hope because of how fucking hot he was. But honestly, based on the woman standing beside him, I was fairly certain he wasn't.

She was hot. Like, unquestionably hot. I would have gone to town on that woman's body if she'd asked me to. Which I guess she kind of was at least hoping for. She wasn't thin or athletic looking; I'd say she was mid-sized, thick thighs encased in tight high-rise leggings and a sports bra that showed off the tanned white skin of her curvy waist. Her hair was a shade that wasn't quite brown but wasn't quite blonde, something in between that was shiny and pulled back in a high ponytail that showed off the plump cheeks on her round face.

The rest of their photos were just as amazing. In the next one, they were sitting on a couch, Finn grinning broadly as he cuddled a small brown dog in his arms while Julie kissed him on the cheek. The one after that was a mirror selfie of Julie in a pair of blue scrubs that made me wonder what she did for a living. She didn't seem crazy enough to be a dental hygienist or something, but was too young to be a doctor—their profile said she was twenty-five. So a nurse, maybe?

But before I could muse on that any further, I'd swiped to the next photo, which was a candid shot of Finn at the beach. He was dripping wet and wearing low-slung swim trunks as he walked out of the water, the same small brown dog at his feet carrying a tennis ball.

And obviously, I completely lost my train of thought.

There might have been more photos, but by that point, I'd clicked on their introduction message again and hit the button to start a chat.

TessTheUnicorn

> Hey, I'm Tessa. Nice to meet you. What's your dog's name?

I didn't expect to hear back right away on account of it being Saturday night, but just a few minutes later when Millie and I had nearly finished crossing the patch of grass, my phone went off again.

Finn&Julie

> TESSA! Julie gave me her phone and asked me to message you.

> I'm Finn, btw.

That was it. But before I could even raise my eyebrows, another message came through... and then another.

Finn&Julie

Also I wanted to message you obvs lol.

But she was hoping to message you back while we were both here.

Except she's gotta deliver a baby.

And she literally was like running out the door when you replied.

So she asked me to message back so you didn't think we were ignoring you.

Cuz we're not.

Actually we're super stoked.

I tried not to laugh as my phone kept going off. Just as I was starting to wonder if Finn knew how to send more than one sentence at a time, he sent one final message.

Finn&Julie

So like, hi! And also my dog's name is Alfie. If he had thumbs, I probably would've gotten him to text back instead because he's smarter than I am. And would probably send it as one message instead of annoying the shit out of you with a bunch of them.

Sorry.

My thumbs work faster than my brain, I think.

Oof. Am I blowing this?

Before I even knew what I was doing, I'd wandered over to a park bench and sat down, which Millie was delighted about. I hooked the handle of her leash around my wrist and she started thoroughly examining the base of the bench while I responded.

TessTheUnicorn

LOL. Hi, Finn. You're not blowing anything, don't worry. Tell Julie it's not a problem. I don't expect immediate responses.

Finn&Julie

That's what I said. But she was worried anyway. She really wants this and you know how Julie is.

It was almost impossible not to laugh, but I kept it hidden behind a smile.

TessTheUnicorn

Well, no… I don't. I've never met either of you.

Finn&Julie

Right, but you do. Cuz I just told you?

There was no holding back a laugh that time. I shook my head before responding.

TessTheUnicorn

That's fair. I guess that's just how Julie is, then.

Finn&Julie

Exactly. So anyway, should we like, chat when Julie is done or whatever? I dunno when that'll be. Depends on how fast the baby comes. But like, I can get her to message you then? Is that okay?

You don't want to keep talking to me now?

I would love to. Just like, shouldn't all of us be talking? I don't want you to think we're like… I dunno. Tricking you into not a threesome or something? Do people do that?

I pressed my lips together, holding in another smile. He was quite thoughtful for someone who said a dog was smarter than he was.

Sort of. And we can wait if you want. But I like to get to know people a bit first before we talk about the threesome aspect of it. So if you want to chat now, we can, and then Julie and I can talk when she's done. If that works for you and her.

Yeah, absolutely! This is fun. So what do you wanna know? How's this work?

I ask you some questions, you ask me some questions… that sort of thing. Just chatting, like we would if we were getting to know each other in any other situation.

Finn&Julie

Ok, cool! You go first?

TessTheUnicorn

Sure. When you say Julie's delivering a baby… like, someone else's baby, right?

Finn&Julie

Oh LOL yeah. She's a midwife. It's her weekend on call and someone went into labour, so she's out there doing the baby catching and stuff. I don't know much about it, but she's really good at it.

TessTheUnicorn

That's super interesting. I can't wait for her to tell me more. What do you do for work?

Finn&Julie

I'm a courier. It's pretty fun, I get to drive around all day and talk to people and stuff.

My turn now, right?

What fruit makes you the angriest?

I blinked at the screen before reading the question again.

"What… *fruit* makes me the angriest?" I said out loud.

Millie looked up from the spot she was sniffing with either confusion or annoyance on her little doggie face. I read the question again, thought for a moment, then frowned back at the screen before typing a response.

TessTheUnicorn

What?

Finn&Julie

Is there a fruit that makes you angry?

Like for me, cantaloupe pisses me off. Every time I see it I think damn, this is gonna be so tasty, and then it's just NOT.

Insta-disappointment.

Millie startled as I burst out laughing.

TessTheUnicorn

Oh, I get it. I'm going to say cranberries. Berries should be sweet and cranberries are just tiny sacks of betrayal.

Finn&Julie

SO TRUE!!!!!!! Ok, your turn.

I wished I had something as unique to ask him as the angry fruit question, but I didn't.

TessTheUnicorn

What's your favourite thing to do on a Sunday afternoon?

Finn&Julie

Go for walks with Alfie. I'll take him on a short hike or something. He's just got little legs so can't do the longer ones with me.

TessTheUnicorn

Aw. I bet he enjoys that, though.

He does. Loves exploring a good trail. Do you have a dog?

No, but my upstairs neighbour does and I walk her sometimes. That's what I'm doing right now actually.

OMG. Send a pic?

"Millie," I said.

She ignored me in favour of sniffing a leaf. I tugged gently on her leash.

"Millie," I said again. "Come on, girl. Help me get laid."

Eventually I got her attention with the promise of a treat, which obviously trumped sniffing a leaf, and made her sit as I snapped a somewhat blurry photo of her. I sent it as she munched on the treat I gave her, then returned to her leaf.

Finn replied as soon as I'd sent the photo.

Ahhh she's adorable! Look at her face. I just want to cuddle her.

"This guy thinks you're a babe, Millie," I said as I typed my response.

She's a cutie. And loves cuddles.

Do you have that in common with her?

For as much as Dottie warned me not to get murdered when I walked by myself at night, I really should have thought of this protective tactic sooner. Finn kept making me laugh, and no one was going to kidnap a crazy lady sitting on a park bench laughing by herself in the dark. Even Millie looked up at me with concern, which was fair. I couldn't remember the last time someone made me laugh the way Finn was. Whether that was intentional of him or not, I didn't know.

But for some reason, I didn't care, and before I knew it, a ton of time had passed.

Finn&Julie

What's the best water you've ever drank?

TessTheUnicorn

The best… water???

Finn&Julie

Yeah. Like for me, the best water I ever had was when my mom and step-dad took me and my sisters to Mexico and I didn't drink anything but beer and margaritas for like four days because I forgot water was a THING.

But then I was so sick and my mom was like Finn haven't you been drinking water and I was like oh shit.

So I drank the bottle of water they had in the room and let me tell you, that shit was premium.

Once I stopped laughing, I typed my response, still grinning down at my phone.

TessTheUnicorn

Jesus. And here I was just gonna say I like a good bottle of Perrier when I'm feeling fancy.

I do love a good Perrier too. I like the lemon one.

Wait. Is there a lemon Perrier?

Maybe it's not the lemon one.

Like the one in the glass bottle and it's orange?

No wait Perrier is green.

Oh. I mean Orangina.

That started another round of giggles, but before I could respond, Millie snorted from my feet. Jumping slightly, I glanced down to see her curled up by my ankles, snoring as she slept soundly on the grass.

"Shit," I said, glancing at the time. I'd been sitting there far longer than I'd thought.

Orangina is also delicious. I hate to do this so suddenly, but I just realized how late it is and need to get Millie home to her mom. Tell Julie to say hi when she's done catching babies and you give her phone back? I want to know what fruit makes her the angriest.

> Grapes. She choked on one once and now she won't eat them.

> But I'll tell her for sure.

> Have a good rest of your night, Tess.

> Can't wait to chat with you again sometime.

Somehow, the final smiley face emoji he sent along with that message made me smile all the way home. It kept me smiling when I got back and Dottie screeched from her bedroom that she was going to call the police on me for breaking into her house, even as I apologized for getting back so late.

And when I'd finally returned to my basement, I was still smiling when I sat down in front of a blank canvas and began redoing the painting for the Mirandas.

Chapter Five

THE BOARDROOM WAS SILENT until a notification pinged on Chuck's laptop. It was quiet for a moment longer, then he gasped.

"Seriously?!" he said. "You're leaving me here alone?"

"It's two days," I said.

"You're giving me less than thirty-six hours' notice before I have to run this ship without my best wench? And you informed me by *official request*?! I'm sitting right here!"

"Last year you texted me from the airport to tell me you were going to Japan for three weeks."

"I wasn't at the airport."

"You were at the airport. In *Japan*. Having already landed. Responding to the text I sent you six hours earlier asking why you weren't at work."

"That was different."

"How was that different?"

"I was visiting my mom's family." He sniffed, typing on his laptop before hitting the final key with an indignant flourish. "And I wasn't the one stuck in this dumpster fire."

My laptop pinged with a notification informing me my vacation request for Thursday and Friday had been approved. "So it's okay for you to leave me alone in this dumpster fire, but not the other way around?"

"You weren't alone," Chuck said. "You had Dinah. And Jia. And whatever that intern we scared away's name was."

"You're right. I wasn't alone in a dumpster fire. I was suffering in hell with the head demon and listening to an eighteen-year-old take bets on if I'd get fired before you got back."

He snorted. "Well, at least you'll still be here Wednesday."

"What's Wednesday?"

"Art class." He motioned to his laptop. "Brenda got back to me. Wednesday at seven. She's ecstatic to have us there. And I'm ecstatic to see the nude models."

"How perfect." Standing up, I closed my laptop. "I'm getting coffee before Loni gets here."

"Throw two sugars and a healthy splash of that butter pecan creamer in mine," Chuck said. "And if there are any of those cotton candy yogurt tubes left in the fridge, can you grab me one of those, too?"

"Jesus, Chuck," I muttered. "You're going to rot your teeth out."

"Hopefully. Then I can claim that getting veneers is medically necessary instead of cosmetic and submit the claim on my benefits."

I rolled my eyes but grabbed us each a coffee, plus the way-too-sweet yogurt for Chuck. Dinah hadn't arrived by the time I returned to the boardroom, which I found interesting because it was now quarter after nine and my understanding from Friday was that our days were supposed to begin at nine.

And Loni wasn't there yet, of course, because there was always a forty-three percent chance that Loni wouldn't even show up for the Monday morning meeting. So as I put the coffee and yogurt in front of Chuck, he swivelled towards me, straightened the sleeve of his black-and-white knitted sweater, then leaned back in his chair and crossed one tailored-dress-pant-clad leg over the other.

"So," he said. "Spill."

"No thank you. I'd like to drink it."

He didn't react to my hilarity. "Why do you need two days off?"

"I forgot about my parents' anniversary."

He flicked an eyebrow up. "And?"

"It's their fortieth," I said. "They're having a big party and my mom called to remind me I promised I'd go."

"*And?*"

I sighed. "And she was upset to hear that *someone* is on a business trip and might not make it back in time for the party. Now I have to figure out if I can convincingly make up a plane crash for him to die in before Thursday."

"Hmm. Diabolical. I like it." He sipped his coffee again. "Or—and I'm just spitballing here—"

"Keep your spit off my balls, please."

He snorted. "Wouldn't it just be easier to, you know, *tell* them?"

"And deprive you of the opportunity to make fun of the comedy of errors that is my life? I wouldn't do such a thing to you."

Chuck snorted with laughter, but in doing so, bumped the table and caused his disgusting cup of tooth-destroying liquid to tip and teeter, spilling a healthy slosh of coffee across the table.

"Are you fucking kidding me?" he swore as he lunged to grab a tissue from the box on the table.

"This is what you get for making fun of me," I said, sliding our laptops out of the way so they didn't get wet as he mopped up the spill.

Of course, that was the moment Dinah burst into the room, panting for breath and clutching a stack of folders and notebooks haphazardly in her arms. She'd clearly overslept; her hair was tied up in a messy bun and there was a line of unblended makeup on her cheek, not to mention a significant lack of coffee in her hands.

"A pen," she muttered. "Why don't I have a fucking *pen* and—" She stopped, a stricken look on her face as she glanced around the room. "Why does it smell like caramel in here?"

"New air freshener," Chuck said breezily.

Dinah looked like he'd told her that a raccoon had broken into a candy factory, fallen into a vat of caramel, then had escaped into our boardroom and was wreaking havoc by leaving caramel-scented shit everywhere. "What?"

"I'm joking, Dinah," Chuck said. "It's just some spilled coffee. We're cleaning it up and—"

"Are you *kidding*?" Dinah shrieked, whirling around to face me. "You *know* Loni hates caramel! She's going to be here in two minutes and if this room smells like caramel she will *lose* it and I don't have a pen and—"

"I didn't spill it," I said indignantly.

"Tessa, I swear to God—"

Chuck handed me a pile of sopping wet tissues and turned to Dinah, placing one hand on her shoulder.

"Dinah," he said, withdrawing a chewed up, white-cased ballpoint pen from her bun and placing it gently on her stack of paperwork. "It's butter pecan, not caramel. And by the time Loni gets here, it will barely smell like anything but hard work and happy employees in this room."

"But—"

"You have a little smear." He picked up a dry tissue from the box on the table and used it to wipe her cheek. "Let me get that."

Dinah flushed pink. "I, uh... thank you."

"No problem," he said in a calming voice. "Do you know, you look phenomenal today, Dinah. Like, you really rock the casual, cozy sort of look *so* well. Your hair is adorable."

She made a noise that sounded like a flattered goat bleating its laughter before it ended in a snort. Chuck's mouth twisted into a lopsided smirk as Dinah caught her breath.

"What would I do without you, Chuck?" she half-giggled.

"Oh, there are a hundred people who could take my place." He took his hand off her shoulder and guided her towards the empty chair near the head of the table. "An incredible woman and stylishly strong mentor like you would have me replaced in a heartbeat, if you wanted to."

"Well, you haven't given me a reason to want to," Dinah said firmly as she plunked her paperwork on the table and allowed Chuck to push her chair in as she sat down.

"Morning, Dinah," I said as I finished cleaning up the spilled coffee on the table. "Just a reminder, you approved my vacation request for Thursday and Friday this week, so I won't be here."

"I know, Tessa," she replied testily. "You don't need to remind me every time you book a day off. I approved it ages ago."

The corners of Chuck's mouth turned down as he tried not to laugh, but Dinah didn't notice.

"Okay," she said as she flipped open the top folder on her pile. "So, before Loni gets here, let's recap the Recycl-Ball plan. We're less than six weeks away. High-level summary. Go."

Biting back the remark that as director, *she* was the one who should be giving the high-level summary for our biggest fundraising gala of the year or at least have some fucking idea of what was going on six weeks before the event, I motioned to my laptop.

"We're going with the masquerade theme," I said. "Using art to upcycle various materials to create an elegant solution that 'masks' the wastefulness of society."

"I've always thought that was clever," Dinah said. "Who came up with that?"

"I did," I said.

She looked like she'd just bitten into a salt-coated lemon. "Right."

"So we've hired artists to come in and create masks on-the-spot for attendees," I said. "But people can choose to wear their own, of course. Then we'll have a fashion show that features some pre-designed—"

"Garbage!" interrupted a loud drawl.

All of us swivelled towards the door as a blast of floral perfume entered the room moments before Loni Less. She was a tall white woman with jet-black hair, save for a platinum blonde streak above her left eyebrow. Paired with the faux-fur stole wrapped around her shoulders and the severe cut of her jaw and cheekbones, she looked every bit the type of person who would purchase one hundred and one puppies simply to skin them for a coat.

Not that she actually would; Loni was the type of vegan who wouldn't eat anything with a heart, which we found out when we ordered a vegan pizza for her and she threw a fit about those poor artichokes that had been murdered for her meal.

"Uh, sort of," I said. "The designers will *use* garbage to—"

"Oh, no," Loni said, her heels clacking on the floor as she rounded the boardroom table. "The idea is garbage. Utter trash. I've decided on a new theme."

"Have you?" Dinah said, her voice so high-pitched that I swore dogs three blocks away began barking.

"Yes," Loni said. She slammed a heavy tote bag onto the table, then put a hand on one stuck-out hip and struck a pose like the cameras were about to zoom in on her. "Love."

Dinah, Chuck, and I all stared at her.

"Love?" Dinah finally said.

"Love," Loni said again, then motioned to the bag on the table. "I found these."

Chuck reached forward hesitantly, opening the bag as Loni rounded the table again.

"Paige Martelle won't know what hit her," she said. "These are edgy. Subversive. Avant Garde. They're on trend."

"These are discount Valentine's Day decorations," Chuck said.

"It's *thrifty,*" Loni snapped.

"And there is plenty of space for exploration," Dinah said. I checked to see if her nose had turned brown, but it hadn't. "Love for the earth. Love for art."

Loni stopped pacing and turned, a look of disgust on her face. "Absolutely not. Love is *trash*. Trash is love." She pointed at me. "Write that down. The rest of you—" She looked around the room as if there were more than four people in it, then lifted an arm in the air, flicking her wrist as she began to snap. "—more. Come on, what do we do with this theme? What's our decor? Chuck?"

"Other than... this?" he asked, pulling a garland of tacky hearts out of the bag.

"Yes! This is just the *beginning*. How else are we decorating?"

"We, uh... we do a callout ahead of time for the gifts and other junk that people's exes leave behind when they break up," he said. "Upcycled mementos that are the physical embodiment of trashed love."

Loni snapped her fingers again. "Sensational. Get that, Tessa. Next?"

"We take it one step further," Dinah said, nearly bouncing in her chair as she sat up straight. "We ask the guests to bring in some of their mementos and do a ceremonial 'burning' as part of the night's festivities."

One of Loni's nostrils sneered up into an unimpressed glower. "Horrific. We don't need everyone smelling of smoke and melancholy. We're *celebrating* trashy love." Another snap, then she pointed at me. "Tessa? What are we *doing* at this gala?"

"Uh... a date auction," I said.

The room went quiet. Loni stared at me.

"Instead of our usual silent auction? You know... like in romance books and stuff?" I said. "We get a bunch of notable people to volunteer to be auctioned off. Artists would make sense, but other local celebrities could work. People... people pay to have dinner or drinks or something with them. That's pretty trashy, right?"

"That... is..." Loni started, then looked off to the side as she wrinkled her nose. "Am I having a stroke?"

"What?" Dinah asked, horrified.

"I smell... caramel," she said, then looked back at me. "And between that atrocity and the absolute deranged drivel that is the idea of *auctioning people off at a gala*, I thought perhaps my brain had malfunctioned."

Dinah looked torn between pure horror at the prospect that I'd just offended Loni and giddily gleeful about Loni hating my idea enough to think she was literally experiencing a medical emergency.

"It's butter pecan," Chuck said.

"It's repugnant." Loni picked up her handbag and shot a withering glare at Dinah. "This has been a vile misuse of my time. I want a proposal and draft schedule sent to me by the end of the week." She glanced at me, then rolled her eyes. "With *classy* draws for our *esteemed* donors." Sniffing huffily, she started towards the door. "A date auction. How primitive."

With that, she was gone, an echo of floral essence and erratic energy the only hint that we'd just been visited by the whirlwind that was Loni Less.

"Well, that went better than usual," Chuck finally said.

"She lasted twice as long as she normally does," I agreed.

"The end of the week," Dinah said. "We have until the *end of the week* to re-plan our biggest fundraising gala of the year otherwise this entire charity is going to go under."

Chapter Six

THE STAFF MEETING WAS always the highlight of my Monday.

Over the years, Chuck had managed to get them dwindled down from all staff to just the ones that Loni wouldn't fire the moment she laid eyes on them: himself, obviously, and Dinah, since she was the director. Then me, since Loni liked me and apparently valued what she deemed as my creative input. But the rest of the staff stayed at their desks, or better yet, didn't start until ten a.m. since Loni was nearly guaranteed to be gone by then.

The reason they were a highlight was because they gave me an excuse to do fuck-all every Monday morning.

Chuck always booked meetings for an hour, but I doubted Loni had ever been in the room for longer than ten minutes. After that, he took it upon himself to clean up all the metaphorical shit she'd tossed into the fan on her way out while calming Dinah down from whatever related panic attack she was having. He had it down to a science that usually only took him about fifteen minutes. That usually left us with at least half an hour for our traditional post-meeting debrief, which involved dissecting Loni's entire outfit and, on the occasions when we actually left the meeting with some kind of task list, complaining about our task list.

What could I say? It was a nice way of easing into the week.

But that day, instead of coming into our office and laughing about how many fake blue minks had to die to make Loni's horrendous faux-fur stole, Chuck burst in with a feverish look on his face and eyes wide.

"Tessa Jacqueline Lane, you have to come see this!" he said.

I dropped my phone on my desk, alarmed. "See what?"

"See *him*." He grabbed my arm, tugging me out of my chair.

"Him who?" I asked.

"God, I'm going to have to order more things online," he whispered, pulling me out of the office and down the hall towards the front desk. "I need you to go and hit on him. Find out if he's into guys at all. If so, I call *dibs*."

"Dibs on who?"

"Lower your voice! He's still out there."

"*Who* is?"

By then, we were at the end of the hall. Around the corner was the lobby and front desk, where I could hear Jia, the nineteen-year-old receptionist-slash-former-student-intern giggling breathlessly as a low, indistinct voice spoke.

"The new delivery boy," Chuck hissed. "Trust me. Go turn on that unicorn charm and get his number because oh my *God*, that man is the definition of a walking orgasm."

With that, he grabbed me by the upper arms, spun me away from him, and shoved me around the corner just as Jia let out another loud giggle.

And thank God she did, because it was the only thing that gave me a chance to escape.

The effect he had on people had to be a scientific marvel. They should have studied him to find out how to bottle the way he made people stop in their tracks and turn into bimbonic puddles of giggling goo.

Especially considering he was dressed like a total fucking dork.

But like, the hottest fucking dork you've ever seen. Somehow, the tailored and pressed navy blue shorts highlighted his muscular thighs and an ass that was just *unfairly* round. The sturdy sneakers on his feet gave way to tube socks pulled up above his ankles, but they were barely noticeable given his sculpted calves. Tucked into his dorky shorts was a bluish-grey polo shirt with navy fabric on the yoke. It was just baggy enough to leave *something* to the imagination, but not much. Not when it was fitted around his toned chest and shoulders and the sleeves were tight around his strong biceps. Topped off with a navy ball cap embroidered with a courier company logo and a black bag slung crossbody and resting on his hip, they could've made millions by putting a photo of him on a Sexy Postal Worker Halloween costume.

The thing is, he had blonde hair. Shaggy blonde hair that peeked out from beneath the ball cap.

And he had a familiar, genuine, room-brightening smile.

And the front of his shirt had a patch on it.

And that patch had a name on it. And even if that shirt *didn't* have a patch with a name on it, I would've recognized him as a man who was angered by cantaloupe and forgot water existed when he was in Mexico.

Finn.

God, he was even more gorgeous in person. I could've gotten lost in the dimples on his cheeks as he shot Jia his million-watt smile. In the strong line of his jaw. The slightly vacant but entirely wholesome expression on his face. I could have stared at him all day.

But I didn't.

Jia's giggle covered my startled gasp, and Finn was passing her a clipboard and pen so she could sign for... something. So while his superhuman ability to make a woman stop in place while simultaneously ruining her panties for the rest of the fucking day absolutely worked on me, he didn't notice before I'd broken past it. Forcing myself to unfreeze, I whirled around and lunged back around the corner, bumping into Chuck. Startled, he let out a low *"oof,"* stumbling backwards as I crashed into him.

"What the fuck?" he asked, grabbing me again and trying to push me back into the lobby. "Go talk to him!"

"I can't!" I said, shoving him back.

"*What*?! But why—"

"I *know* him," I breathed. "I can't let him see me here."

Chuck's eyes widened and he let go of me. Quickly, I scurried past him, though he tailed close behind until we got back to our office.

"You *know* him?!" he exclaimed as soon as he slammed the door closed behind us.

"Yes," I said. "Maybe. Sort of."

"Have you slept with him?!"

"No! Not... not yet. No. Not ever, now."

"Wait, what? What do you mean, not yet? And what—"

"He and his girlfriend messaged me on MatchMi." I flopped into my desk chair, disappointment surging through me.

"He... wait. You've been messaging a guy like that and didn't even tell me?!"

"I started talking to them on Saturday." I grabbed my phone, tapping the screen and opening the app. "I was going to tell you this morning."

The next thing I knew my phone was being plucked from my hands. "I don't believe you."

"Hey!" I said indignantly, trying to take it back and only managing to grab a handful of his ass as he turned away to look at the screen. He batted my hand away mindlessly.

"Let's see—*oh*!" he said, his voice going low.

I rolled my eyes. "I told you. His name is Finn."

Chuck collapsed into his chair, crossing one leg over the other as he tilted his head at the screen. "My God, he's just as beautiful here as he is in person. He could be one of those men who stand outside of Abercrombie & Fitch. Do they still have guys who do that? It was the only reason I used to go to the mall."

"I have no idea. I've never bought anything at Abercrombie & Fitch."

"Me neither, but I spent an inordinate amount of time in the store as a teenager." He swiped on the screen. "What did you say your record was for making a guy come in one night? Four?"

"Four's usually the max, yeah."

"Not him," he said, practically stroking my phone. "I bet our buddy... What was his name?"

"Finn."

"Finn here could go *all* night. He's a *god*, Tess."

"He's pretty hot."

"That *smile*. His *hair*." He swiped on my screen, then sighed. "Oh, he has a dog! I'm in love."

"Alfie."

Chuck looked up at me with a raised eyebrow. "Huh?"

"The dog." I reached for my phone. "His name is Alfie."

"Adorable." He snatched the phone away before I could grab it. "And a girlfriend, too, of course. What's her name... Julie? Julie. Wow. She's beautiful. A... nurse?"

"A midwife."

"Maybe she'd be into a threesome with two dudes?"

"You've always said you don't actually want to *have* a threesome."

"True. It's far too much pressure for me." He sighed and swiped on the screen again. "I guess I'll settle for living vicariously through you."

"I'm not sleeping with them."

You would've thought I told Chuck I pissed on puppies in my spare time. The look he gave me just then was one of utter betrayal paired with significant concern for my sanity.

"I can't," I said before he could say anything. "It's like, Unicorn Rule Number One. Never have a threesome with someone you have to see in any other capacity ever again."

He pressed his lips together, unimpressed. "I feel like you just made that up."

"Did I?" I asked. "Did I really, Chuck? Or did I have a threesome that ruined a lifelong friendship with people who weren't even *involved* in the threesome?"

"That was one time."

I glared at him and he lifted his hands in surrender, though his eyes were still sparkling with laughter.

"Okay, okay, I'm sorry," he said. "But come on. I overheard him talking to Jia and he's just filling in for Georgina while she's away because her son is getting out of jail. That *barely* counts."

"He would still know where I work."

Chuck stared down at my phone, his groomed eyebrows slowly pinching closer together. After a moment, he looked up.

"You were already on the fence about them, weren't you?"

He knew me too well for his own good.

"Maybe," I said. "Now I'm on the side of the fence where it's not happening."

"How could you possibly not want to find out what this man looks like when he's drilling you into the mattress and—"

"I do. I *deeply* want to find out."

"Ah," he said. "So she's the problem?"

"She's not a *problem*." I folded my arms across my chest. "I just think I might break her if we went through with it."

"Break her how?"

And God, wasn't that just the fucking *question*.

Julie was an enigma in an entirely obvious way. She was so inexperienced and naïve that part of me wanted to corrupt her. But she was also so quirky and sweet that I, strangely, also wanted to *protect* her.

And a big part of me didn't like that feeling.

Which sucked, because Julie really *was* great. She'd messaged me after she got home from delivering a baby on Sunday afternoon, thrilled and excited and slightly exasperated at the questions Finn had asked me.

Finn&Julie

I was hoping he would give me some info about you I could use to sound way cooler in this conversation. But all I've learned is that if you had to pick a vowel to feel sorry for, you'd pick the letter "i." I don't even know what that question was meant to accomplish.

TessTheUnicorn

I thought maybe it was some kind of tricky psychological question. Like maybe I feel the most sorry for "i" because it's the middle vowel that gets less attention than the first couple of vowels that get used more and doesn't even have something special about it like "y" does.

Finn&Julie

That's clever. Unfortunately that was 100% not the reason he asked.

TessTheUnicorn

Huh. Too bad. I thought he might be onto something there since I'm a middle child.

Finn&Julie

Well, I guess it did help me learn something! I'm the youngest of four. I have three older brothers.

TessTheUnicorn

Really? I have two brothers.

Finn&Julie

OMG did your parents also have crazy high expectations of you because you were the only girl too???

And the conversation took off from there. I'd spent a ton of time talking to her on Sunday, commiserating about growing up with only brothers and getting to know each other.

The thing was, in her original message, she'd been concerned she might be a bit too inexperienced. I'd noted that, but I hadn't exactly *flagged* it. There was nothing wrong with being inexperienced. The fact that she even thought to mention it was enough assurance for me and there weren't any other major red flags.

But sometimes things that wouldn't usually be an issue were. Julie saying she didn't have a lot of experience wasn't a deal breaker.

But that kind of implied she had *some* experience.

She was sweet. Wholesome. A little naïve. Empathetic. Grew up in a house full of boys, but was not even close to a tomboy. She'd been on the path to marry her college sweetheart—she didn't have a high school sweetheart because her parents had been strictly against dating while she was in high school—until they'd broken up for reasons she glossed over.

Finn&Julie

And then I met Finn. His mom works at the hospital our midwife collective works out of so they invited us to their Christmas party. He went to the party with her because his step-dad was out of town and well… the rest is history, I guess!

TessTheUnicorn

How long have you been together?

Finn&Julie

Just over a year.

I'd raised my eyebrows at that. A year wasn't very long for couples looking for a threesome. But before I could think of a response, Julie messaged back again.

Finn&Julie

He's not like anyone I've ever been with before. But he's been patient and willing to explore with me. Everyone thinks we're total opposites, but I didn't KNOW things could be like this before him. Like… fun. And exciting. And enjoyable. It's been incredible.

TessTheUnicorn

How is he different from other people you've had sex with?

Finn&Julie

???

OH. I meant "been with" as in "been in a relationship with."

And that.

That had set the alarms off.

"Tessa?" Chuck asked as I tried to sort out my thoughts. "Are you saying you'd break her in a metaphorical sense or a physical sense? Because the last time I checked, you weren't overly into whips and chains or anything, so I don't think you could physically *hurt*—"

"Metaphorically, obviously," I said, rolling my eyes at him before frowning. "Or, well, maybe physically. Like… I'd overwhelm her. There's 'inexperienced' and then there's 'inexperienced with a history of sexual repression oh and also she lost her v-card *last year* at the age of twenty-five to the guy she's proposing a threesome with.'"

"Oh," Chuck said, his voice pitching low as he drew the sound out.

"Yeah. Based on what she said, she's not completely naïve. Like, she's tried some kink-adjacent stuff with him. But there's a big difference between being tied to the headboard with a silk scarf and adding a third person into your relationship. Especially when that person is *me*."

He burst out laughing. "Why would it be so bad for it to be *you*?!"

"Because I'm a cynical thirty-year-old unicorn who is completely unlike her sunshiney, patient boyfriend that's 'exploring things' with her." I put my phone down on my desk with a sigh. "I'd break her."

"Maybe she needs to be broken a bit," he said. "You know. A couple of cracks here and there to let her inner freak come out? It sounds like that's what she wants, actually."

"Yeah, but on what planet am *I* the right person for that job?" I asked. "You'd think they'd want less of an asshole to help some sweet little newbie bisexual discover herself."

"Or maybe you're the perfect person for the job," Chuck said. "Once upon a time, *you* were a sweet little newbie bisexual who needed to discover herself."

"Yeah, and look what happened when I had the exact wrong type of person to break me in."

"Exactly."

I frowned. "What?"

He raised his eyebrows at me expectantly. When I didn't magically understand what the fuck he was talking about, he sighed. "You would make sure you *aren't* the wrong kind of person to break in sweet little Julie, Tessa Barbara Lane."

"Why are you assuming I would want that kind of responsibility?"

He shrugged and unfolded his legs, turning towards his desk so he could grab his coffee. "Because you're the perfect person for it. And because you need a little baby bisexual to take under your wing."

"I do not."

"You do."

"I absolutely do not. I have no wings. And if I did, I wouldn't want baby bisexuals under them. I want to fuck and then go home to my cave of a basement and drink beer." I grabbed my coffee and sipped it. "Like, she might believe she can handle all this, but what if she can't?"

"Hmm. What's your gut telling you?"

I laughed dryly. "My gut has proven it's completely incapable of being trusted."

"Well, I guess you'll just have to listen to my gut, then," he said, spinning back around towards me. "And guess what my gut is saying?"

"You'd spend less time in the bathroom if you got your sugar intake semi under control?"

"Don't be ridiculous." He wagged a finger at me. "My gut is saying you can only get so much of a read off people while on an app. Instead of wasting your time debating things, just go meet them."

"Yeah, except that doesn't change the fact that Finn is our replacement courier and—"

"—and what?" Chuck asked, his tone unimpressed. "You're going to give up fucking an actual literal god-on-earth and his adorably hot girlfriend because he *might* make things weird? Without even doing him the common courtesy of getting to be part of that decision? If there's anyone you should make an exception to that rule you just made up about not fucking people you know tangentially in real life, it's him."

"I didn't just make it up," I said. "It's one of the rules."

"That you made up," he said. "Nevertheless, sometimes we say fuck the rules, Tessa Alessandra Lane. Message those beautiful people back and tell them you'll meet for a drink. What's the worst that could happen?"

"I waste my time or I get stood up."

He sighed heavily. "Tessa. Darling. If they don't show up or if they suck, you go home with the hot server you're into."

I twisted my mouth to the side. "I mean... yeah."

"See?" Chuck said. "You have nothing to lose. The actual worst thing that could happen is you have sex with one sexy person instead of two."

Chapter Seven

Chuck was an idiot.

The actual worst thing that could happen was not having to hook up with the hot server instead of having a threesome.

The actual worst thing that could happen was getting stood up *and* it being the hot server's night off.

Which is what I texted to Chuck after I'd been sitting in Bar One for nearly forty minutes.

In fairness to Julie and Finn, they weren't forty minutes late. I tried to show up fifteen or twenty minutes before my couples did so I had time to get to a table and grab a drink. And it wasn't like I was unreasonable. Buses could run late and Ubers could have a hard time finding somewhere to pull over and unexpected construction could randomly pop up. I didn't mind if people were a few minutes late or, in one case, where I got a flurry of frantic messages on MatchMi from a couple who were stuck in traffic caused by a car accident and didn't want me to think they were standing me up.

When they'd arrived, the woman had looked so relieved that I was still there that she nearly cried. And they definitely made up for their lateness later that night. The memory of the way she'd used her tongue on my clit while her husband was pounding me was a sure-fire way to get me turned on in no time.

But Finn and Julie would not be able to make it up to me as there was no series of apologetic messages as I sat there waiting for them, which had astounded Chuck after I texted him to let him know the hot se rver wasn't there.

Chuck

You're joking. But he WORKS there.

Me

He's still entitled to days off, smartass. And I looked so fucking cute today.

Chuck

What are you wearing?

Me

I didn't know you felt that way about me.

Chuck

You know what I mean. I just wanted to know if it's jazzed up cute or the standard cute Tessa fare of tight jeans, a tank top, and that old leather jacket.

Me

Excuse you, I look fucking amazing in this outfit. And my jacket isn't OLD.

Chuck

You've had it since high school.

I turned my phone around and took a selfie of me flipping off the camera, then sent it to him.

Chuck

LOL. You do look amazing, like always. Are you sure they aren't coming? Like maybe they're stuck in traffic.

Me

They were supposed to be here twenty minutes ago. Pretty sure I've been ghosted.

Chuck

See, this is why you should give them your phone number instead.

It was my turn to roll my eyes, but I did it in person as I sipped my beer.

Me

I don't give my phone number out to people I have no intention of seeing more than once. It just leaves room for them to stalk me.

Chuck

Maybe you could use a good stalking. Preferably from a tall, handsome courier with a bubble butt and—

"Oh my God, Tessa, you're not gonna believe what happened," said a deep, excited voice.

I jumped and looked up from my phone as the table shook. A tall white man with broad, muscled shoulders encased in a grey Henley shirt plunked himself into the booth across from me. His bright blue eyes were full of eagerness and familiarity, even though I'd never met him before in my life.

Well, not face to face.

"Uh—" I said.

"So, Julie and I are in my car, right?" he said, leaning forward. "And I was like 'Jules, you gotta put the address in the GPS' and she's like 'You know where we're going, we've been there before.' And I was like 'You *know* I do better when I've got the GPS' because I'm used to it, right?' 'Cause in my work truck, we use GPS for everything 'cause of all the packages, right?"

"Sure," I said.

"Exactly!" He grinned and flipped his palms up as if he'd said the most obvious thing in the world. "So she's like 'Nah, we're just going to Wonder Bar, it's so easy, I'll just tell you' and I'm like 'Okay whatever,' you know? So *then*—"

"Thanks, babe," interrupted the curvaceous woman who had just approached the table with an anxious look on her face. "Throw me under the bus."

He looked up at her. "What? Nah, babe, it was my fault." He turned back to me. "She said Wonder Bar and I *thought* she said Bar One, and I knew where that was 'cause this is part of my usual route, you know? But then just after I paid for parking, she's like 'Oh my God no, it's *Wonder Bar*' and I was like 'Ah shit,' 'cause this—" He gestured at the room around us "—is not Wonder Bar."

I had to fight back a smile, partly because of his earnest excitement and partly because somehow, the man who could only seem to text one sentence at a time was also the man who couldn't seem to stop talking. "That is very true."

"But it's fine 'cause Wonder Bar's super close and so I was like 'Whatever, we'll just walk over.' So *then* we're a little late, right, 'cause like it wasn't *as* close as I thought it was—"

"It was not close at all," Julie said.

Finn didn't seem to hear her. "—and I felt bad 'cause like, I don't like being late, you know? So I hold the door for Julie and she's like, 'I dunno where Tessa is so I'll just message her,' but then I see this hot woman with wavy brown hair and I'm like 'Oh that's her!' So I just go over and I sit down and I'm like, 'Tessa, you're not gonna believe what happened.' And I tell her about going to the wrong bar and then I'm like 'But we're here now and I hope you still wanna have a threesome.' Then just as I say that, Julie walks up and she's like 'Finn, oh my God, we're at the wrong bar and that's not Tessa' and I'm like oh *shit* so then we like, *ran* back to Bar One and then I got here and I saw you and I was like 'Oh my God, Tessa, you're not gonna believe what happened' and—wait." He looked at me closely. "You're Tessa, right? 'Cause if I did this *again*—"

I couldn't help it. I burst out laughing as I nodded. "Yeah, I'm Tessa."

He let out a relieved sigh, smiling broadly as he leaned back in his chair. "Can you imagine if I did that *twice*?!"

"It was bad enough it happened once," Julie said as she slid into the booth.

"And that lady's boyfriend was there," he said. "But I didn't know that."

"You sat beside him."

"I thought Tessa maybe brought someone so she wasn't meeting us alone," he said. "Like, so she doesn't get murdered by some stranger."

"My upstairs neighbour would love you," I said. "She's always telling me not to get murdered or kidnapped or something. Joke's on her, though. My ass is too big to kidnap efficiently."

Julie's eyes widened. "But... You're not... I mean, you're..."

"Fat?" I asked. "Yeah, I know. It's great."

"No!" she said, shaking her head. "I was going to say 'hot.'"

I sipped my beer. "I said I was fat, not ugly. Both can be true."

"Both are very true," Finn said, then looked at Julie with a smile. "Right?"

Julie nodded quickly, her cheeks turning just red enough that I felt a bit guilty. "Of course. Sorry. I... I didn't mean to imply—"

"Don't worry about it, babe," I said. "Really. We're all here and we're all hot, so we're off to a good start."

That got a smile out of her. Well, most of a smile. There was an apologetic wateriness to her eyes that just... ugh.

It was just so fucking *sweet* how flustered she was.

I studied her as the server came over to take their drink orders. She was way hotter in person than in her photos. That wasn't me being an asshole; I'd fully admitted she was fucking *delicious* in her photos, but it barely compared to seeing the unposed and unprepared version of her sitting in front of me. Her not-quite-blonde and not-quite-brown hair was pulled back into a ponytail and in the light of the bar, took on a reddish-gold sheen, a challenging colour that I would have both loved and loathed if I ever made an attempt at painting her.

"Anyway," Finn said after the server had turned to go back to the bar. "Sorry we're late. I hope you're still interested in having a threesome with us, but if not, I get it. It's completely my fault."

I sipped my beer. "Well, I was a little pissed. But you tell a pretty good story, so maybe I'll keep considering it."

The corner of his mouth lifted, a dimple appearing on one cheek as his eyes widened. "Okay, awesome. So what do we gotta do to make that, like, not just a consideration?"

"Finn!" Julie said, her voice a breathless hiss as she glanced at me nervously. "I... I'm sorry. Sometimes he's not house-trained."

I raised my eyebrows. "Well, I guess it's a good thing we're not in a house."

"I... oh," she said.

Ugh.

That should have bothered me. I mean, it usually did. The anxious scolding and embarrassed cringing... literally, the last time I'd sat in this booth with a couple who did the same thing, I nearly sent them home.

I wanted forwardness. I wanted honesty. I wanted to fuck and move on with my life. I didn't want jittery almost-virgins who reprimanded their partners for talking about the thing we were there to talk about. And I *absolutely* didn't want to feel like I was obligated to be patient with her just because she was less experienced.

And yet...

"You can relax a little," I said, trying not to smile. "I appreciate the forwardness. This is what we're here to talk about. I wouldn't have asked to meet you if I wasn't at least pretty sure that I wanted this to go further."

Julie took a breath and let it out, then nodded, her ponytail bouncing slightly as she did. "Right. Of course. I just hate being late and I'm excited and this is all so..." She paused, biting her lip for a moment before releasing it and looking at me with a thrilled glimmer in her eyes. "This is *amazing*."

"Super amazing," Finn added, nodding eagerly.

"Good," I said, and God help me, I couldn't stop myself from smiling. "The whole purpose of this is for us to get to know each other a bit better and decide if this is something we want to do. It's one thing to chat on MatchMi, but it's different in person. So why don't you start by telling me about yourselves?"

Julie nodded. "Okay. Well, I'm Julie. I've been a certified midwife for almost two years now and I love it. Um..." She twisted her mouth to the side. "I feel like I told you so much about me already. Can Finn go while I try to think of something interesting about me?"

"Everything about you is interesting, babe," Finn said, slinging an arm around her shoulder.

Julie's cheeks turned pink. "I still need a second to think."

Finn nodded, then took his arm back from her shoulders and shot another million-watt smile at me as he leaned forward.

"Hey, what's up, I'm Finn Goodman," he said, his voice so enthusiastic and charming that I thought he was about to follow his statement up with a request for me to like and subscribe to his channel. "I'm twenty-six, I'm a driver for CanDeliver Courier, and I grew up in Richmond. I have a dog named Alfie. But I told you that already when we chatted. My favourite colour is purple and my favourite food is peanut butter and if I had to be an animal, I would for sure want to be a slow loris."

"A... what?" I asked.

"A slow loris," he repeated. "It's like, this super cute little rodent thing that lives on an island." He dug into his pocket and pulled out his phone excitedly, but before he could unlock the screen to, I assumed, show me a picture of a slow loris, he looked up again. "Either that or an otter."

"An otter? Why?"

"So I could just like, swim around all day and put rocks in my little otter pocket, you know? Come on, that'd be *so* fun."

God, he was so ridiculous.

Like, in the best way. It might have made me sound like an asshole, but I couldn't have meant it more affectionately if I tried. Not to mention that he was just like... wow.

I knew he was hot. Like, I'd seen the photos. I'd thirsted over the photos. And I'd seen him in person, wearing that fucking postal worker-esque uniform that was making me wonder if I had some kind of *thing* for uniforms. But I'd barely caught a glimpse of him then. Sitting in front of him, I could see all the little details that added up to create this image of perfection: the way his hair was tousled and messy in the most enticing way. The blueness of his eyes, which was so deep it was almost oceanic. His general exuberance. The muscles hinted at by the perfect fit of his grey Henley. All of it added up to create a man who was a complete panty-dropper.

Seriously. My jeans were probably the only thing keeping my panties attached to my ass because my willpower would have completely let me down.

And the hilarity of it all was the fact that this ideal specimen of a human was literally named Finn *Goodman*.

I loved it.

And that was a huge fucking problem.

I'd wanted them to suck. I'd wanted at least one of them to be draped in red flags and problematic behaviour so I could call the whole thing off without having to tell Finn my workplace was one of the stops on his route. I mean, not that he seemed like the type to do anything nefarious with that information, but if I didn't *have* to risk telling him where I worked, I wasn't going to.

But they didn't suck. They were hot and sweet and funny and even my cynical ass was enjoying being around them.

Which meant it was up to me to tell them I had a rule against fucking them.

"Wait, that's not a slow loris," Finn said, frowning at his phone screen.

Julie glanced over. "Yes, it is."

"Really?" He twisted his mouth to the side. "I thought they were the smiley ones that take selfies with people and stuff."

"I think you're thinking of a quokka," I said.

"*Oh*!" Finn slapped the table. "Yeah! A quokka. I'd be that. Or an otter."

"I can easily see you being either of those things," I said.

He grinned. "What about you?"

"What about me what?"

"What animal would you be?"

"A raccoon," I said. "Weirdly adorable, motivated by food and/or garbage, and generally harmless until someone fucks with me and I use my little raccoon hands to claw their eyes out."

"I love raccoons," Finn said so earnestly that I actually believed him. "Julie says she'd want to be a hedgehog."

Julie shrugged self-consciously. "I just think they're cute."

"Perfect. A quokka, a raccoon, and a hedgehog. This will be the weirdest threesome ever."

Julie's eyes brightened. "So you're still interested in having a threesome?"

"I am," I said. "But there is something I need to mention that might make you not interested in said threesome."

Julie glanced at Finn, concern creasing her forehead. "What's that?"

Sighing, I took another sip of my beer, then set it down carefully on the table. "So, I have a few rules about threesomes. I brought up a few of them when we chatted and there are a couple in my profile, but one that doesn't come up very often is that I don't do this with people I'm connected to in some real-life capacity."

"Oh," Julie said, looking crestfallen. "Do you and I know each other from somewhere?"

I shook my head, then grimaced apologetically at Finn. "I know you from somewhere, though."

"Yeah, I know," Finn said.

I raised my eyebrows. "You do?"

"Of course. From MatchMi. Remember? We were chatting there."

So ridiculous. He was so ridiculous. And so hot.

"Right," I said. "But I also know you from somewhere else."

"Really?" He looked skeptical. "I know sometimes I'm not the most observant person, but I remember pretty much everyone I meet. Once I've met them, I mean."

"Well, we didn't exactly meet," I said. "It's just that yesterday, you delivered a package to my workplace. And like I said, I don't hook up with people more than once. But if we do this, there's a chance we might run into each other sometimes. I don't want things to be awkward or for that to cause issues when we're all expecting that this is a one-time thing."

Finn nodded slowly. "Can I say hi to you?"

"What?"

"Like, if I see you. We can still be friends, right? Even if we have sex once?"

I'd never had anyone ask that before.

It took me a moment to process the statement. On the few occasions I'd randomly run into couples I'd formerly hooked up with, I'd ignored them just as hard as they'd ignored me. Aside from a quick meeting of the eyes, neither of us acknowledged that we even knew each other.

"I don't see why not," I finally said.

Finn smiled, then looked at Julie. "That wouldn't bug you, right?"

She shook her head. "No, not at all. I mean, I understand why you wouldn't want to do this with people you know, but it doesn't bother me at all if you and Finn run into each other. Or if we end up keeping in touch or something."

"We won't," I said, forcing myself to say it gently for some reason. "That will definitely just lead to complications. But if you're both okay with the potential that we might see each other outside of this, then... then I guess it's not a problem."

The dimple appeared in Finn's cheek again. "Cool. So what else do we need to talk about?"

Chapter Eight

"So that was how we discovered I don't like having things in my bum," Julie said in the most matter-of-fact tone I'd ever heard.

There were tears in my eyes.

Literal, legitimate tears from laughing so hard.

And on one hand, that might have made me a bit of an asshole. Like, I was nearly pissing myself because in the midst of me asking Julie and Finn how they decided they wanted to have a threesome and to tell me about their sex life and what their limits were, she'd brought up the panic attack she'd had the first time she'd put a butt plug in.

But on the other hand, Julie and Finn were both laughing too, even though Julie's face was red.

"I just couldn't stop thinking about his mom processing my file!" she said, giggling as I wiped my cheeks and tried to catch my breath. "Like I know she wouldn't *say* anything if I had to go to the hospital because we lost something in my butt, but she'd know. And *I* would know she'd know."

"But did it feel good otherwise?" I managed to ask. "I mean, I get the aversion to putting toys in your ass, but chances are pretty slim that you'd lose a finger or a cock up there."

"Slim, but not zero," Julie said in her most serious voice. "I can clench my butthole pretty darn tightly."

It was a few minutes before we could compose ourselves again after that.

My second beer was nearly gone by that point. Julie was partway through her second glass of wine. Finn's piña colada had been empty for a while, but when the server had come back around, he'd asked for a glass of soda water. But despite the fact that I almost never had a second drink with my couples, I wasn't feeling drunk.

Talking with them was easy. Smooth. Natural in a way that was completely unnatural and probably should have been alarming. And it had been from the moment we'd gotten down to business.

"So," I had asked earlier, just after the server brought the first round of drinks. "Tell me how you decided you want to have a threesome."

The question didn't seem to faze either of them, which was a good sign.

"Well, it's like I mentioned," Julie had replied, glancing at Finn, who used his teeth to pluck the cherry on top of his drink from the stem, seemingly without realizing how deliciously depraved it looked. "Before him, I didn't have a lot of, um... experience, I guess."

"I popped her cherry," Finn said through his mouthful of maraschino cherry.

A statement like that could have made him seem like a total douchebag, but it didn't come out nearly as douchily as it could have. Especially since Julie laughed and elbowed him playfully.

"He did," she said. "And he was wonderful about it. He's been wonderful about *all* of it. My ex... I mean, not to get into the details, but obviously we never... you know. But I'm glad about it now because I couldn't imagine anyone better than Finn."

"That is something that made me worry a little," I said. "Not that I'm into anything really kinky or out there, but a threesome can be a pretty big thing, especially for someone who hasn't had much experience."

I was half-surprised and half-impressed when Julie started nodding before I even finished talking.

"I expected that," she said, then looked up at me with a sweet smile on her face. "And honestly, I appreciate you being concerned about it. It makes me feel more comfortable with you."

The fact that her statement bolstered my pride should have been worrying, but I couldn't deny the pleased warmth in my chest as she said it.

"But that's kind of how the whole thing came up in the first place," Julie continued, glancing at Finn. "He's never made me feel like I'm weird for not having sex before meeting him and never made a big deal about me being new to all this. And he's totally been game to trying new things with me and letting me explore all this stuff that I feel like everyone else learned years and years earlier than I did."

"And how's that been for you?" I asked Finn.

He looked up at me, his lips wrapped around the straw of his piña colada. Letting the straw fall from his mouth, he thought for a moment.

"I'm not sure what you're asking," he said.

I raised an eyebrow. "Uh..."

He shifted in place, straightening up. "I mean, like, *obviously* it's been great. I get to have sex with this gorgeous woman as often as she wants it." He grinned at me. "I'm not an idiot. I have absolutely no complaints about that. But as for how it's been, I dunno. I *think* I'm doing it right, but she doesn't have anyone to compare me to. Which is kind of where you come in. Hopefully, I mean."

I tried not to laugh. "Well—"

"I mean 'hopefully' as in join us," he said. "Not as in hopefully you come, because that's not a hope, that's a given. I'm like a pizza joint."

"A—" I blinked, trying to wrap my head around what he'd said.

Julie stepped in to ask what I hadn't processed yet. "What do you mean, you're like a pizza joint?"

There was a proud look on his face as he put his arm around her shoulders.

"You know, babe," he said. "I'm not satisfied until you're satisfied."

"*Oh*," I said before I could stop myself. "I thought you were trying to say you were going to come in thirty minutes or less."

Thankfully, Finn didn't seem offended by my quip. He raked his teeth over his lower lip, a wicked glimmer appearing in his blue eyes as he grinned at me.

"The thirty-minutes-or-less guarantee applies to you, not me," he said. And those words... whew.

I'd never been so turned on by a pizza-related pun before.

"I'll hold you to it if we go through with this," I said as though I hadn't already decided I was absolutely going through with this. "But I was asking if *you're* happy with your sex life. Not that it's a bad thing, but it sounds like a lot of what you're doing is based on what she wants. Are you getting what you want, too?"

Julie looked concerned, but Finn just smiled again.

"I'm not satisfied until she's satisfied," he repeated. "So yeah, I am."

"Alright," I said. "Good."

Julie smiled and I saw her arm shift as if she was touching Finn's thigh under the table.

"Anyway, to answer your original question," she started. "I was finding I was really curious about threesomes. I think part of it was knowing that I was bisexual and feeling like I kind of discovered that too late, you know? And at first I kept feeling like I didn't actually *want* to have a threesome because what if that made Finn feel like... you know. Jealous or something."

"Are you generally jealous of things like that?" I asked Finn.

He pulled Julie in comfortingly. "Nah. I've never been with anyone who wanted to do this before, but it's not like it bothers me. I like sex and stuff and I want her to also like sex and stuff. And I like making people happy. If this is gonna make you happy and her happy, it's gonna make me happy, you know?"

The fact that he included me in that desire for happiness felt good.

Our conversation had continued on organically from there, which was both unusual and not. Whenever I met with a new couple, I had questions I wanted answered, but it wasn't like I sat there with a list of questions to ask them one-by-one. Sometimes, I got those answers in the course of our conversation—asking people how having a threesome came up for them usually also answered *why* they wanted to have a threesome, for example—but most of the time, I had to help guide the conversation with my questions, at least a bit.

With Finn and Julie, I felt like I was learning about *them*.

Like when we started talking about our limits and Julie said she wasn't into butt stuff, which they'd discovered because she had a panic attack while they were experimenting.

"My mom works in administration at the same hospital Julie's midwife collective is based out of," Finn explained when we'd stopped laughing long enough to catch our breaths. "She sees all the admissions and stuff."

"So if we had a sex-related injury, she'd *know*," Julie added. "It was weird enough seeing her at work all the time when Finn and I first started dating, but I don't think I'm quite at the point where I could handle her reading all the details of me getting something stuck in my bum."

"And does that go for you, too?" I asked Finn, stifling another laugh.

"I mean, yeah," he said. "I'm not going to put things in her bum if she doesn't want me to."

"No, I meant *your* bu—ass. Your *ass*." I cleared my throat, trying to compose myself enough to get through the rest of the conversation. "What limits do you have?"

He shrugged.

"You have no limits whatsoever?" I asked.

"Well, I mean, eventually I'll probably need sleep," he said. "And like, a sandwich or something."

Another laugh I had to fight back. "Right, yeah, but what about like… sexual limits? Things you don't want to do?"

"Oh." He thought for a moment. "Well, I don't want anyone to pee on me or anything."

"That's reasonable. Anything else?"

He licked his lips as he thought, the expression on his face going serious for a moment. "Um, well I don't like whips and stuff. Like, on other people. If someone wanted to try one on me, that'd be fine, but I can't… I can't hit girls."

"Even if she asked you to?"

He shook his head. "I just can't. It would bother me too much. I don't like hurting people. But other than that, as long as it's reasonable, I don't mind at least considering it."

"So… bondage?" I asked. "Getting tied up?"

"Yeah, we've tried that." He smiled at Julie, who hid a smile behind her hand. "I liked it better when I was tied up."

We went over everything: what they wanted out of this and what they didn't, which we were all on the same page with. Positions they'd like to try and ones they didn't, to which they gave fairly run-of-the-mill answers; namely, they were open to pretty much everything that didn't require a full-time choreographer to orchestrate. Fantasies they had, which was undeniably interesting when Julie started talking in a low, sweet voice about how much she wanted to see Finn fuck me.

"The amount of times people have said they just want me to focus on the woman is…" I was saying to them, then sighed and turned to Julie. "Babe, you're gorgeous, but if I want to hook up with just another woman, I'll hook up with just another woman. If we do this and he puts his dick in me, are you going to be pissed?"

"Probably not," she said without a moment of hesitation. "I can't just say no, it'll all be fine, because we've never done this before, so I don't know for sure. But I've wanted to watch him be with someone else for ages now. I just..."

She trailed off, glancing down at the table.

"Just what?" I pressed.

Her voice came out soft, not quite breathy but not quite steady, something almost lyrical, in a way.

"I've pictured this so many times," she said. "Just kneeling on the bed beside him and watching some other woman's face as he slides inside her, imagining how she's feeling right at that exact moment with him filling her and thinking like, God, that must feel so good. Because I know exactly what it feels like to have him inside me and the idea of someone else experiencing it while I watch is just..."

I wasn't sure when I looked over at Finn, but at some point, I had. Blue eyes met mine and held my gaze as Julie spoke. His smile had faded a bit, though not in a bad way. It had just gone from something that had made sunlight burst throughout the room to something more like a candle, a flicker, a gentle spread of enticing light that, when paired with Julie's words, sent an unexpected tremble of excitement through my stomach.

Then the corner of his mouth flicked up a bit more and, like a bad fucking cliche, my breath caught in my throat.

Fuck.

"So I don't think I'll be mad if puts his dick in you," Julie finished, and I tore my eyes away from Finn. "And if I am, it's not like it would be your fault. I take full responsibility for it."

"Right," I said. "That's... right. Perfect." I cleared my throat and turned back to Finn, whose expression hadn't changed but appeared far less lewd without Julie planting a fantasy into my head as I looked at him. "And what about you?"

"What about me what?" he asked.

"Do you have any fantasies?"

"One of you on my face and the other on my dick," he said instantly. "But really, anything she wants you to do to her, I want to see you do to her. And anything you want me to do to you, I want to do to you."

That did nothing for the warm arousal starting to pool in my stomach, but I tried to ignore it.

"What about you, though?" Julie asked. "What's off-limits that you didn't mention online?"

"No hitting me with things, no tying me up, no spitting on or around me, and if things get to be too much for any of us, we yell the word 'probiotic,'" I said.

"What does yogurt have to do with this?" Finn asked.

"It's the safeword," Julie said.

"Is that clear enough?" I asked. "We can pick another one, but not to sound like a total hoe, I try to use the same one with everyone so I don't accidentally scream 'pineapple' when I actually mean 'foliage.'"

"No worries, it's clear," Finn said.

"And Finn is really good at noticing when things seem to be too much," Julie added. "Even if the word isn't said."

"Good," I said. "Next, this is a one-time deal, so if we do this, you get a hotel room. I don't go to your place and you don't come to mine. You're on the hook for that, not me."

"Why?" Julie asked. "Not that it's a problem. I'm just curious."

"It's your territory," I said. "I'm already the outsider. I don't need to feel like I'm invading your personal space, too."

"I was kind of hoping you'd invade our personal spaces," Finn said.

There was another break for a round of giggles. Sipping my beer, I took another breath.

"Also, you need condoms," I continued. "Non-negotiable. I have an IUD and I get tested regularly, but I'm not fucking you without a condom. You bring them. And note I said *them*, plural." I raised my eyebrows at Finn. "Got it?"

He grinned. "Yes, ma'am."

"Last thing," I said. "Don't fall in love with me."

They laughed and I laughed and no one needed to know that I was completely serious.

"Is there anything else we should know about?" Julie asked.

There was, and it was something I'd asked plenty of people about before. But for the first time ever, I was somewhat... well, *nervous* about it.

Which was un-fucking-acceptable, so I told myself to get over it and looked at her intently

"This is going to make me sound like an asshole," I said. "But you need to understand that it's something that can be a huge issue and I need to make sure, okay?"

She nodded, her eyes large and round with earnesty.

"You've never been with a woman before," I said. "I know you said you're certain you're bisexual, but people say a lot of shit to get me to do this. If you're not completely sure, that's *fine*, but I need to know before we start if that's a risk."

Some people would be insulted by me questioning their sexuality, as they damn well should be, but Julie just smiled. There was a sadness behind it, something that sparkled in her eyes, but she smiled.

"My mom always wanted me to be a nurse," she said. "I didn't want to be one. But I wanted to make her happy, so I decided I'd be a midwife because I always liked babies and the whole idea of pregnancy fascinated me. It felt like a good compromise, you know? So just after I graduated, I started working right away because there's *always* a demand for midwives. And I was with my ex at the time, and his sister was pregnant, so she asked if I'd be her midwife."

Her hand was resting on the table and Finn put a protective hand on top of it.

"It's probably obvious on account of the whole 'waiting till marriage' thing, but my family was pretty conservative, and so was my ex's," she said. "But I found out at his sister's baby shower they were *far* more conservative than I realized."

"How did that happen?" I asked.

She sighed. "One of her cousins started making jokes about me not having given birth before becoming a midwife. She made a comment about how it was almost the same as having a lesbian for a midwife, but at least I wasn't attracted to women. Which was awful, obviously. And I was so uncomfortable that I... I just started talking about how it would never be an issue for anyone because one, we're professionals, and two, it's not like things are particularly attractive in the middle of labour. And that got everyone teasing me for saying vaginas could be attractive."

"They sound like fucking gems," I said.

She snorted softly. "Yeah, well. I was embarrassed, obviously, but I said like, yeah, of *course* vaginas are attractive. Because all girls check out other girls, right? Like, it's totally normal to be kind of attracted to other women. And then all of them started staring at me while I was like, 'Um, obviously *everyone* stares at boobs and wants to kiss girls in bikinis because women are just hot and we've all been conditioned by the male gaze to think women all want to kiss and touch other women, but like also, it's totally normal to want to do that.'" She sighed, tilting her head back. "Anyway, that's how I found out that *not* everyone gets turned on by thinking of other women."

"Oh, no," I said.

"Mm-hmm." She sighed. "So I realized I was bi, my ex's sister realized she didn't want some degenerate like me delivering her baby, and my ex realized that he must be projecting feminine vibes or something and made it his mission to be the manliest man who ever manned and broke up with me."

The three of us fell silent. Julie looked sad, even as Finn squeezed her hand, and I had the incessantly odd sensation of wanting to wrap my arms around her and tell her it would all be okay.

Which was fucked up.

"Well, I'm glad he dumped you," I said.

Julie's eyes shot up, wide with shock. Even Finn looked stunned.

"It was his loss," I said, lifting my glass to my lips and taking a sip. "Being with him would have been a complete waste to the people of the world who want to stare at your boobs and kiss you in your bikini and show you that it's completely normal to be attracted to whoever the fuck you want to be attracted to."

She laughed, the sound just the slightest bit watery. "You think so?"

I held her gaze for a moment, then smiled as I let my eyes flick down her body. "His loss is my gain, babe. Finn's too, obviously."

Her lips parted and I watched her chest rise as she sucked in a breath. When I looked back up at her face, her cheeks were pink.

"If this is, um, your way of saying we... we're going ahead with this—"

"It is," I said, catching the very subtle but very obvious way she shifted in place that told me she was as fucking delighted as I was.

"—then I'm glad, too," she whispered. "Because I haven't stopped thinking about what it's going to be like to kiss you since we first saw your profile."

"And I haven't stopped looking at your boobs all night," I said, and they jiggled as she laughed. "I can't wait to get you naked."

"Me neither," she breathed.

"So, uh, just so we're clear," Finn said, his voice a little louder than ours but hoarse in that delicious way some men's voices get when they're turned on. "Is this happening right now? If not, that's totally cool, but if it is, I'm just gonna need a few minutes before I can stand up."

I leaned forward, reaching across the table as I nudged Julie's wine glass towards her.

"Finish up," I said. "I know a place nearby."

Chapter Nine

THE HOT SERVER WAS one of the biggest reasons I usually met my potential hookups at Bar One, but he wasn't the *only* reason.

No, Bar One was part of the carefully delineated system I'd developed over the countless couples that came (and came... and came...) before Finn and Julie.

The bar itself had a good vibe, with music loud enough to cover a conversation, but not so loud that we couldn't talk.

The lights were dim, the drinks were reasonably priced, there was a cheap overnight parking lot on the same block, and it was conveniently located two blocks away from the Onyx Hotel, which was the pricey place I'd suggested to Landon and Eva the previous week.

The Onyx was perfect because it wasn't sleazy. I could have found a by-the-hour place, but a couple's first threesome was a special moment in their lives. My sentimental little heart just felt like they deserved something better than a cheap motel with sketchy door locks and barred windows that made it seem like there was something wrong with what we were doing. And there wasn't.

Also the Onyx had king-size beds and threesomes are way better on those than on a queen-size or a double.

Plus, I was thirty. *I* deserved better than a place that probably had bedbugs and questionable red stains on the carpet.

Most of the time, I told my couples we weren't going to hook up the same night I met with them. And most of the time, I lied. It was more of an excuse to walk away safely if I didn't vibe with them the way I'd hoped or to give them an easy out if they changed their minds.

Not that any of them ever did, but the option was there should anyone need it.

But the vast majority of the time, I knew I was going to fuck my couples that night. The only downside to my completely justified deception was that a lot of them failed to bring the required supplies—a.k.a. condoms—to their meetings since they didn't think it was going to happen.

Which is where the Shoppers Drug Mart, located exactly halfway between Bar One and the Onyx, came in.

"We'll wait out here," I said as we reached it and Finn let go of Julie's hand. "Pick up whatever brand is your favourite."

"Yes, ma'am," Finn said.

"And grab some lube, too. Just in case," I added. "But not the tingly warming kind."

He grinned. "Got it."

"And some Gatorade for all of us."

"Gatorade?" Julie repeated, frowning.

"Well, we'll probably be working up a sweat. And Finn will need to replace some, uh, bodily fluids."

"Right," she said, her voice high-pitched. "That makes sense."

I smiled innocently at Finn. "I'll take blue, please."

"Red for me," Julie said, her cheeks pink.

He walked towards the store cheerfully while I led Julie to a bench across from the entrance to wait. She watched Finn go, then turned to me with sparkling eyes.

"I'm so excited," she whispered. "But I'm so nervous. Is that normal?"

And oh, God, was that intoxicating. The breathiness of her voice, the trill of excitement making it shake, the way I could almost see anticipation skittering across her skin, like emotions were vibrating out of her and she couldn't stop them. I remembered those feelings, the exhilaration of those moments, and I fucking *lived* for that.

"Totally normal," I said. "But you know what's making you nervous?"

"What?" she asked.

I looked at her lips pointedly. "Kissing me for the first time."

She raised her eyebrows, though it wasn't enough to hide the knowing eagerness on her face. "Because I've never kissed a woman before?"

I shook my head. "That first bit of physical contact trips people up, regardless of how many women they've kissed. Everyone thinks it's this big pivotal moment that will change everything, and it will, kind of. But it can be nerve-wracking because you're going to have to watch your partner kiss another person, or you're going to have your partner's eyes on you when you kiss someone who isn't them. So you know how to make it easier?"

She knew, but pretended she didn't. "How?"

I tilted my head, inviting her forward. "You come kiss me while he's in there."

"Isn't that kind of like starting without him?"

I shrugged. "You know him better than me. Is he more likely to be upset that we 'started without him' or more turned on by seeing his girlfriend blatantly making out with some chick on the sidewalk while he buys condoms and Gatorade so he can fuck the hell out of both of them in a few minutes?"

Somehow, both of us knew Finn well enough to know the answer to that, and when he walked out of the Shoppers a few minutes later, he nearly dropped the reusable bag he was holding.

I mean, who could blame him? Julie's tongue was somewhere near my tonsils and my hand was already under her shirt, indulging in the softness of her belly as I crept it up towards her ribcage and the underside of her breasts. I was hoping the bagginess of her sweater shielded the action from the eyes of people driving by.

But also, I didn't care.

From the corner of my eye, I watched Finn move the reusable bag in front of his body. He glanced from left to right before subtly shifting his hand to adjust *something* before clearing his throat. Fighting a grin, I sank my teeth into Julie's bottom lip and tugged it, shivered at the sweet gasp that drew from her, then let it go as I pulled away and blinked innocently at Finn.

"Sorry," I said unapologetically as I stood.

"You shouldn't be," he said. "But if you are, I'll take one, too."

"From me or from her?" I asked.

Finn glanced at Julie, then at me.

"Yes," he said decisively, and before I could so much as giggle, his lips were pressed to mine.

And oh, *God*.

He wasn't shy. Not even a little. I'd barely drawn in an excited breath before Finn's tongue was in my mouth, filling it with the vaguest hint of coconut and the sweetest sensation of anticipation. A hand moved up to my cheek, cupping it as he deepened the kiss, claiming my lips as unapologetically as I'd claimed his girlfriend's.

It stunned me, that kiss. The ease of it. The way it felt intentional and unintentional at the same time, his lips working against mine like he knew what he was doing but had no idea just how fucking *good* he was at it.

Which, frankly, was very on brand for Finn.

Right before he had dipped his head, I'd heard a car honk. A bus was about to drive by. A group of people were chatting as they walked. But the *moment* he took my lips, they all disappeared. The world disappeared. Julie disappeared.

And that was a fucking problem.

He pulled away, ending things too soon and too late at the same time. Before air was even back in my lungs, I watched him dip his head to kiss

Julie as deeply as he'd kissed me. Both of them blatantly disregarded the cars and buses and pedestrians on the street, just like I had.

When they parted, Julie's face was red. Mine probably was, too. And if my panties were any indication, hers were also starting to soak through.

Finn looked at me and grinned before extending his hand to mine. "We should probably get a room, hey?"

Chapter Ten

"Where should we start?" Finn asked after we got to the hotel room.

It wasn't an unusual question. A lot of couples seemed to think that I should be the one to direct everything, which was fair. I wasn't always the only person in the room who'd fucked more than one person at a time before, but I often was the most experienced and thus the one who knew how to start things. So I shrugged off my leather jacket and put it on the chair near the bed, then reached out and took Julie's hand.

"I think we should start with you getting naked, Finn," I said as I guided her to the foot of the bed.

That charming lopsided smile spread across his face, then brought his hands to the front of his grey Henley shirt.

"Yes, ma'am," he said, and he lifted the shirt over his head in one smooth motion.

And *fuck*.

That man could have been on the cover of anything. Magazines. Romance novels. My bed, repeatedly. He had the perfect amount of muscle—the type that said "Yeah, I could probably bench press you, but I won't turn down a slice of pizza." In other words, I could see definition in his stomach and biceps and pecs and those broad, gorgeous shoulders, but he didn't look *hard*.

Well, not like that, anyway. Because part of him was definitely hard.

When he'd pulled his boxers off, my eyes had trained onto that rigid, thick dick of his so fast that NASA would have been jealous of my radar system. He was on the bigger side, because of course he was. Because of course the walking cliche that was *Finn Goodman* had a big dick.

When the only thing he was wearing was his smile, he turned to me and Julie. As much as I wanted to stare at his dick until some unsuspecting hotel employee came in the next morning for a wellness check when we didn't vacate the room on time, I tore my eyes away and looked at Julie. She looked at me, her eyes sparkling, and bit her lip.

"Wow," I said.

"Right?" she whispered.

"Thanks," Finn said brightly. "Now what?"

And wasn't that the fucking question.

Now I wanted his dick inside my pussy and my mouth and my ass all at the same time.

Now I wanted Julie's pussy on my face at the same time I wanted my face buried in her tits.

Now I wanted to take everything, all of it, all at once and come again and again and *again* while these two gorgeous people spoiled my body like the greedy bitch I was.

But according to stupid shit like the limitations of the laws of physics or whatever, I couldn't do that. So instead, I nudged Julie to stand up.

"Now you undress her," I said to Finn. "Slowly. Showing her off to me. By the time she's naked, I want her to be dripping down her thighs."

"Why aren't *you* undressing anyone?" Julie teased.

Licking my lips, I put my hands behind me so I could prop myself up as I leaned back on the bed.

"Because I'm a lazy fuck who likes to watch people get naked," I said. "And because we all know the second I touch you, I'm going to pin you to the bed. And I won't be able to stop until I've licked every inch of that stunning body and made you come on my tongue, Jules."

She blinked, lips parted as her breath hitched.

"Oh," she said. "O-Okay. That makes... that... that's a good reason."

I licked my lips again, then looked at Finn. "Let me see you strip her."

"Yes, ma'am," he said, then pulled Julie forward and set to work.

He looked like he was torn between having the time of his life and being tortured beyond belief. He was a kid on Christmas morning, wanting nothing more than to tear into the most pristine and enticingly wrapped present under the tree, but who's been told he has to be careful, to not rip a single inch of the paper because his mom wants to save it for later.

He handled her with care, caressing her smooth white skin with his fingertips each time he slipped a piece of fabric off her, sneaking in kisses wherever and whenever he could. Each time, he lingered, eager ecstasy mixing with impatient yearning before removing the next piece of Julie's clothing.

Her cardigan fell to the floor, followed by her t-shirt. I wasn't sure if Finn was teasing me on purpose, but he switched to her jeans next, sliding them down her legs and shoving them to the side once they were off. Then, once she was in a plain blue bra and white cotton panties, he took her hand and spun her like a slow-motion ballerina, showing her off to me just as I'd told him to.

Maybe it was just a me thing, but I found it completely unfair how hot everyone was. I felt like I was the opposite of demisexual: I was attracted to everyone until I got to know them. Tall, short, thin, fat, athletic, man, woman, nonbinary: it didn't matter. My type was "willing, eager, and not too much of an asshole."

But I did have a special spot in my heart for women like Julie. For girls with thick, jiggly thighs and little bellies and wide hips that had stretch marks scattered along them. I fucking loved marks like that, how they marked spots for me to kiss and made paths for me to explore with my tongue. Looking for them was like a scavenger hunt—almost everyone had them *somewhere*—and finding them always made me smile.

Things like that made people real.

"Fuck," I breathed as I stared at her. The skin on her chest started to turn pink and when I looked back up, she was blushing.

"You like?" she asked with a shy giggle.

"Babe, you're fucking sensational," I said.

"That's what I keep telling her," Finn said as he finally stopped kissing her and bent to slide her panties down her thighs. "I dunno if she believes me, though."

"You should believe him," I said to Julie.

She blushed even redder. "Okay."

Once Finn tossed her panties to the side and I took a moment to drink in the sight of her naked, it was time for one of my favourite parts.

Getting myself naked.

And maybe it shouldn't have been.

Maybe some people thought I should have been shy or suitably humble about my body. That was the messaging, wasn't it? It's okay to not hate yourself, but God *forbid* you think of yourself as hot, because that's egotistical and vain and inappropriately selfish.

But it was more important to me to be honest instead of appropriate, and the honest truth was that I was hot and I didn't care who knew that I thought of myself that way.

The most controversial thing I'd ever done in my entire life was to choose to love my body as it was. And given the plethora of controversial decisions I'd made, that was saying something. But I loved everything from the not-quite-curly-not-quite-waviness of my hair to the crease between my belly and my hip. And if others didn't, they could go fuck themselves.

Because they sure as shit wouldn't be fucking me.

But that didn't apply to Finn or Julie. Both of them seemed very intent on fucking me as Finn practically yanked me off the bed and both of them set to work undressing me. As Finn's fingers began to work the button of my jeans loose, Julie tugged my tank top up and off, then leaned in.

"I have been waiting all night for this," she whispered, then kissed me, passion and heat moving from her lips to mine, making my head spin with a captivating dizziness before pulling back and setting to work unclasping my bra.

As she did, I was distracted by the man who had apparently knelt in front of me to tug my jeans down to my ankles. He pressed a small kiss on my bare thigh and I looked down into pleading blue eyes that were patiently waiting for my attention.

"Can I touch you?" Finn asked in a soft and serious voice.

"Absolutely," I said.

He smiled, his lips parted. "With my mouth?"

Oh, God yes.

"You can touch me however you want, Finn," I said.

I had to stifle myself from making a noise as he nuzzled me, burying his face against my still-covered pussy and darting his tongue out to trace my lips through my panties. Feeling the heat of his breath, watching the way he was bewitched by me when I wasn't even *naked* yet...

Fuck, it was hot.

My attention was torn away from Finn when I felt my bra come loose and the straps slide down my arms. Sighing in relief, I looked up at Julie, who dropped my bra and reached forward to cup one shaking hand around my breast.

"Better catch up, Finn," I murmured as I felt him inhale deeply between my legs. "Julie's already finished up here."

He groaned, though I wasn't sure if it was a complaining type of groan or an excited one. Probably the latter, given that he immediately brought his hands to the waistband of the black thong I was wearing and peeled it down my thighs. I thought he'd stand up then, but my panties were barely at my knees when I felt lips pressed against the bare skin of my mound.

Gasping, I looked down at him, eyes wide as he started to tease me with his tongue, then looked at Julie again. Her lips were parted and her eyes half-closed, giving her a look like she was drunk with desire.

Even though I always asked to make sure, that moment when I confirmed a couple really *wouldn't* have any issues with jealousy was always a relief. And that was very true of Finn and Julie. Honestly, if Julie hadn't been such a sweetheart and Finn wasn't the personification of actual sunshine, I would have worried they'd fight about who got to touch me more or which one of them got to eat my pussy first.

But they didn't. They worked together, Finn joyfully helping Julie through those tentative moments of firsts: first time sucking on another woman's nipples, first time putting her fingers in a pussy that wasn't her own, first time making another woman moan as she played with her clit...

I understood exactly what she meant about Finn being patient as she discovered what she liked in bed. Watching him show her what he did, the things he knew she liked and how they looked from his point of view rather than hers... fuck. It was hot. It was one of those moments that felt almost too personal for me to witness, but I wouldn't have traded it for anything. I wouldn't have given up the moment Julie withdrew her fingers from my pussy and Finn captured her hand, pleading with her to let him suck my wetness off her fingers. Or the moment they knocked their heads together when they both attempted to suck my nipples at the same time.

And I definitely wouldn't have given up the moment that Julie took a deep breath as if to steady herself, pushed her brownish-reddish-blondish hair over her shoulder, and dipped her head down to kiss my pussy. My hips bucked in surprise as she dove in and I gasped, eyes widening.

"Everything okay?" Finn asked from where he was kneeling beside me.

"Yeah," I said. "I was just—*oh*!"

Julie glanced up at me, eyes questioning as she paused with her lips surrounding my clit.

"It's okay," I said. "Keep going."

The corners of her eyes crinkled and she sucked on my clit again, making me shudder.

"Is she good at it?" Finn asked. "She looks like she's good at it."

"She's good at it," I said.

He groaned, but he was smiling. "God, I can't wait to do that to you when she's done."

"Yeah?" I asked.

He nodded. "The way you tasted on her fingers was just... mmm."

"But what about you?" I asked, glancing down at his cock, which was so hard that it looked like it hurt.

He followed my gaze, then grinned again. "I'll get there when I get there."

"You don't wa—*ah*," I gasped, my eyes fluttering closed as Julie slipped a finger inside of me again. I reached down, resting a hand on the back of her head as I let her tongue distract me for a moment, then re-opened my eyes and looked at Finn. "You don't want a blowjob or something first?"

He laughed. "No guy in his right mind is ever going to turn down a blowjob, but no. This... this right here is what I want. If you sat there and said I couldn't come even once tonight, I'd tell you 'yes, ma'am' and it would *still* be one of the best fucking nights ever, you know?"

I was going to say something cynical, but Finn's gorgeous eyes were full of sincerity and Julie was flicking her tongue against my clit. So instead, I reached for him.

"It would make me really happy for you to kiss me while I stroke your cock," I said.

Finn licked his lips, shifting forward and leaning down to press his lips to mine.

"Yes, ma'am," he whispered, and then he groaned against my lips as I wrapped a hand around his thick, throbbing cock.

Chapter Eleven

WHAT JULIE LACKED IN experience she made up for in eagerness, though eagerness only took one so far.

As in, it was taking me somewhere, but not to the finish line.

I hadn't expected it to. She was doing amazing for her first time going down on a woman. With a bit of time and practice, she was going to be an absolute goddess at it.

But my hookup with her and Finn was a one-night thing, so I couldn't dedicate too much time to letting her practice if I wanted to get off.

She was straddling my leg, her wetness slick on my skin as she greedily buried her face in my pussy, when I reached down and clasped a handful of her hair in my hand. I didn't pull, just guided, nearly regretting it when she lifted her head and looked at me like I'd just taken away a meal she wasn't done eating.

Which was true, in a way.

"My face is getting jealous of my leg," I said. "So you should probably come sit on it instead."

Finn had moved on from my lips and was sucking on my nipple while I stroked his cock, making him groan as he circled his tongue around my nipple. But when he heard me ask Julie to sit on my face, he shot up, his eyes wide and excited.

"Yes," he said. "Yes, do that, babe."

Julie giggled at his enthusiasm, the slightly offended look on her face disappearing as she moved up the bed. I shifted down, shoving the pillows out of the way. Finn moved to take Julie's place, leaning down to lick the spot on my leg that she'd been straddling, then kissed his way up to my pussy and took his turn tasting me. Moaning, I spread my arms, beckoning Julie forward. She looked nervous, but ducked down and kissed me, the taste of my pussy strong on her lips.

"Mmm," I said. "I can't wait to taste you."

"Right," she breathed. "G-Good. Okay."

There was a moment of hesitation, but she finally threw her thighs on either side of my head. Her slit was hovering above me, barely within reach of my mouth, and I waited a moment before caressing her leg.

"Sit on my face," I said.

Julie shifted, lowering herself slightly. I waited again, then frowned as I tilted my head back so I could look up her stomach and past her breasts.

"I said *sit*, Julie," I snapped, then hooked my arms around the back of her thighs and pulled down until she was pressed firmly against me, her dripping pussy coating my lips and chin and my mouth overflowing with the taste of her.

I think she gasped. I don't know. I could barely hear anything with her thighs covering my ears and my senses being overwhelmed by the sweetness of her pussy. But as soon as I set to work, I heard a muffled sort of noise, and then another, followed by the unfortunate loss of a mouth between my legs and the sensation of the bed shifting as someone moved.

And since I was pinning Julie to my face and was subsequently trapped beneath her on the bed, that could only mean Finn was moving.

Tilting my head as much as I could, I looked up. My view was mostly obstructed by Julie's body, but I could see her turn her head and watched as Finn kissed her. His lips moved as he said something and even though I couldn't see or hear her, Julie must have responded, because a huge smile spread across his face a moment later. The bed jostled again as he stood and moved above me, leaning back against the headboard as Julie leaned forward to take his cock into her mouth.

As many threesomes as I'd had, I'd never watched a blowjob from this angle.

Which would have to change in the future, because this was one *hell* of a view.

I watched as his thick tip disappeared into her mouth, pink lips sealing around his shaft. She wrapped one hand around him, but was able to get a surprising amount of that not-insignificantly-sized cock in her mouth. Given what I knew about Julie, I imagined Finn was probably the first guy she'd sucked off, but *damn* if she wasn't good with her mouth.

Not as good as me, though.

Finn actively trying not to come was probably the only reason I made Julie come first. The groans I could hear coming from his mouth were desperate and needy, but the choked sounds coming from Julie's as I teased her clit with my tongue were more urgent and had barely anything to do with the cock halfway down her throat. I cupped her ass, squeezing it hard as I devoured her.

When she tapped a hand on Finn's hip and pulled back, letting his glistening cock fall from her mouth as she cried out stifled words, I knew I'd won. Seconds later, her hips bucked again and all the effort she'd put into not putting her weight on my face disappeared, leaving her to smother me with her body. I tried not to moan, knowing if I did, I'd probably run out of air before she was finished coming, but it was hard not to.

Not when I was quite literally covered in the epitome of bliss.

When her quivers had faded and I was about to suffocate, I slapped her ass lightly and pushed up, getting her to move just enough that I could slide out from beneath her. Wiping my face as I took a deep breath, I turned to watch her resume bobbing her head on Finn's cock, sloppy sounds coming from her mouth as he clutched her hair. His eyes met mine, heavy-lidded and half-drunk on pleasure already, and I got to my knees so I could stretch up and let him taste his girlfriend's orgasm on my lips.

"You next?" I asked.

He ran his tongue along my lip, then nipped at it. "I'm not coming until you do."

"Is that a challenge? I'm going to be offended if I don't get more than one load out of you tonight, you know."

He smirked and kissed me again. "Oh, I'll give you as many loads as you want. After you, though."

"Is that so?"

"Yea—*ahhh*," he said, which I think he meant to say normally, but Julie attempted to swallow his cock just then and his eyelids fluttered closed for a minute.

I tried not to laugh. "I think if that's what you want, you're going to have to make Julie stop sucking your dick."

He made a noise that was half laugh, half pain. "Uh... yeah. I guess so."

As he panted for breath, I kissed him again.

"I think we both know you're not going to do that, Finn," I murmured against his lips. "I think we both know you're going to watch as I get down there and join her until you come all over us."

"Oh, *God*," he groaned, but he didn't seem too upset about it.

I mean, who would be? Two women, one man, and both of us on our knees in front of him as we shared his dick? Sure, Finn was a selfless people-pleaser, but even he couldn't resist the thought of that. And I couldn't blame him. I didn't have a dick, but watching two people focus on your pleasure as they knelt in front of you was one of those lascivious moments of obscenely carnal filth that anyone would enjoy bringing up in their memories time and time again.

God knows I did.

So I gladly pulled away from Finn's mouth and dropped to my knees beside Julie, bumping her with my hip and making her glance over at me.

"Share," I ordered, and she released his cock with a wet pop before grinning.

We did the typical sharing-him-like-an-ice-cream-cone thing for a while, the thing that guys always seem to want but don't realize until they try it that it doesn't feel as good as they think it will. But that doesn't matter. It was about the visual: my and Julie's lips sliding along his shaft and meeting at the head of his cock. Shimmering wetness coating his shaft and tip. Two tongues finding all the sensitive little spots around his crown and fighting over the drips of pre-cum he was already letting out.

But the visual alone wasn't going to make Finn come, especially when I watched him tilt his head back again and breathe deeply as he fought back against the pleasure we wanted to give him. So it was time to put my mouth where my mouth was.

Or however the saying goes.

The easiest way to do that was to pay attention to as many of those sensitive, orgasm-inducing spots as possible. My personal favourite was to get the other person's mouth on a guy's balls while I worked his tip. Given how close Finn was, I figured that would finish him… as long as I could get Julie's mouth where I needed it.

Luckily, I had an elegant solution to make her do just that.

"Julie," I said.

She raised her eyebrows questioningly on the other side of his cock.

"Suck on his balls," I said, then grabbed her head and pushed it down.

She didn't question it, just parted her lips and sucked her boyfriend's balls greedily into her mouth. Finn cried out, slamming one hand against the headboard as I wrapped my lips around his cock.

"Tess," he said. "You're gonna make me come."

That was kind of the point, I wanted to tell him, but my mouth was full.

He put his other hand on the back of my head, not quite pushing me down, but I took more of him in my mouth all the same. It wasn't much more—his cock really *was* on the bigger side—but it was enough that Finn started panting for breath.

"Fuck," he said. "Oh, *fuck.*"

His other hand moved from the headboard to Julie's head, twisting through her hair as she and I worked together to make him come. Wet sounds came from both our mouths and I bobbed my head faster, picking up the pace as his stomach began to twitch and his hand tightened in my hair.

"*Plecaicomenorth,*" he said.

He thankfully understood that the choked noise I made was a question because he cleared his throat and tried again.

"Please-can-I-come-in-your-mouth," he said in a rush, followed by a groaning sound. "Please, I don't want to pull out."

I made another noise, hoping he understood that one meant "Yes, absolutely, I can't wait for you to shoot your load down my throat." He must have, because a few seconds later, he couldn't hold it back.

"Oh my God, Tessa," he moaned, then tightened his hand. "Fuck, Julie, I—"

And then his cock pulsed against my tongue as he spilled his load.

More impressive, though, were the *noises* that spilled from him. I could honestly say I'd never been with a guy as vocal as Finn, and I fucking loved it. He moaned, he gasped, he whispered our names, he cried out, and it was so fucking hot that I could barely stand it.

When he went still, I pulled back, swallowing as he sighed and rested against the headboard. Julie took her mouth off him, turning to me with playful eyes as Finn sank down on the bed.

"I think we did good," she said.

"I think we did very good," I replied.

"I *know* you did good," Finn mumbled, and I laughed as Julie leaned in to kiss me.

Most of the time, guys needed a bit to recover after they came. That was fine by me, since they usually just watched as I fucked their girlfriends until they got it up again. I thought that was going to happen when Julie kissed me, so when Finn suddenly grabbed me and pulled me away from her so he could capture my lips instead, I let out a surprised gasp.

"What's wrong?" he asked, eyebrows furrowing in concern even as he pulled away.

"I thought you'd need a minute," I said.

His tongue poked out of his mouth, licking his lips in an absolutely indecent way.

"Not a chance am I letting the two of you have all the fun," he said in a low voice. "Now get your ass over here, Tessa."

I don't know why he bothered telling me to do it. Not when he grabbed me, lurched forward, and tossed me down onto the bed like I was as insubstantial as an inflatable sex doll.

Me.

He *tossed* me.

God, it was a damn good thing I wasn't going to see them again, because that was the kind of thing that could make a girl fall in love.

Especially when Julie landed beside me, her arm bumping against mine as she let out a low "*oof*." Before I even registered her presence, Finn was over me. His hair flopped messily on his forehead and a hungry look spread across his face as the light from the room glowed gold around his head.

"My turn," he growled playfully, and then a mop of golden hair was all I could see of him as he buried his face against my pussy.

And fuck.

Fuck.

The man was everywhere. Fucking everywhere. His tongue was inside me and he was pinning one of my hips down to the bed, even as

I squirmed uncontrollably beneath the attention of his mouth. But somehow, he also had a hand between Julie's legs, and she was moaning and writhing as he levelled the same amount of attention on her pussy as he was on mine.

And considering it felt like *all* the attention was on my pussy, I had no fucking idea how he was doing it.

He switched between us, grabbing Julie's leg and hooking it over mine so that when he slid two thick fingers into my pussy, he could easily shift over and start eating her pussy while still nestled between my legs. Soft, muffled groans underscored the wet sounds of his enthusiastic attention, punctuated by the high-pitched gasps he kept drawing from both me and Julie.

It wasn't until he had switched back to my pussy again and I'd cried out, grabbing a handful of his thick gold hair as his tongue began spoiling my clit again, that Julie touched me.

I felt her hand slip between our bodies and looked over. Our fingers entwined and our eyes met, so close that I could almost see my flushed skin in the reflection on her pupils.

As much as I enjoyed the whole "getting fucked into oblivion" part of threesomes, these little moments of intimacy were the showstoppers. I wasn't supposed to have those moments. They didn't belong to me. They belonged to couples, to him and to her when they were alone. But being there as a third... it was like cheating.

Like, cheating as in a life hack, not cheating like the kind of thing that ends marriages.

It was cheating in the way that I'd done nothing to earn those moments, but I got the exhilaration of them all the same. The look of sheer joy on Julie's face, the sweat making her forehead shine, her swollen lips semi-parted as she breathed... I'd never had to take her to dinner or whisper sweet nothings or promise her anything except a good time to get that moment.

But it was mine. And as a little smile spread across her lips, those were mine too.

It didn't take long for the two of them to make me come. Not when Julie was sharing every breath and plea and moan with me while Finn showed off his absolute genius for eating pussy. Pleasure built up, bursting through the place it pooled deep in my core and radiating through my body until my back was arched and Julie was whispering encouragement against my lips.

Finn kept eating me out all through my orgasm, stopping just as I tore my mouth away from Julie's to plead with him to stop because I was too sensitive. When he pulled back, eyes sparkling, a huge grin spread across his face as I sighed and let my legs flop down on the bed.

"Fuck," I said.

"He's good, isn't he?" Julie murmured.

"He's so good. Holy fuck. You lucky bitch."

She giggled and Finn smiled, then pressed a quick kiss against my belly before turning to Julie and diving in.

The next few hours were a sharp haze. Most of it blended together in my mind, memories of sensations and feelings and orgasms instead of words or actions. But some moments stood out, cutting through that enchanting cloud so I could hold on to them for later. Like when I sank down on Finn for the first time while Julie watched, her hungry eyes taking in every moment of his throbbing cock disappearing inside of me. She bit her lip, slipping her hand down her body and playing absentmindedly with her clit as I began to ride him until Finn realized what she was doing.

"Babe, please," he said, staring at her with an expression that was half puppy-dog-eyes and half all-encompassing ache.

"What?" Julie asked.

"You know what."

Her shoulders raised with tension and Finn's pleading expression deepened. "I want it so bad. Please. You did it with her. You know it's going to be okay."

I raised my eyebrows, stilling as the prickling feeling of a red flag began to wave inside of me, but Julie must have caught the expression on my face and shook her head.

"It's okay," she said. "It's something we talked about and I've just always been... nervous."

Which was how I found out that Julie had never sat on anyone's face before mine.

It was the only fantasy Finn had expressly mentioned: one of us on his cock with the other on his face. I couldn't blame him. That position was hot as fuck, and I loved being able to lean forward and play with the other person at the same time.

"We can switch if you want," I said. "You can ride his cock while I get his tongue again."

But Julie shook her head, took a breath, and crawled over to get in position. The last thing I saw before she settled down was Finn with an expression like he was gazing into the light at the end of the tunnel, where pearly gates and intense orgies between angelically hot people were taking place for all of infinity.

It wasn't the last thing I heard, though.

"Come on, Jules," came Finn's muffled voice from between her legs. "You'll sit on Tess's face properly, but not on mine?"

"Move down a little," I urged. "I promise, he'll like it."

"But what if I—"

"Babe, he tossed you across the bed like a rag doll. He's completely capable of making you move. So if he suffocates, that's his own fault. And really, there are far worse ways to die."

She laughed, shocked, and then Finn's arms were around her thighs.

"I *said*," he growled. "Sit. The *fuck*. Down."

And then he pulled her down with so much force, I wouldn't have been surprised if he broke his own nose.

He didn't, though, thankfully. He made Julie come on his face and me come on his cock, then fucked her while she and I made out, then fucked me while she sat on my face again, then... a bunch of other stuff, probably. I think he came twice more, though it might have been three times. I couldn't even count how many times I came, and Julie might just have never *stopped* coming.

All in all, it was a massive success.

We only stopped when Julie shakily said she couldn't handle any more. To be fair, I don't think any of us could have. Finn would have kept going for the rest of the night if we'd asked him, but that was because the man would've probably fucked himself into a dehydration coma just to keep us happy.

He really was a people pleaser.

Together, we lay on the bed, catching our breaths and chuckling as we recounted our favourite parts of the night. I stayed until Finn and Julie snuggled together and kissed gently, which was my usual cue to let them have some "couple time" while I got ready to leave.

Which was, apparently, news to Julie.

"You're not staying?" she asked, her eyes wide when I returned from the bathroom and started to dress.

"Nope," I said, hitching my jeans up and buttoning them. "No offense. Both of you were lovely and this was fantastic, but I don't stay the night. One-and-done, remember?"

"Right. That's fair."

She sounded almost disappointed, which made something prickle inside of me. I thought it was my usual red flag radar tingling, but it hurt a little more than most of those prickles did.

"Sorry. I thought I was clear on that," I said.

"You were." Julie looked up and smiled. "You absolutely were. I just… I know you said you don't do long-term things, but—"

"Julie," I said. "I don't. Don't ask me to."

"I *know*," she said, raising her hands. "I just meant that if you ever wanted to do this again as a casual thing… I mean, at least you know we're interested."

I smiled back, hoping it didn't come across as patronizing, and then wondered why I was worried about her thinking I was being patronizing. Sliding my tank top on, I crossed the room to her, then grabbed her wrist and pulled her in to kiss her. It made her giggle, and I nipped at her lip.

"I won't. Too much of a risk that you'll both fall in love with me," I said, brushing her hair off her face. "Thanks, though.

She smiled. "Can we keep in touch? Like friends?"

Fuck.

The answer to that was no, but it was hard to say that when they were standing right in front of me. Especially when I knew there was a chance of seeing Finn when he delivered things to my office.

"Maybe," I said. "We'll see, okay?"

"Okay."

I gave her one last kiss for some reason, which was weird because I never really kissed people once the fucking was done, then turned to Finn.

"Thank you. I can't decide if your dick or your tongue was better, so good job on that."

He chuckled, his cheeks blushing red. "Thanks."

"Alright." I turned to grab my leather jacket. "I'll see you around, maybe. Have a good—"

But before I could finish, that huge hunk of muscled golden retriever energy shot off the bed, still naked as the day he was born, and threw his arms around me in an affectionate, all-encompassing hug.

"Like you're getting away without a hug," he said. "I hope we see you again, Tess. Send us a message sometime, yeah?"

"I... yeah," I lied. "Yeah, I will."

He smiled and pressed a kiss to the side of my head. "Thanks for everything. You're awesome."

And honestly, for as many couples as I'd walked away from with no intention of ever contacting them again, that made them among the most difficult.

Part 2

Confession: Forty bucks is
forty bucks.

Chapter Twelve

Sometime on Tuesday while I was having the life fucked out of me, Loni decided that the end of the week was Wednesday. Using Loni logic, that meant that the end of the week had *always* been Wednesdays and had definitely not been a thing she just randomly invented after a few too many multi-thousand-dollar bottles of wine.

It wasn't the oddest thing Loni had ever done, but like most things Loni did, it left Dinah in a frazzled state of fluster, her heart rate keeping up with the hummingbirds as she tried to figure out how it would be possible to move Fridays to Wednesdays for the foreseeable future. At the same time, she was busy yelling at me about the proposal and draft schedule for the Recycl-Ball not being done yet, despite the fact that proposals and draft schedules were exactly zero percent of my job description.

"I don't even know how to do that, Dinah," I said, wincing as she screeched at me. "I can help you with it, but—"

"I don't have time to do it myself! What good are you if you can't even manage a proposal and a draft schedule?"

I shrugged. "Beats me. I can go get coffee or something, if you want."

"When do you need it, Dinah?" Chuck asked.

"I need it—" She looked down at her wrist, which was bare. "—twenty-six minutes ago."

"I'll have it to you this afternoon," Chuck said. "Now, why don't you—"

"THIS AFTERNOON IS NOT GOOD ENOUGH!"

"Okay," Chuck said brightly, clapping his hands together. "Time for Operation Oh Shit, Tessa Isla Lane."

"What in the fuck is Operation Oh Shit?" Dinah asked.

Neither of us answered. That was because Operation Oh Shit was my and Chuck's version of Code Red. Or Code Blue. Or whatever code is the code where everything was burning down for real and we needed to actually take things seriously for a while. We exchanged a look, then I stood up and left the office to go to Starbucks down the street while Chuck took control of CARE's limited resources to do what needed to be done.

I definitely got the better end of the deal with Operation Oh Shit, but it was because we figured the most useful thing I could do when Dinah was in ultimate panic mode was to stay far, far away from her. And I always brought Chuck back a caramel macchiato and whatever baked good looked like it had the highest sugar content.

Of course, like most Operation Oh Shit situations, Chuck was able to handle it just fine. By four o'clock, he had everything figured out and CARE was running as smoothly as it usually did.

Which was about as smoothly as a rusted-out truck speeding down a dilapidated gravel road, but still. Things were back to normal.

The only downside was that I didn't get a chance to tell Chuck all about the previous night, which he took great offense to despite the fact that he was the one who called for Operation Oh Shit.

"Priorities, Tessa Veronica Lane," he said that night as we walked to Brenda McClane's studio for the art class he'd signed us up for. "What's more important, our workplace's biggest fundraising event of the year or you telling me every dirty detail about Finn's dick and sweet little Julie?"

I rolled my eyes, but spent most of the walk telling him about Finn and Julie, finishing just as we reached the studio.

"They sound amazing," Chuck said, opening the door for me.

"They were," I replied. "Honestly, that was one of the best ones I've ever had."

"Seriously?"

"Mm-hmm." We started up the stairs to Brenda's studio. "Surprising, since she'd never been with a woman before, but Julie was so into it and Finn..."

"Mm-hmm?"

"He was great."

"In bed."

"Yeah, but also just in general." We'd reached the top of the stairs and were walking towards the studio door. "He's sweet. And patient, like Julie said. And like, legitimately hilarious. I don't know if he *meant* to be hilarious, but I haven't laughed that much in a long time."

We were just about at the door to the studio. Chuck stopped before opening the door, giving me a strange look.

"It almost sounds like you liked him," he said.

I rolled my eyes. "A hot, funny, golden retriever boy who could probably bench press me? Yeah, Chuck, I liked him, if by 'like' you mean wanted to let him pin me to a bed and—"

The door to the studio flew open before I could finish, revealing a short white woman who had frizzy brown hair peppered with grey. There was a spot of grey paint smeared on her cheek and a splatter in the same colour on the thick lenses of her round glasses.

Brenda freakin' McClane.

She had been renowned in the Vancouver art scene before she retired. Her work used to be in galleries and museums across the country, usually accompanied by a very artsy black-and-white headshot of a pale woman with slicked back hair and sharply focused eyes, a hand resting coyly on her chin as she stared at the camera. Whether that headshot actually showed *Brenda* was questionable; I could see a slight resemblance to the embodiment of chaos packaged in a teensy human shell standing in front of me, but only just.

These days, Brenda ran an art studio and taught classes in her spare time. But she had a long-standing love of the environment and, more importantly, a close friendship with one of Loni's rich family members. CARE, who was notorious for being unable to afford to support any relevant artists, had thrown tons of grant money her way to create a series of trash sculptures a few years earlier, which Brenda did mostly as a favour to the Less family. Those sculptures were part of the reason CARE had any legitimacy whatsoever, so keeping Brenda happy was important.

"*There* you are!" Brenda shouted. "I thought you were going to bail on me and we'd have to cancel!"

I glanced at Chuck, confused. It wasn't quite seven yet; it wasn't like we were late. "Uh... nope! Here we are."

"Sorry, Ms. McClane," Chuck said. "I thought this was a group class."

She laughed. "Oh, it is. We were waiting on you. Come, come. Follow me."

Chuck and I exchanged another glance as she stepped out of the studio with a bundle of fabric in her arms, then followed her.

"Have either of you done this before?" she asked.

"Well, Tessa is our resident artist," Chuck said. "So she has. But this is my first official time."

"A virgin," Brenda said. "Don't worry, we'll be gentle. Remember, there are some beginners in this class, so don't take the results too personally."

The results...

I figured it out before Chuck did. He still looked confused when we reached the bathroom. Brenda turned to us and held the robes out.

"We just have the one bathroom," she said. "But I'm assuming you have no problem disrobing together."

"What?" Chuck said.

Brenda ignored him. "Oh, the students will be so excited. It's hard enough to get *one* model; two is practically a dream! It's a full house tonight. I was worried that it wouldn't be enough notice to schedule a special class but I almost had to turn people away." She shook the robes at us. "Here you are. Just come into the studio once you're ready. I'll have your checks ready for you at the end of the class."

With that, she turned, leaving each of us clutching a terry-cloth robe as we stood in front of the bathroom.

"We're not doing this," I said when I was sure she was out of earshot.

"Why not?" Chuck asked.

I stared at him incredulously. "You *want* to model nude?"

"*Model*? We're here to *draw*."

"Really? Because Brenda seems to think we're here to model for her."

"She does not."

"Oh, right. How silly of me. How could I be so mistaken?" I held up the robe Brenda had handed me. "Remind me again what are these for, then?"

He pursed his lips. "Uh... to make sure we don't get paint on our clothes?"

"It's a drawing class."

"Maybe it's just part of the process?"

"Ah, yes, of course. Getting naked to draw nude models is what I've done in *every* figure drawing class I've ever attended. How could I have forgotten such an important detail?"

"See? Totally normally," Chuck said.

I glared at him. "I was being sarcastic."

"Well, she can't *possibly* think we're the models, Tessa Debbie Downer Lane."

"Aside from the fact that she literally said two models was a dream for her."

"She must have meant the models who are probably already in the studio. I was *very* specific in my email to her."

"What did you say?"

He pulled his phone out of his pocket, tapped the screen, and then jutted his hip out as he began to read. "Dear Ms. McClane, Hope this email finds you well. My co-worker, CARE's resident artist Tessa Lane, mentioned she was looking to broaden her artistic experience and I knew we simply had to talk to the best of the best—you, of course! Do you have any figure drawing classes looking for an excessively experienced artist (Tessa) and an absolute beginner (myself)? We would love to sit together and use our collective assets to help model—"

"Are you not hearing this?" I interrupted. "Are you not hearing how this sounds? Chuck, you couldn't have been more misleading if you'd tried!"

"Well, it's not like she said she thought I was asking to model!" he said. "Look, her response said 'Dearest Chuck, I can't express to you how ecstatic I am for your offer to work with one of our classes! It's so difficult to find willing participants sometimes. My students would be delighted to have you sit for us—'"

"Chuck."

"Okay, fine!" He threw his other hand up, forgetting he was holding the robe and nearly hitting me in the face with it. "I may have misinterpreted her response a little."

"You mean a lot."

He sighed. "How mad do you think she'll be if we back out now?"

"Livid. It'll probably cost CARE one of its only assets."

"Fuck." He grimaced, then glanced down the hall and sighed. "What if we just... did it?"

"Are you serious?" I asked. "Of all the things I wanted to do tonight, sitting naked in a room in front of you and a bunch of strangers for three hours was not one of them. My limit is two strangers, and they're usually both naked, too."

"Right," he said. "Of course."

"Do *you* want to?"

"Absolutely not." He sighed, looking at his phone. "Two Operation Oh Shits in one week. And you won't even be around to witness it when Dinah and/or Loni kills me tomorrow."

"You weren't even a little suspicious when Brenda didn't mention how much the class would cost?"

"I thought she did!" He tilted the phone at me. "I read it as her saying 'the class costs forty dollars each' and not 'we'll pay each of you forty dollars an hour.' I thought that seemed like a reasonable—"

"Wait." I grabbed his phone. "Did you say forty bucks an *hour*?"

"Uh... yes."

I read the email on his phone, which did indeed say she was offering us forty dollars an hour, then up at him. "I mean... hypothetically speaking, forty bucks is forty bucks. An *hour*."

He hummed. "Hypothetically speaking, I might be willing to let you see me naked for forty bucks an hour."

"Hypothetically speaking, I might be willing to look at you naked for forty bucks an hour."

We stared at each other.

"This won't make things weird for us?" he asked. "Like as friends?"

"No," I said. "As long as you don't judge my ugly underwear. I wasn't planning on anyone seeing them tonight."

"I won't judge your ugly underwear if you don't judge the fact that I'm not wearing any."

I wrinkled my nose, then nodded. Without another word, I handed Chuck his phone and opened the bathroom door.

Chapter Thirteen

"STOP LOOKING AT MY coochie."

"I'm not looking at your coochie."

"I can feel you looking at it."

I let out as dramatic a sigh as I could without moving too much. "You don't even *have* a coochie, Chuck."

"I meant my back coochie."

"You shouldn't have posed with your ass in my face then, dumbass."

"I didn't think you were going to squat down!"

"Trust me, it's one of the biggest regrets of my life."

"Rude."

"Mr. David, could you please rotate your arm back to where it was previously?" called one of the students. I wasn't sure which, since I had Chuck's so-called "back coochie" about four inches from my face in what felt like a nightmarish game of twister.

"Sorry," Chuck said, moving his arm again.

I hadn't expected Chuck to be as comfortable as he was with this, despite never having done it before. As soon as we'd gone into the bathroom, I started undressing.

"Just jumping right in, huh?" he muttered.

I stopped taking my pants off and looked at him. "Now is the time to back out if you don't want to do this."

He shook his head. "It's fine. As many times as I've been naked in public, I've never *gotten* naked with someone else like this."

"How many times have you been naked in public?" I asked, which was how I learned about the exhibitionist streak Chuck had in his college days that manifested by way of dancing naked in a cage at a bar every Friday and Saturday night for a few months.

"Well, I'm not going to judge you for being naked or something," I said. "I might be an asshole, but I'm not *that* much of an asshole."

He snorted. "Like I was worried about that. I just don't need you falling in love with my hot body and getting jealous of my top-tier modelling skills."

"Trust me. There isn't a chance of either of those things."

And that was the truth.

First of all, Chuck and I knew we were meant to be friends. Everyone always thinks that people who were friends like we were would eventually admit we were both in love with each other, but that wasn't going to happen. There was no big reason behind it. We just weren't each other's type in a non-platonic sense. That always seemed to surprise people, though it really shouldn't have. I mean, if I as a bisexual woman could be friends with other women without pining away for them and Chuck as a pansexual man could be friends with other men without falling in love, why was it so hard to believe that we could be friends with each other?

So there was no chance I was going to fall in love with Chuck just because I was seeing him naked.

Second of all, Chuck was a terrible model. I mean, he was good-looking, don't get me wrong. Having met both his parents briefly at the CARE Recycl-Ball one year, I could honestly state there had been no chance Chuck *wouldn't* be attractive. His mom was Japanese and had passed on her thick, dark hair and smooth skin, while his dad was white and had passed on his killer smile and strong jaw. So he already had his looks going for him. And while Chuck might not have been the guy who was at the gym twenty-four seven, he was naturally on the slimmer side and had unexpectedly nice arms for someone who kept them encased in sweaters most of the time.

Not to mention that he was like… meticulously groomed. I mean, I would have been happy knowing that just from having seen his eyebrows and impeccably clean-shaven face every single day. But now I also had the unwelcome knowledge that there was not a single body hair on his body that didn't look like it was intentionally left where it was.

So no, Chuck wasn't a terrible model because he was ugly or something.

He just sucked at standing still.

"Next pose, please," Brenda called, and I stood up as quickly as I could, shaking my legs out.

"I'm running out of ideas," Chuck whispered.

"Already?" I whispered back. "We haven't even finished doing gestures yet."

He shrugged helplessly and I rolled my eyes.

"Are you okay with doing touching poses?"

He looked wary. "Like… touching *how*?"

I rolled my eyes. "I'm not planning on grabbing your back coochie or anything. Just turn around and we'll stand back to back."

"…and press our back coochies *together*?"

I rolled my eyes. "No, genius. Just… just turn around and I'll—"

"Mr. David? Ms. Lane? Have you got another pose for us?" Brenda asked pointedly.

"Sorry!" I exclaimed.

I directed Chuck to turn around with his feet shoulder width apart and his hands extended to the side, then faced the opposite direction and mirrored his stance, pressing my palms to his.

"Ooh," Brenda said as we settled in. "I like this. Everyone, take note of the positioning. This is a very standard pose, but the addition of a second body adds a level of complexity. Note how the shadows fall from each model and..."

I tuned out as she kept talking, glancing around the room. Brenda hadn't been lying when she said it was a full house. There were a few empty spots, but everywhere else was occupied by people frantically sketching me and Chuck.

My heart had skipped a beat when we walked into the studio and moved into the center of the room, but I kept a cool face as Brenda asked us to disrobe. Determinedly not looking at Chuck, Brenda, or *any* of the students, I'd shrugged the robe off before taking the first pose I'd thought of.

I didn't know if Chuck had any nerves in the first place, but mine had faded almost instantly. It was anticlimactic, in a way; there was no intense moment of fear or second thoughts or worry. Part of it was because I was busy thinking back to some of the figure drawing classes I'd attended, trying to pick out the poses that would be easiest to hold and that I'd found most helpful to practice drawing.

But most of it was probably because I was pretty comfortable in my own skin. A lot more than I would've been ten or so years earlier, when I was taking classes like this regularly.

"Alright everyone, that's it for gestures," Brenda said a short while later.

"That's it?" Chuck whispered. "We didn't even make our forty bucks!"

I rolled my eyes and smacked his arm as I turned around. "That was the *warmup*."

"We'll take five minutes for everyone to set up and our models to have a break," she said. As the students bustled to re-sharpen pencils and sip their water and stretch, Brenda walked over with our robes. "Mr. David, Ms. Lane, do you have some positions in mind to hold for the longer poses?"

"We do," I said.

"We do?" Chuck said.

I elbowed him before grabbing my robe from Brenda. "Yes, we do. But if you have requests, we're happy to consider them."

"I do," she said as Chuck and I shrugged the robes on. "The final pose you did where you were interacting with each other was especially helpful. I was hoping you would consider doing more poses together rather than seeming like two solo models. If you're comfortable with it, that is."

I shrugged. "It's fine by me. Chuck?"

"Sure. Just no grabbing my back coo—"

"Say 'coochie' one more fucking time," I grumbled, and he burst out laughing.

Brenda laughed along, though I was sure she had no idea why. "That's wonderful. One more question for you, and please, feel free to say no…"

I glanced at Chuck. We met eyes and didn't need to exchange words to know we were both thinking the same thing.

"…we have a few students who arrived after we'd started," she finished. "Would you be willing to allow them to come into the room? They've been waiting outside the studio, but I will tell them to leave if you're not comfortable with it."

That wasn't what I was expecting.

Probably because I had a dirty mind and thought the whole thing sounded like a bad erotic fantasy. But I was relieved it wasn't what I was expecting, and Chuck seemed to be, too.

"I have no problem with that," he said. "Tess?"

"Bring 'em in," I said. "The more, the merrier."

While she went to let the latecomers in, Chuck and I grabbed some water and I hastily explained to him the poses I had in mind for us to take. We still weren't quite done when Brenda clapped her hands and said it was time to start.

Which was unfortunate, because Chuck was really, *really* bad at this.

"Like this?" Chuck whispered as I fought with his inherent awkwardness while trying to position him the way I'd pictured.

"No, stop moving your head. Look that way and just move your—"

"Here?"

I closed my eyes briefly, taking a deep breath before letting it out. "That's my tit, Chuck."

He gasped, whipping his head back with a look of horror on his face as he snatched his hand away like he'd been burned. "Sorry."

"It's fine. Just stop moving."

Grabbing my boob must have been the trigger he needed to just let me position him before posing myself. We weren't quite facing each other, though if I looked out of the corner of my eye, we could make eye contact. One of his hands was resting on my hip and one of mine on his arm as we half-twisted in the other direction.

"Are you finding this hot at all?" he muttered once we were settled and the students had started to draw us.

"Oh, fuck no," I mumbled back. "Please don't tell me you are."

"Not even a little."

"Good."

A brief snort of air was the only hint I had that he wanted to laugh. "I was just worried you might be attracted to me."

"No, Chuck. I know you far too well for that."

"Rude."

"It's why you love me."

"Sometimes I wonder."

Laughter threatened me, so I fought back a smile and took the chance to glance around the room for the first time in a while.

Which is, of course, when we saw each other.

Well, I mean, he'd obviously seen me first. Because he'd walked in with the latecomers and was now sitting at one of the previously empty seats and was fighting back a semi-amused expression that I'd seen more than once. He had one hand over his sketchpad, familiarly fuckable fingers gripping a pencil, and the sleeves of his shirt were rolled up like they always were to show off the contrast between his tanned white skin and greyscale tattoos.

"Oh my God," I muttered, trying not to move my lips.

"What?" Chuck replied, not at all bothering to muffle his voice.

The man sitting in front of me half-grimaced and half-smiled as he shrugged as subtly as he could.

"Sorry?" he mouthed.

I failed to hold back my laughter, though I did manage to contain it, meaning that I made an odd sort of snorting sound mixed with a high-pitched giggle. Considering that laugh wanted to be one of those keeling-over-tears-running-down-your-face kind of laughs, I considered it a success.

"What *is* it?" Chuck repeated, and I felt him move beside me.

"Mr. David, can you please keep your head facing the direction it was originally?" Brenda asked pointedly.

"Sorry," he said, snapping his head back to where it was, though he was glaring at me out of the corner of his eye. "Tessa Jennifer Love Hewitt Lane, tell me what the *hell* that God-awful sound was."

I didn't know how to tell him without everyone in the room hearing it. We were in an art studio with a bunch of frantically focused art students, after all. But luckily, Brenda chose that moment to start talking loudly about proper shading techniques or some shit like that.

"You know that server at Bar One I keep telling you about?" I breathed as quietly as I could.

"What?" Chuck asked, bewildered. "The backup plan guy?"

"Yeah, that one."

"Uh... I guess."

"Listen to me carefully, Chuck. Don't move your head."

"I didn't move it!"

"No, I mean when I tell you what I'm about to tell you."

I couldn't *technically* see him roll his eyes, but his pupil disappeared from the corner of his eye before looking back at me. "Consider me encased in anticipatory carbonite."

"He's currently drawing us naked."

Despite my near-certainty that Chuck would immediately turn his head and Brenda would admonish him again, he was true to his word. The only movement I saw was the widening of his eyes before he tried to look in the direction I was facing without moving, which didn't go especially well because his skull was in the way.

"I can't see him."

"Obviously."

"But I want to see him."

I pressed my lips together. "You'll just have to wait until we have a break."

Chuck huffed. "Like hell I will."

I frowned. "What—"

"Brenda?" Chuck called.

She stopped speaking to the class mid-sentence, tension hanging in the air.

"Yes, Mr. David?" she asked.

"This is so embarrassing," he said. "But I have just the slightest little crick in my neck and I hate to impose on everyone's experience, but would you mind if I just stretched it out real quick so we can continue posing? I just need a few seconds, tops. I am so very sorry for the inconvenience."

As it turned out, Brenda didn't mind Chuck moving so long as she had a sufficient amount of simpering and apologetic notice.

"Oh, of course!" she said. "Please, go right ahead."

"You're an angel, Ms. McClane." He made a show of rolling his head back and forth before twisting to look over one shoulder, then the other, where he lingered half a moment longer than was necessary before sighing with imitated relief before repositioning himself. "Much better. Thank you for your patience, everyone."

Soft responses of "no problem" and "anytime" and the non-committal "murmblemulfurmbumble" echoed from the students around the room. Then, as Brenda began speaking to the students again, Chuck looked at me.

"You're talking about the blonde with the forearm tattoos and fuckable hands?" he whispered.

"Yeah."

He groaned. "Don't tell me that."

"Okay. That wasn't him."

"I am naked in a room full of people right now," he said. "How dare you make me look at someone that delicious?"

I held in a laugh. "He's an excellent backup plan, eh?"

"Jesus, Tessa." He sighed almost longingly. "What kind of people are you bagging that *he's* the backup plan? How is that not Plan A? How have you not fucked that man in an alley yet?"

"What was that, Mr. David?" Brenda asked suddenly, and both Chuck and I jumped as we realized she was behind us. Well, half-jumped. We jolted, but stayed in place.

"Did you need to stretch again?" she continued. "I apologize, I didn't hear you."

"Um... yes," Chuck said unconvincingly, then did a quick shake of his head. "All done, thanks."

Another murmblemulfurmbumble went around the room. I risked a glance at the server from Bar One, who was still wearing an apologetic smirk. I couldn't tell if he'd heard us or not, but it didn't matter.

I mean, at worst, he'd heard Chuck ask why I hadn't fucked him in an alley yet. Like, oh no. Now he knew I thought he was hot and might want to go down on him and/or ride his fingers until—

And that was enough of that line of thought, I told myself, seeing as I was standing naked in a room full of people.

At least, until Chuck had to open his big mouth a while later after we'd moved into our final pose of the night.

"So you're banging him in the alley when we're done?" he asked, trying to speak without moving his lips.

"Why would I do that?" I replied as subtly as I could.

"Because he's hot?"

"I... yeah, but..."

"But?"

I sighed. "I have to pack tonight. I'm flying to Burnsley in the morning."

"Flying to... Tessa. You beautiful, sensual, confident little chicken nugget. It sounds like you're trying to talk yourself out of getting laid tonight."

"I got laid last night."

"And has that *ever* stopped you before? Come on. You're the efficiency master when it comes to hook ups. I bet you can fuck him in the alley and still be home in time to pack and get a good eight hours in before you leave."

I twisted my mouth to the side. "I am really efficient when it comes to sex."

Chuck stifled a laugh. "So? In the alley?"

"Why? You want to watch?"

"I mean, if you're offering..."

"Why in the hell would I be offering that, Chuck?"

"Well, I know you haven't fucked just one person at a time in a while. But if you're planning on inviting me to be part of the threesome, just know that, respectfully, I want nothing to do with you."

"I can honestly say I cannot think of a single reason I would want to invite you to a threesome with me."

"Because you're a kind and generous person and, as an accomplished and renowned artist, it's part of your mission to ensure art can be enjoyed by all, so you'd want to share a finely sculpted Adonis—"

Thank God Brenda picked that moment to clap her hands together and declare that it was the end of the class, because I couldn't hold back the laughter any longer.

"I don't know what's funnier," I giggled as Chuck and I stood up. "You referring to me as kind and generous... or assuming that I'd share with *you*."

Chuck huffed, but he was fighting back a smile of his own as we reached our robes and shrugged them on. "So you're going to go for it, then?"

I glanced at the server from Bar One, who was packing up his supplies. "You know... I just might."

But I did not.

I was going to. It didn't escape my attention that the server from Bar One was filling his backpack a bit more slowly than everyone else. And I definitely noticed him lingering as Brenda came over to thank us for our time and invited us to look around at some of the drawings the students had done.

And when I caught his eye after Brenda handed us our checks and not-so-thinly veiled hinted that if we wanted to pose for her again, she would be ecstatic to have us back—which was surprising considering how bad Chuck was at it—before letting us know we could leave the robes in the bathroom after we finished changing? When I saw that little question in the server's eye and the slight flick of his eyebrow?

Yeah, I gave him my subtlest nod and head-jerk to indicate he should hang out in the hallway while I got dressed. As efficient as it would have been to just pull him into the bathroom and fuck him before I got re-dressed, there was the annoying issue of Chuck also needing to use the same room.

But then it all went to hell.

"...details about the location of any and all additional tattoos that might be on his beautifully sculpted body and—"

"Oh, *fuck* no," I said.

Chuck's nattering about the server was cut off as he made a high-pitched noise of offense. "Excuse me? I thought we were friends."

"Not that." I stared down at the screen of my phone, my mouth dry.

Just the sight of his name was enough to draw every bit of joy from my being. The sight of his name followed by a message saying twelve missed calls? I was lucky the granola bar Brenda had given us for a snack halfway through the art class didn't end up spewed all over the bathroom floor.

My distress must have shown on my face because Chuck stopped what he was doing and walked over to check on me.

"What is it?" he asked, uncharacteristically serious.

"It's... oh, fuck," I said, squeezing my eyes shut. "She must have called him."

"Who's she? And who's *him*?"

The words stuck in my throat, but I forced them out. "Mom called Brad."

My mother had called my fucking husband.

Chapter Fourteen

"Oh, fuck," Chuck said, then grabbed my phone out of my hand. "He called twelve times?! What can be so important that he called twelve ti—oh."

"Thirteen times." He held the phone out to me, an apologetic look in his eyes. "Do you want to answer it?"

"Of course I fucking don't," I grumbled, but took the phone anyway and tapped the screen. "Hello?"

"Hey, beauti—"

"Do not call me 'beautiful,'" I said. "This is your millionth reminder that you do not get to call me by pet names anymore."

Brad sighed. "Hello, Tessa."

"Hello, Bradley. What do you want?"

"Great, thanks. Work's been insane for the past few months but two days ago Dimitri officially offered me the promotion, so—"

"I'm hanging up now."

"Wait, don't."

"Click. Sorry, can't hear you."

Despite his frustration with me, he chuckled. "So convincing. How's it going, Tess?"

"Cut the shit. I don't have time for small talk."

"Clearly, since you've been ignoring my calls all night."

"As much as I wish it were true, I wasn't ignoring your call. I was in an art class."

That was a mistake. Brad clutched at that little tidbit of information like it was a thousand dollar bill floating in the wind. "Art class? For what? You're already an amazing artist."

"I don't have time for flattery, either."

"You know I'll always believe in your talent, Tess. You *are* an amazing artist."

I glared at Chuck, but only because he was the only person in the room, and if I glared at myself in the bathroom mirror, I might make myself cry. He looked affronted as he pulled on the grey-and-blue knitted sweater he'd been wearing. Then he mouthed something that was far too complicated for me to lip-read, but that I assumed was "Do you want me to hang out here with you or should I go to the hallway and give you some privacy and also I'm not actually offended, I'm here if you need anything at all because I know how much talking to that shitstain messes with your head and I'm worried about you," to which I nodded.

He responded with a brusque nod of his own, then slipped out of the bathroom and let the door close behind him.

"Your brown-nosing is both noted and unappreciated," I said to Brad.

"Call it whatever you want. You're still my favourite artist of all time."

I rolled my eyes. Well, it was more like a glance up at the light to keep the tears behind my lashline where they belonged, but that was irrelevant. "Fine. What do you—"

"So why were you taking a class?" he pressed. "Was it like a personal development thing? Can I help? If you want money for more classes or if you want to go to one of those retreats again, I can—"

"No."

"Tess, I want you to succeed. Legitimately, I do. Tell me how I can help."

There was a lot wrong with that statement, though none of it was a lie. Brad did want me to succeed. He believed in me to a fault. But considering he was the reason my art had fucking *sucked* for the past five years, it was hard not to snap back at him that if he wanted to help, he could go back in and never introduce himself to me in the first place.

I didn't say that, though.

"I don't need your money," I replied.

"I know you don't, beautiful. I just—"

"I was at the class to model."

The confusion in his voice was so obvious that I could almost picture the expression on his stupid face. "Modelling? Like…"

"For a figure drawing class. Not that it's any of your business but considering a room full of strangers just stared at my and this other guy's businesses for three hours, I guess it's pointless not to tell you."

"Wait, your *business*? Were you… and what do you mean, you and another—"

"As much as I'm enjoying this totally inappropriate interrogation, if you don't tell me why you called, I'm going to hang up for real this time," I said. "I have… plans."

"You have plans after ten on a work night?" he asked, and there was something in his voice that I immediately recognized as what one would call "a gigantic fucking trap."

And yet, there was no way to avoid it.

"I have the day off tomorrow," I said.

"Hmm. Why's that?"

"I have shit to do."

"Like packing your suitcase because you have a flight to Burnsley for your parents' fortieth wedding anniversary?" he asked.

"No," I said.

"Tessa."

"It technically lands in Kelowna."

Another chuckle. I hated that I could still make him laugh. And I fucking loathed that part of me felt warm when I did.

"Touché. So which flight should I be booking?"

"None of them. You're not coming."

"Oh, okay," he said lightly. "I just thought since your mom called and tore me a new one for being on a quote-unquote 'business trip,' I should make an appearance. You know, since apparently I've known about their anniversary party for quote-unquote 'months.' Oh, and that my quote-unquote 'family' misses seeing me because you've come up with an excuse for my absence every time you've gone back home in the past two years. So I figured that, in order to maintain the charade you've asked me to maintain, you'd want me to attend the party with you."

"Do you know how obnoxious you sound when you say 'quote-unquote' like that?"

"Tess. You know I'll cover for you until you don't want it to be a cover anymore—"

"It will never not be a cover. The only way I see it not being a cover anymore is if and when I find someone else I want to marry and need to tell my family about it so they'll attend the hypothetical wedding I probably won't want anyway."

"So you're saying there's a chance," he said.

"Brad, for the millionth time. Listen carefully."

I caught sight of myself in the bathroom mirror, grimacing at the sight of my pale face and furrowed eyebrows, and turned away again.

"We're not getting back together. Ever. You can offer to pay for all the art classes you want. You can say all the beautiful words you think I should hear. You can believe that going out of your way to impress me by pretending that we're still married so I don't have to tell my family that I was wrong and that you were the worst mistake of my life will make a difference. The fact that I even have to pretend to have any sort of connection to you anymore makes me want to go to Olive Garden and eat as much pasta as I can just so I can throw it up on a blank canvas that I'll sell as an art piece expressing how disgusting the idea of being with you is. Getting back together will never, ever happen. I do not regret leaving you. And I do not love you. I never will again."

Brad didn't laugh, but despite the harshness of my words, he didn't react with anything except compassion, which made me want to scream.

"I understand, Tess," he said. "But I'm still going to spend every single day of my life hoping that will change. There's no one in the world I want the way I want you."

"Sucks to be you, then, because it's never fucking changing."

"I know. But a guy can hope."

"A guy shouldn't hope. A guy should get over it and leave me alone."

"But then what will you tell your family?"

"That you died."

"If that were true, I feel like you already would have instead of letting me help your parents after the fire and—"

"You fucking *swore* you wouldn't hold that against me."

He sighed. "I'm not holding it against you. I understand why you couldn't. And I understand why you still can't. I understand *you*, Tess. I want you to be happy, even if that means we play this game for the rest of our lives. You've always deserved better than how they treated you. I wish you could see that the way I do."

"Shut up, Brad." My voice threatened to crack and I closed my eyes. "Please don't come. I'll make up some excuse. Like a plane crash or something on your way back from your business trip."

"Uh... that ship might have sailed. I didn't realize I was supposed to be on a pretend business trip, so when she asked where I was, I said I was in Vancouver."

I groaned. "Fuck. Seriously?"

"Sorry, beautiful. Maybe give me a head's up next time?"

"That would require talking to you."

"Look, I've already checked my schedule and other than having to take a conference call at eight on Friday morning, I can be there," he said. "I'm assuming Dylan's staying at their place so we can just book two rooms at the Mountainview. Depending what time you're leaving, I can fly out and connect with you in Vancouver, or we can just meet in Kelowna and drive out together."

Closing my eyes, I tried to think of something—anything—I could do to stop this from happening. The only thing worse than spending three-and-a-half days with my family was doing it while pretending Brad and I had the perfect marriage. But aside from coming up with a story featuring aliens, time travellers, and a significant amount of fettuccine alfredo—mainly because I was starving and really wanted fettuccine alfredo now that I'd mentioned it—I couldn't think of an excuse.

I mean, yes, I could have just not gone. Or told my family the truth. Or told Brad to change his number so my mom didn't have it anymore and I could convince her he'd sadly fallen down a well and could no longer attend any family events. But at this point, with my mom having already talked to him, it was just going to disappoint my parents even more.

And God knows that for some fucking reason, despite everything, I hated disappointing them.

"I get into Kelowna at noon," I said begrudgingly.

"So you leave around eleven? I can make it to Vancouver in time. What flight—"

"No. Just... just fly from Seattle. I'll wait for you in Kelowna."

"You'll be waiting for a couple of hours then," he said.

"You say that like a few extra hours without you is a bad thing."

"Did you rent a car already?"

"Yep. I'll pick it up and go to Olive Garden while I wait for your slow ass. You can Uber there."

He laughed. "Okay. I'll call the hotel."

"Like hell you will," I said. "I will call the hotel and book you a second room so there isn't some 'misunderstanding' like there was last time."

"It *was* a misunderstanding," he said. "And even if it wasn't, trust me, Tess. I'm almost forty. There's no fucking way I could handle sleeping on the floor for three days again."

"Served you right," I muttered.

"It was worth it to know you were comfortable."

"Oh, shut up, Brad," I said, then hung up on him.

My phone buzzed barely thirty seconds later with the details of his flight, because of course it did. Because of course Brad had probably been sitting in his stupid fancy office with his stupid laptop open in front of his stupid face, all prepared to buy his stupid plane ticket to spend the weekend pretending to be my stupid husband.

Well, sort of. He wouldn't be pretending to be stupid.

Sighing, I put my phone in my purse, my stomach curling with nerves as I finally shrugged off the robe and got dressed. I was so shaken up by my call with Brad that I'd completely forgotten about the server from Bar One until the bathroom door opened a crack and Chuck poked his head in.

"I'm assuming the lack of angry cat noises coming from your mouth means you're done?" he asked.

I almost hissed at him, but just nodded. He opened the door the rest of the way and came in.

"So I have good news, bad news, and worse news," he said.

"Oh, God."

"The good news is that I learned your hot server's name."

"Really?" I asked.

Chuck nodded. "He was hovering around the hallway waiting to say hello."

I sighed. "Is the bad news that it's 'was' and not '*is*' hovering around the hallway?"

"What? No. The bad news is that his name is Charles."

I burst out laughing. "Please don't tell me he goes by Chuck, too. That's the worst Charles-related nickname."

"None taken, thanks," he said icily. "And no. He goes by Charles because he's a classy, elegant, stunning specimen of a human being with a fabulously enchanting smile who—and this is the worst news—is both mindful and respectful of boundaries."

I frowned. "How is that the worst news?"

"Because he thought me sitting in the hallway while you hid in the bathroom was an indication that you didn't want to be approached after he stared at you naked for three hours, so asked me to pass on a hello and he hopes to see you again at Bar One sometime."

Leave it to Brad to ruin fucking everything.

Chapter Fifteen

I wasn't expecting sympathy from Chuck after I explained why Brad had called, but I wasn't expecting a subtle look of exasperation to cross his face.

"Tess... if you just *told* your family—"

"I don't need this right now."

"You're putting yourself through hell to maintain the charade that you're still married to this asshole, and for what?" he pressed. "You don't even *like* your family. Why are you still trying to impress them?"

"Because."

"Because...?"

"Because I said so." I picked up my purse, not looking at him. "Since Brad ruined any shot I had at getting laid tonight, I want to go home and drink until I pass out. Maybe if I'm lucky I'll get alcohol poisoning and miss my flight."

"And you really think that's healthier than just coming clean and telling your family you don't have the perfect marriage?"

"Since when are you a fucking doctor, Chuck? Oh wait, you're not." I grabbed the bathroom door and yanked it open. "So kindly back off with your judgement and holier-than-thou attitude."

"Uncalled for," he said as I left the bathroom. "Completely fucking uncalled for."

I gritted my teeth. He wasn't wrong, which was the worst part. Chuck followed me out of the bathroom, tense silence accompanying us until we reached the bottom of the stairs and stepped out onto the sidewalk.

"Sorry," I said gruffly.

"I'm sorry, too," he replied, then put an arm around my shoulder as we walked. "The Tessa Diana Prince Lane I know is a complete badass who I respect and admire completely. Seeing her struggle with this one thing that is so very unlike that bad bitch I know is frustrating. And yes, choosing to fake an entire marriage to your family instead of telling them the truth should probably clue me in that there is something about this that I may never understand but should at least respect."

"It's okay," I said. "I'm sorry I said you had a holier-than-thou attitude."

"It's okay. I'm more pissed that you don't believe I'm a doctor."

"You aren't a doctor."

"True. Most of the time I roleplay as the patient. I do love a good prostate check."

I snorted. "You're disgusting."

"You love it."

Disgustingly enough, I did kind of love Chuck's particular brand of hilarity that walked the line between high brow humour and poop jokes. It was probably one of the only things that could make me smile after a conversation with Brad.

"Tess, you do know you deserve to be happy, right?" Chuck said suddenly.

"Of course I do," I said. "And I *am* happy."

"Mmm. And you're a fucking liar. Such a good combination."

I let out a high-pitched scoff. "I'm not a liar! What the hell?"

He took his arm off my shoulder, probably because it was awkward to walk like that with someone a good seven or eight inches shorter than you, but looped my arm through his and pinched it close to his body so I couldn't run away.

"I'm just saying, you don't owe him anything. I know he helped your family—"

"He didn't just help, Chuck." I tried to shake him off my arm, but he just squeezed it tighter. "He did *everything* for my parents after the fire. Like, yeah, they had insurance, but no one ever tells you that insurance probably won't cover every single thing you ever owned."

"Yes, but—"

"And then rebuilding the house. The insurance company wanted to use a budget builder that would've built something less than half the value of my parents' previous house, probably with a ton of construction issues. Brad was the only reason they were able to fight that."

"Well, yes, but just because he's a real estate specialist or whatever—"

"*And* there was the whole 'hiring the best fucking company in British Columbia to design and build the house' thing," I continued. "Not to mention the fact that my parents probably would've divorced if it hadn't been for him calming them down and walking them through the whole process."

"You understand that the cost of that shouldn't have to be you continuing this charade for him, though. Right?"

"He never asked for that." I sighed. "I asked him to. You know that. I couldn't bring myself to tell them while I was going through the divorce. It was embarrassing and I just... I kept putting it off. Like, I deserved a break from the stress of the divorce before dealing with the stress of everyone knowing. Then the house burnt down and he stepped up for everyone."

"Because he wanted you back."

"Yeah, but he was the only person keeping it together and now..."

"Now he's like a second son to them," Chuck said.

"Third. I have two brothers."

"Right. I forgot about little... Duggan."

"Dylan. And he's twenty-seven. Not so little." I sighed and shook my arm again, finally managing to dislodge it from Chuck's grip. "The only reason I'm not the family disappointment is one, because I brought Brad to them and everybody loves Brad, and two, because they don't know what a fucking disappointment I am. It's just... it's easier this way."

"Easier," he repeated. "It's *easier* to suffer than to just tell your parents that Brad is a dirtbag who didn't treat you like the goddess you are."

"Yep. Maybe if I'd told them back then, but I just..."

He raised his eyebrows. "Just what?"

I pressed my lips together, hating the vulnerable fear that was starting to crack through my usual crusty exterior. "I lost my nerve. Every single time. And I haven't found it yet."

We reached an intersection and paused, waiting for the light to change so we could cross. Chuck was silent for a bit, but just as the little man appeared to give us the right of way, he took my arm again.

"You didn't lose your nerve," he said. "You might have misplaced it, sure, but you're still the nervy curvy wonder you've always been. You could call your mom right now and tell her the whole story."

"You know, you're right."

He was so shocked he almost stopped in the middle of the road as he turned towards me. "What?"

I tugged him forward so we didn't get flattened by a car. "Yeah. I'll call her right now so that when I show up tomorrow, everyone will have the whole entire weekend to tell me what a mistake it was to leave him, even after I tell them what he did to me."

He tried to look offended but couldn't hide his laugh. "The mockery is unnecessary."

"Mockery? What mockery? They love criticizing me and every choice I've ever made in my life. It's the perfect anniversary gift for them. I won't even have to come up with an excuse for forgetting to buy them an anniversary gift. It's too bad Zain's birthday isn't for a while. He would've loved being insufferable about all this, too."

"Mmm, is that so?" Chuck asked knowingly. "Is it because he has some romance-y type feelings for his best friend's little sister?"

I gagged. "Yeah, right. Of all the things Zain's ever felt about me, romance-y is not one of them."

We were nearly at the point where we needed to part ways so Chuck could go home to his trendy condo and I could go back to my cave-like basement suite when he turned to me and pulled me into a hug.

"I mean this in the nicest way possible," he started. "But have you considered therapy?"

"Have you considered embezzling funds from a trashy art charity to help me pay for it?"

He laughed, likely in spite of himself. "Why can't Brad pay for it?"

"I'm not asking Brad for anything. Look where that got me last time."

Chuck sighed and released me, his eyebrows furrowed with sympathy. "I wish I could fix this for you. You don't deserve all this hassle."

"I mean, I kind of do. All of it is pretty much my fault."

"It is not. He's the one who was almost ten years older than you and still thought—"

"I meant after. From the 'couldn't bring myself to admit I was divorced to my family' thing to the whole 'not being able to admit everyone was right when they thought he was too old for me' thing." I sighed. "Those things were all my fault."

"That doesn't mean you deserve it."

After giving me shit one last time for leaving him at the office by himself for two days, we each went in our separate directions. Once I was on my own, the rest of my walk was made in silence.

Which was probably not a good thing, since it meant I had time to think.

It had been a few years since I'd last seen Brad. He'd come with me to the first Thanksgiving at my parents' after they rebuilt their house. Mom had cried when she saw him, thanking him for everything he'd done, which was—to be fair to a man who deserved no fairness—a lot. But like Chuck said, he'd only done it because he was trying to get me to go back to him.

And I refused.

Just like I was refusing to tell my family I'd been divorced for five years.

I'd been divorced longer now than Brad and I had ever even been married.

I wish I could make it make sense. On one hand, I couldn't stand my family. I did everything I could to stay away from them and keep them out of my life. On the other, I craved their approval. I craved being part of them. I craved knowing my parents were proud of me and my brothers liked me and that I was worth caring about.

Even if I wasn't.

I was six or seven when my parents took us on a vacation to Vancouver. I couldn't quite remember why, though I think my dad was attending some kind of work convention. And for some reason, Mom thought it would be a good time for us to take a family trip together.

For some other reason, she took me and my brothers to the art gallery.

She must have had a coupon because my family was *not* the kind of family that went to art galleries or museums or anything like that. According to my mom, my older brother, Josh, had complained the entire time, and Dylan had thrown a tantrum halfway through the tour, but I didn't remember that.

I didn't remember anything except the art.

I was absorbed by it: shapes and colours, textures, big paintings mounted on walls and perfectly carved sculptures and things I didn't understand but wanted to. When we reached the end of the tour, I'd been sullen right up until we got to the gift shop and I begged my mom for a sketchbook set I saw.

She caved, surprisingly, even though Dad grumbled about it when we got back to the hotel because Josh and Dylan started whining that I got a present and they didn't. He'd had to take them down to the hotel gift shop and buy them some overpriced candy to keep them quiet.

By the end of our vacation, I'd filled that sketchbook. When we got back to Burnsley, Mom went to the dollar store and bought me a stack of cheap notebooks with blank pages. I filled all of those, too, and all the replacement ones, and the ones after that. Doodle after doodle, drawing after drawing; all I knew is that *this* was what I wanted to do, and since Mom kept buying me sketchbooks, I thought everyone else knew, too.

Until I drew Zain.

I was about thirteen, so he and Josh must have been sixteen or seventeen at the time. The two of them were inseparable and as such, were the bane of my existence. Josh was insufferably annoying as he mocked me incessantly, and Zain was just as bad. He was as snarky as he was clever, more than a little conceited, and loved to pick fights whenever he could.

Needless to say, I had a massive crush on him. He was beautiful, or at least, beautiful to a thirteen-year-old girl who was just starting to notice boys.

Well, and girls, but at the time, I wasn't entirely clear on what those feelings meant. Small towns like Burnsley didn't tend to have a lot of guidance for kids who were queer when I was growing up.

Zain had dark, intense eyes, light sepia-brown skin, and lips that were often curled into an unimpressed smirk. His hair was thick and by then he'd started wearing it a bit longer, enough that it flopped messily onto his forehead.

I told myself that, as an artist, I had to practice drawing different people and places and things. And since I'd drawn everyone else in my family multiple times, Zain was a new face to practice. So while he and Josh watched wrestling or something in the living room one day, I sat at the dining room table with my sketchbook, sneaking glances at him every so often as I drew.

I was in the middle of shading Zain's nose when my sketchbook disappeared from under my pencil.

"Hey!" I shouted, looking up frantically.

"Whatcha drawing, Teacup?" Josh said, flipping my sketchbook towards him.

"Give it back!" I pleaded, but it was too late, of course.

"Is this... Zain?" he asked.

"No," I said.

"Why does it say 'Zain' on it, then?"

Zain glanced over from the couch, one of his nostrils raising in a curiously disgusted sneer. "What?"

"It's... not... no!" I stammered. "It's, I just, I—"

Josh burst out laughing and started towards the living room. "Man, check this out. She drew you!"

I slid off the chair and lunged after him, screeching as I desperately tried to get my sketchbook back. I almost managed, too, but Josh was much taller than me already and held me back with one arm as he tossed the sketchbook across the room to Zain.

"You're going to wrinkle it!" I cried. "Please, give it back."

Zain caught the book and glanced down at the page, dark hair falling across his eyes and forehead.

"Why are you drawing me?" he asked.

My face *burned*. "Because I need to practice drawing all sorts of people and you... you were sitting there."

"What do you need practice for?" Josh asked.

"Because I'm going to be an artist," I said.

Josh and Zain looked at each other, then almost unanimously burst out laughing.

"Oh, shut up!" I shouted.

"Tessa!" Dad said, appearing suddenly in the entryway to the kitchen. "Don't tell your brother to shut up."

I froze, tears springing into my eyes as my dad scolded me.

"What is going on in here?" he asked, glancing from me to my brother. "I can hear you bitching at each other from outside."

"Tessa thinks she's gonna be an artist when she grows up," Josh said, snorting.

"I am," I said. "I'm going to go to art school and learn to paint and my paintings are gonna be in the art gallery. In Vancouver. And other ones, too."

Dad looked at me. "Honey, art school would be a waste of time."

For a moment, my stupid childish mind thought he was going to say it was because I was so good at art already that I didn't need school. Then he chuckled, just like Josh and Zain, a condescending smile on his face.

"Only *really* good artists can make a career of it," he continued. "But maybe you can paint flowers on teacups and sell them at the farmer's markets or something. Call it the Tessa Teacup Collection."

The look on my face must have said everything. Josh dissolved into laughter again, though Dad did scold him for stealing my sketchbook and made Zain hand it back to me. I took it silently, my face red as I grabbed my pencils off the dining room table and disappeared to my room. When I got there, I flipped the book open to the drawing I'd been working on. The spine was cracked and a long line of pencil streaked through the center of the drawing, from the tip of Zain's nose and through his chin, all the way to the edge of the paper.

"I'm going to be an artist," I said to myself, even as tears started to drip down my face. "I'm going to be a *fucking* artist."

Five years later, I was sitting at the dining room table while Mom was cooking dinner one night. Josh, who was still living at home, was in the living room with Zain. Dylan was sitting with them, though they were ignoring him as much as they ignored me, when Dad walked in after work.

"Hi honey!" he said cheerfully to my mom in his loud, booming voice. "Hey, Teacup! There's mail here for you."

Confused, I looked up from the drawing I was working on and picked up the envelope with my name on it, slid my finger beneath the flap, and pulled the folded letter out.

"What is it?" Mom asked interestedly.

I screamed, scrambled out of my chair, tripped and narrowly missed crushing the letter as I crashed to the dining room floor, then finally managed to spit out that it was my acceptance letter to UBC.

They were excited, right up until I told them it was for the Visual Arts program.

In Vancouver.

Mom had barely been able to hide her skepticism and Dad?

Dad was livid.

"University should be preparing you for a career," he'd said. "I'll be damned if I'm paying that kind of money for you to colour all day."

I tried to tell them I could use my degree for things like graphic design, even though I had no intention whatsoever of being a graphic designer. Or I could be a photographer; there were always people who needed wedding photos or graduation photos or things like that.

They saw right through all that, which was fair. I wanted to be an artist, not an actor.

"But I've already been accepted," I protested as my dad refused to pay my tuition like he had for my brother.

"Maybe you can switch degrees," Mom suggested, as if it was the most helpful thing in the world. "To Education or Nursing."

"I don't *want* to be a teacher or a nurse!"

"Well, I'm not paying for you to be—" Dad held up his hands next to his head so he could make exaggerated air quotes "—some snotty hippy 'artist' who'll end up on the street thinking your fucking doodles can buy dinner."

No one made a sound. Even Josh, for once in his fucking life, was silent as he watched from the living room. Beside him, Zain—whose hair was longer than ever and whose forearms had the beginnings of the tattoos he'd collect over the coming years—was watching with blank disinterest, and Dylan hadn't even looked up from his phone as my dad reduced my passion to nothing. Mom's shoulders were tense and her lips were pressed together in a line as she waited to see what I would say.

"Fine," I said, my voice so confident that it was obvious I was faking it. "I'll pay for it myself."

A beat went by, then almost in unison, Dad and Josh burst out laughing.

I went to my room with my acceptance letter, refusing to come out for dinner even when Mom pleaded through the closed door. I refused to answer it when they sent Josh down to have a friendly brother-to-sister chat about the cost of tuition and why art school was a bad investment, which he would know because he was halfway through his business degree and was poised to be a sales manager at the same industrial machinery company Dad worked for. The next morning, when I came up for breakfast before school, I avoided my mom's attempt to kiss me on the cheek and stiffly informed her I'd be late coming home because I was meeting with the guidance counselor to talk about student loans.

It wasn't until a few days later that my parents came down to my room, knocking before pushing the door open to see me sitting on my bed, typing furiously on my laptop as I ignored them.

"Can we talk, Teacup?" Mom asked.

I kept typing.

Dad sighed. "Okay, Teacup. We get it. Time to grow up."

I kept typing, even as Mom smacked him on the arm.

"Tessa," she said. "You're right."

I almost kept typing. Not because I was trying to be particularly snarky or because I thought I'd misheard her, but because I thought maybe I was dreaming. Or dead.

I'd never expected to hear either of my parents say I was right about anything.

But I stopped, slowly at first, my fingers clacking out the final few letters one by one. Then, I frowned at my screen for a moment before looking up at her.

"What?" I asked.

"You're right," she repeated. "Your father and I discussed this and—"

"Wouldn't say it was much of a discussion," Dad muttered, and Mom slapped his bicep again.

"—if you really, truly think this is what you want to do with your life, we'll pay your tuition like we are for Josh," she finished.

"What's the catch?" I asked dully.

"There's no—"

"You damn well better work your ass off," Dad interrupted. "Because if I'm paying for friggin' *art school*, I don't want to hear that you've changed your mind halfway through and I sure as shit am not bailing you out if things go south. You're either going to be a success or you're on your own."

And so now, I was on my own.

Part 3

Confession: The threat of a toothy blowjob can solve most problems

Chapter Sixteen

THE BEST WAY TO eat fettuccine alfredo is like an uncivilized goblin.

There was something inherently satisfying about shovelling creamy, cheesy noodles into your mouth like a goddamn heathen instead of daintily twirling it around a fork. Like, just grabbing a huge-ass forkful and shoving as much in your mouth as you can while still being able to chew it. And the nice thing about alfredo sauce is that it's white, so when it inevitably dribbles down the front of your shirt, it's not permanently stained.

That's why you can't eat spaghetti like a goblin. The clothing casualty rate is just far too high.

I'd also fight anyone who said fettuccine alfredo was better with chicken or shrimp or whatever. Honestly, adding protein is a waste. It just takes up space that *could* be filled with more pasta.

"But Tessa," the hypothetical dumbass I was fighting would argue. "What about having a balanced meal?"

And to that I'd say: "I'm eating a bowl of garlicky pasta covered in cream and enough parmesan to constipate a herd of raccoons and you think my concern is how *balanced* the fucking meal is? Now shut up and bring me one of those chocolate brownie lasagnas for dessert."

Of course, having said that, I didn't eat fettuccine alfredo like a goblin in public. No, when I was sitting in that Olive Garden in Kelowna, I was eating my never-ending bowl of fettuccine alfredo like a proper human being.

Mostly.

There were only a few bites left when a good-looking man with light brown hair, dressed in jeans and a casually unzipped sweater overtop what was probably a severely overpriced designer shirt, wandered up with his carry-on suitcase rolling behind him.

Brad.

"Hey, beautiful," my ex-husband said as I twirled a proper human-sized bite of pasta on my fork. "That looks delicious."

I finished twirling my fork, then shoved it into the pile of pasta still on my plate and scooped a huge forkful into my mouth. Noodles were hanging out and slapping my chin as Brad sat down across from me, doing his best not to show how disgusted he was.

Unfortunately for him, I knew exactly how to gross him out.

"Enjoying your lunch?" he asked.

I slurped the noodles into my mouth much louder than was strictly necessary. Brad tried with everything in him not to shudder, but I saw his mouth twitch and he had to look down at the empty place setting in front of him.

"'S great," I said once I'd chewed enough to speak.

"Delightful," he said.

I swallowed the rest of my alfredo. "Are you getting food or can we get this shitshow on the road?"

Brad shook his head. "Even if you weren't purposely trying to make me puke, I ate on the plane."

I shrugged and ate another bite, though I scaled back on the goblinness that time.

"How was your flight?" he asked as I chewed.

"Horrible."

"You had a lot of turbulence?"

"No, I was heading to Kelowna and knew you'd be here."

Infuriatingly, he smiled. "I missed you too, Tess."

"I didn't miss you."

"I can pretend."

"Don't."

The server chose that moment to return to the table. I ate the last bite of my pasta as she asked Brad if he wanted a drink or to order something, which he politely declined.

"Would you like another bowl of pasta?" she asked me.

"No, I'm done, thanks," I said.

"Some dessert?"

I shook my head. "Just the bill, please."

"You can bring the bill to me," Brad said.

"No, thank you," I said. "I can pay for my own lunch."

"It's my treat, Tess."

The server looked from me to him and back at me. "Um... so just the bill, then?"

I glared at Brad for a moment longer. He looked back at me, patience in his green eyes. It was disgusting how gorgeous he still looked. Not that thirty-nine was old, but it was an age that Brad wore *well*. When people talked about men in their forties aging like fine wine, they meant guys who were aging like Brad. There were a few flecks of grey starting in his light brown hair, but it was still thick and shiny and perfectly styled. A few more wrinkles around his eyes, but the only reason I could see them was because I'd spent so long memorizing every line and curve on his face. That stupid fucking dimple was just as enticing as it had always been and the slight bit of stubble coating his cheeks and chin made him look casual and carefree and gorgeous.

The fucker couldn't even have the decency to look like shit after spending the morning on an airplane.

"Sure," I said. "And can you add one of those chocolate brownie lasagnas on it to go, please?"

"Absolutely, that's not a problem at—"

"And a strawberry cheesecake. Also to go."

The server glanced at Brad. "Anything else?"

"Make it two of those brownie lasagnas," he said, shooting her a charming smile. "And a couple of plastic forks, please."

When we got to the rental a few minutes later—which had been upgraded to an SUV even though I wanted a small and sensible sedan that had decent gas mileage—I handed Brad the keys and got into the passenger seat. He took them without comment, stopping to put his suitcase in the back before getting in the driver's seat. By then, I'd pulled out my phone and was staring at it determinedly.

"Work?" he guessed as he pulled out of the parking lot.

"Yep," I replied, opening MatchMi to see if I had any new messages from potential couples.

"How's that going?" he asked.

"Fine."

"What have you been working on?"

"Stuff."

He laughed softly. "Tess, come on. It's going to be a long weekend if we don't talk at all."

"Sounds like my perfect weekend."

"It'll be a lot easier to pretend we're still married if we know at least a bit about each other's lives."

He made a good point. I sighed.

"My work at CARE is going fine. We're working on this year's Recycl-Ball, which is when I connect with most of our donors, and it's a shitshow because Loni decided she wanted to change the theme even though we're, like, six weeks away."

He thought for a moment. "First weekend of May?"

"No, the Thursday. Cheaper to rent out the country club on a weeknight, apparently."

"You're still enjoying it there?"

"I wouldn't be there if I didn't," I lied.

He nodded, awkwardly quiet. "And you're, uh... modelling now?"

"Mm-hmm."

He cleared his throat. "Nude?"

"None of your business."

"Beautiful, I just said I want to make it easier to pretend—"

"On what planet would I tell my family about nude modelling?"

He sighed. "Fair. What about painting?"

"I paint."

From the corner of my eye, I saw him glance at me. "Any shows coming up?"

"No. I'm... taking a break from that. Right now I'm doing custom commissions for high-end interior design clients."

"But you'll be going back to shows soon, right?" he pressed. "That's where you'll get recognition, Tess. People need to see the work you—"

"I don't need your advice."

He cut himself off immediately. "Alright. Anything else I should know about?"

"No."

"How's your family doing?"

I sighed. "Fine. Mom's talking about retirement and Dad's still of the opinion that he'll retire after he dies. Josh and Audrey are in the midst of wedding planning. Dylan's still Dylan."

"Silent and looking like he's over it at all times?"

"As far as I know. He's still doing the e-sports and streaming thing."

"He must be seeing a lot of success with that if he's still doing it. Is he still living at home?"

"No, he moved up to Kamloops with a couple of his gamer friends. Or at least, that was the last I heard."

"And what have you told everyone about me?"

"You're busy with work, you travel a lot, you're still doing real estate acquisitions, and we still live in Vancouver together. We spent last Christmas with your family. Everyone's going to give you hell about not coming around for a couple of years, but it's not my fault you're always on business trips."

"Would you believe I've hardly been on any this year?"

"No, because I told everyone you travel constantly, so you better come up with some places to have visited."

"Can do."

We fell silent for a bit, the radio playing in the background as I looked back at MatchMi. There were a few new messages, but none that showed promise. A couple trying to save their relationship by opening it. A guy who was clearly way more into it than his partner was. Three single guys with the oh so generous offer to have a threesome with me if I brought my own friend.

And a message from Finn and Julie.

It wasn't the first time I'd gotten a message from a couple after I'd hooked up with them. Most of the time, I didn't bother opening them, or if I did, it was only to block their profile from messaging me again. It was a standard thing. Something I'd done a million times.

One and done. They all knew that. And I never had a problem enforcing it.

But seeing their name pop up...

I hesitated.

"Are you seeing anyone?" Brad asked suddenly.

My jaw twitched and I tapped the screen to close MatchMi. "I see lots of people. Every single day. They're everywhere, for some reason."

He didn't laugh. "You know what I mean. Are you dating anyone?"

"Why would you need to know that?"

"Why wouldn't I want to know that?"

"Because you don't need that information to lie to my family convincingly."

"I guess I'm just curious what my chances of winning you back are," he said.

"Still zero, Brad. Same as always."

"There has to be some chance—"

"Zero. Negative zero, now."

"Negative zero isn't real."

I glared at him. "There is no chance. I don't want you back."

"You say that, but here I am."

I stared out the window, my jaw clenched.

"I'm gonna prove it to you, Tess," he continued when I didn't say anything. "One day. I'm going to show you I deserve you again."

"Sure you will."

"I will."

"Shut up, Brad."

He actually listened that time, thankfully. But I subtly unlocked my phone, then the settings tab and turned off my notifications for MatchMi. Just in case *someone* looked at my lockscreen.

Brad would be disgusted if he knew about my lifestyle and all the people I was sleeping around with.

Well, maybe not disgusted. Maybe shocked was a better word. Or offended. And honestly, part of me wanted to tell him. Part of me wanted to make him sit there and listen as I told him in excruciating detail what it had been like to watch Julie choke on Finn's dick while she was sitting on my face, or how it tasted to make out with her and Finn's cock at the same time.

I wanted to see the pain on his face, hearing all the things all those anonymous people had done to defile his precious little ex-wife. All the things he would *never* get to do with me because he was a piece of human garbage.

But, unfortunately, I did still need him, because for some reason, I couldn't let go of wanting my family to like me. I couldn't handle the pain of admitting I'd been wrong.

If I could just get over that, everything would be so much easier. If I could just sit down like Chuck said and say, "Mom, Dad, I divorced Brad and I know you're going to be disappointed but it was the right thing for me to do and as your daughter, I hope you understand and support me and my happiness."

And then my dad would say something about Brad getting custody of my family in the divorce and they'd all laugh. Someone would tell me I was making the wrong choice because Brad was the perfect husband and how on *Earth* could I give him up?

And I just hated looking like a failure.

We didn't talk much over the rest of the drive. Brad spoke up here and there, telling me little tidbits about his life that I didn't care about, but could use to make my ruse seem more realistic. I grunted in response and played stupid games on my phone, doing everything I could to distract myself from the feeling of being driven to my own execution.

But eventually, we got to Burnsley, and I could almost hear the sound of darkly looming drums counting us closer and closer to Hell.

"It's too early to check into the hotel," Brad said as he turned off the highway. "Do you want to just go straight to your parents' place?"

"Not really," I muttered.

"Well, we can either go hide in a coffee shop somewhere and procrastinate. Or we could go to your parents' and use the excuse that we've been travelling all day and have to check into our rooms to leave sooner."

It was a good idea. I sighed and pulled up my messages to let my mom know we would be there soon.

The driveway was full when we pulled up to the house, so Brad parked on the street. I recognized one of the cars as Josh's new BMW—Mom had sent multiple photos of it, bragging about how he'd gotten a promotion at work and decided to treat himself—but wasn't sure who the other car belonged to. I doubted it was Dylan's. It was too practical.

Steeling myself, I took a deep breath, then reached for the door handle. Just before I could open it, Brad put his hand on my arm.

"Wait," he said. "Forgetting something?"

"Why I'm doing this?" I replied. "Yeah."

He smiled, a lopsided smirk as he let go of me and dug into his pocket. I groaned when he withdrew the small velvet box.

"You couldn't have let me pretend I forgot them at home?" I asked as he passed it to me.

"How would you have forgotten them at home?"

"Took them off while painting and forgot to put them back on."

I flipped the box open, my heart aching as I looked at my wedding rings. They were the most beautiful rings I'd ever seen in my life. Brad had picked them himself, dropping far too much money on a giant fucking custom made art-deco style set he knew—rightly so—that I'd love.

One of the hardest parts of the divorce was taking those fucking rings off. I loved them. I loved what they used to represent.

Now, I hated them more than anything in the world.

Besides the man who gave them to me.

"I'm always going to try being the best for you, Tess," Brad said softly. "If you won't let me show you I can be the best husband in the world, I understand, but then I'm going to be the best damn ex-husband you could ever ask for."

I took the rings out and slipped them on my finger, then handed him back the box.

"If you wanted to be the best ex-husband, you'd stop trying to get me to change my mind," I said, then opened the door of the SUV and got out.

Chapter Seventeen

Silent and unsmiling, Brad and I walked up the front sidewalk. I took a deep breath, then knocked on the door three times before turning the knob.

As it turned, we each slipped into our roles the same way someone might slip into a pool they thought would be too cold but turned out to be just the right temperature. Tension morphed to familiarity, dread into cheerfulness, and by the time I'd swung the door open fully, the part of me that wanted to run away screaming was suppressed, tied into the knot in my stomach.

"Hello?" I called.

"Anybody home?" Brad added, despite the fact we could hear people talking from the kitchen.

"Lorelei, grab the gun, I hear an unfamiliar voice," came my dad's booming response.

A swell of laughter burst from the back of the house and I heard the scraping of a chair on tile. Brad chuckled as he took off his shoes and put them on the mat near the door. By the time I'd kicked off my sneakers, Mom had rounded the corner.

"Teacup! You're here!" she squealed. "And you—*finally*!"

She threw her arms around Brad's shoulders.

"Good to see you, Mrs. Lane," he said as he hugged her. "Happy anniversary."

"It's been years, Bradley," she scolded, though she was smiling as she squeezed him back.

"I know," he said, and I could have sworn the apologetic tone in his voice was genuine. "I'm sorry. Work has been insane."

"You need to make time for what matters," Mom said as she let go of him. "Like your family. And my daughter."

Brad nodded solemnly. "I always have time for Tessa. And things should be a little easier now. I just got the promotion I've been trying to get for the past few years and—"

Mom had started towards me, likely for a hug, but cut Brad off with a screech as she slapped my arm instead. "A *promotion*?! Tessa, you didn't tell me about that!"

I winced, then grimaced harder as she yanked me in for a hug. "I, uh... wanted him to tell you in person. So we could see your reaction. I wouldn't want to deny you the opportunity to slap me in excitement."

She cackled in my ear before letting me go. "Well, come in. I wish I'd known you were coming early. We were just having coffee with the Hameeds, but I can get Gary to grab some extra chairs from outside and we'll order pizza for dinner," Mom rambled, then clapped her hands together. "It'll be like a pre-party for the party on Saturday!"

"I texted you to say we were coming," I said. "We're too early to check in at the hotel."

She waved her hand airily. "My phone's on the charger. You should've called the house phone."

I tried not to roll my eyes as we followed her to the kitchen. "I don't know why you even bothered connecting it when you built the house. You never answer the house phone."

"Well, yes. It's usually telemarketers."

"Why do you even have a landline, then?"

"Because what if we need it, Tessa?" she asked. "What then?"

"Of course," I said. "How silly of me."

She didn't respond, mostly because we stepped into the kitchen and everyone acted like Elvis himself had entered the building.

Growing up, Mom always talked about how much she hated our kitchen. There was never enough counter space, she'd always said, and far too much dining space. We rarely ate at the kitchen table, so it became the place where we did homework and crafts and piled stacks of junk mail and paper that had nowhere else to go. So when the house burnt down and she had the chance to redesign it from scratch, she'd made a lot of changes.

The living room wasn't right beside the kitchen anymore; it was at the front of the house, just beside the front door. The kitchen itself took up the entire back end of the house. There was a huge island right in the middle with a sink on one side and a breakfast bar on the other, three tall stools tucked underneath it as seating. She had a ton of counters and cabinets, a stove built into the wall, the highest-end appliances and a huge pantry with a frosted glass door.

It was her dream kitchen, but she still hated every inch of it. It was too big now, with too many counters and cabinets crowding the space, and it wasn't like she had any kids or grandkids in the house to cook for anymore.

Nestled into the nook next to the big window that overlooked the backyard was a kitchen table that sat, at the most, six people. Naturally, there were seven people crowded around it, plus an empty chair that must have been Mom's.

"Brad!" Josh shouted as we walked in. "Hey, man!"

"Hey, short stuff," Brad replied.

Josh snorted back a laugh as he stood up. He was a good six inches taller than Brad, but that had been their *thing* since the very first time I'd brought Brad home. They did that awkward dude hug where they sort of shook hands but also pulled each other in and clapped each other on the back with the other arm.

"Good to see you, bud," Josh said.

"Congrats on the engagement, dude." Brad peered around him to Audrey, Josh's fiancée, who couldn't get up from the table because Josh was standing in the way. "Do I get to see the ring, Audrey?"

She shimmied a bit, then stood up and held her hand out. "It's been so long that I'm not used to people asking to see it anymore!"

Brad took her hand and admired the ring. "Gorgeous." He clapped Josh on the bicep. "You did good, man."

"'Course I did. Have you met this girl? I had to lock her down any way I could!"

They all laughed. Josh squeezed past Brad to get back to the table and Dad leaned back in his chair.

"Who the hell is that?" Dad asked. "Some old bastard Tessa dragged in from the airport?"

Brad laughed and shifted to the end of the table so he could greet my dad. "Must be. She was always too good for that Brad guy, anyway."

"Well, maybe if that Brad guy came around a little more often, I'd recognize him." Dad stood and patted Brad heartily on the back as they shook hands. "Good to see you, son."

"And you, Mr. Lane. It's your fortieth anniversary, hey? Got any tips?"

I glanced around as they riffed off each other. Dad had been sitting at one end of the table. Beside him, looking like an artificially de-aged version of Dad, was Josh. Audrey was sitting with him, of course, and Dylan was tucked into the corner staring at his phone and ignoring everyone else. Then beside him was, for some fucking reason, Zain's mom and dad, Dr. and Mrs. Hameed.

And then, for some additional fucking reason, Zain sat at the head of the table.

If Zain and Josh hadn't become best friends when they were so young, I don't know if they ever would have. Josh was the loud, outgoing, sporty one. He'd always been extroverted and popular and obnoxious. Zain, on the other hand, was… well.

Some people might have said his quietness made him mysterious, but I knew him too well for that. He wasn't so much quiet as he was indifferent to everyone he thought he was better than, which was most people. I'd been on the receiving end of his dry, snarky taunting more than once growing up. Where Josh never hesitated to make whatever joke he could, Zain would stay silent until he had the perfect response to cut someone down.

Then there was the fact that the two of them just *looked* like they wouldn't be friends. Josh was your standard white guy. Brown hair, an average build, usually dressed in a cheap suit or some kind of polo-shirt-and-jeans combo. Kind of like Brad, but taller.

Zain was shorter than Josh and had thick black hair that fell over his forehead. His dad was originally from Pakistan and his mom from the UK, where they'd lived until his dad moved the family to Burnsley so he could take over for the town's retiring optometrist. There were countless tattoos on his arms and probably elsewhere, though it wasn't like I had a reason to know that for sure, and I wouldn't have put it past him to have a hidden piercing or two.

Frustratingly, he was everything my type and more.

More frustratingly, he was staring straight at me as everyone else continued talking to Brad.

No one else—except Mom, of course—seemed to realize I'd even entered the room. I mean, Dad had gotten up and left to get the folding chairs from the garage without even saying hello to me. But Zain sat there, dark brown eyes boring into mine, an unreadable expression on his face as everyone else chattered loudly. I couldn't explain why, but my throat went dry and the oddest feeling crept up my spine. I thought maybe it was dread, sure that he was going to smirk and throw some biting remark at me that everyone else would think was just good-natured teasing.

But then a heartbeat passed and Zain smiled.

"Hey, Tessa," he said.

It wasn't loud, but his smooth voice spread through the room like oil paint cut by a palette knife. Brad stopped talking mid-sentence and there was an awkward moment of silence before Josh turned to me.

"Teacup!" Josh said with about half the enthusiasm as he'd greeted Brad. "How's my baby sis?"

"Not a baby anymore," I said.

"That's right," Mrs. Hameed said. "She's ready to *have* her own babies, Joshua."

I laughed. It was not a convincing laugh.

"How are you doing, Tess?" Audrey asked.

Even though she had horrible taste in men, I liked my brother's fiancée. I didn't know her well on account of the whole "not spending a lot of time with my family" thing, but I'd always loved how she dressed. She was smart and friendly and always had the most beautiful clothes I'd ever seen. That day, she was wearing her dark brown hair clipped back with a beaded barrette and was dressed in a simple brown dress paired with a leather jacket a few shades lighter than her tanned skin.

"Doing just great," I replied, shifting around the crowded table so I could talk to her more easily. "How are you? How's wedding planning?"

"And here we go," muttered Josh.

Audrey glared at him before looking back at me. "I was going to say 'fine' but with that attitude, 'not happening' is starting to look more and more appealing."

Dylan, in a rare show of emotion, laughed from the other side of the table. "You deserved that."

"I did," Josh agreed, having the decency to look embarrassed. "Sorry, babe."

She didn't look at him. "It's going fine, Tessa. We're just getting to that stretch where we're making all those big decisions and everything's beginning to look very real. You know, where the bride has a million things she's expected to do and the groom isn't expected to do anything and also doesn't seem to understand that our patriarchal society puts far more pressure on the bride to do those things."

God, I loved Audrey. I had no idea why she was with my brother, but I loved that she was.

Dad returned with the folding chairs and there was a loud commotion as everyone shifted their chairs, clustering together so we could add two more spots at the table. Despite my hope that people would move so I could sit with Audrey, I ended up beside Mrs. Hameed.

Which was fine. I liked Mrs. Hameed, for the most part. As soon as Josh and Zain became friends, Mom made sure Mrs. Hameed felt welcome in the community, since they were pretty new to Burnsley. She had a British accent and was always impeccably dressed. That day, she was wearing a pale pink hijab and wore a darker shade of the same pink on her lips.

"How are you doing, Tessa, dear?" asked Mrs. Hameed in her soft but commanding voice after Brad and I had settled in our spots.

"I'm great, thank you," I said. "It's wonderful to see you again. I didn't know you would be here."

"Oh, it was very last minute," she said. "Zain came into town with Rayan and Ashley for your parents' party so he doesn't have his car, but he wanted to visit Josh. So Ahmed and I said we'd bring him over and then your mom invited us in for coffee."

"I said I could get a taxi," Zain said from beside her. I couldn't blame him for sounding a little grumpy; it was no fun being in your mid-thirties and feeling like you had to rely on your parents for a ride.

But Mrs. Hameed waved his flat statement off. "So please update me, Tessa. How have you been doing?"

"Great," I said, probably a bit too brightly. "Keeping busy, you know. How about you?"

"Oh, you know. *Mostly* wonderful," she said, smiling widely.

From the corner of my eye, I saw Zain tense, but he didn't so much as glance in our direction.

"What's been so wonderful?" I asked.

She beamed. "Well, Rayan and Ashley just found out they're expecting again!"

"That's great," I said. "Congratulations. This is their... third?"

"Yes." She picked up her phone, which was lying on the table, and unlocked the screen, bringing up her photo album. "Mia is seven and Sami is five. I thought Ashley was all done having babies, but it looks like Number Three had other plans! And I'm certainly not going to complain about having another grandchild. I'll take as many as I can get."

"Josh," Zain said. "Has Brad seen your new car?"

"Oh, yeah!" Josh said, pushing his chair back from the table. "Man, you gotta come see it."

"Hell yeah," Brad said, then put his arm around my shoulder. "Want to come, beautiful?"

"Nope," I said.

Brad shrugged and stood to join Josh and Zain as they inched around the crowded table.

"Anyone else?" Josh asked.

"Boys and their toys," Mom said, chuckling as all the other men stood up. I mean, obviously they did. Brad was going, and Brad was everyone's favourite person, so everyone wanted to be around him.

"I swear, if Josh ever had to choose between the car and me, he'd probably choose me, but he'd have to stop and think about it first," Audrey said, rolling her eyes.

"That sounds like Josh," I said, trying not to laugh.

"I think Gary would be the same way with his golf clubs," Mom said. "Teacup, you really should get that husband of yours to give the boys lessons."

Ugh.

"Yeah, no kidding, Tessa," Audrey said, laughing. "That man would move the stars for you."

"I guess he's alright," I said, trying to sound like I wasn't ready to puke at having to speak positively about Brad in any way. "But tell me more about the wedding. You've got your dress and everything?"

Her annoyance with Josh seemed to fade instantly and a beaming smile spread across her face. "I do. And Josh and Zain are going to get suits fitted Saturday before the party, which is why Josh is being such a shit today. He thinks it's too early."

"It's different for men," Mrs. Hameed said. "They don't have to do anything months in advance. He could go get a suit three days before the wedding and it would be fine."

"Yes, but that does nothing for *my* stress level," Audrey said, and we all laughed.

"Zain is the best man?" I asked.

Audrey nodded. "And then Dylan and my brother, Ben, are groomsmen. But that's something I wanted to talk to you about, actually."

Oh, *no.*

Every single muscle in my body tensed. At the same time, I tried to look like every single muscle in my body hadn't tensed. I stared at Audrey, hoping my eyes weren't wide enough to look like a deer about to be mowed down by a semi in the middle of December and knowing I was probably failing.

"Oh?" I forced myself to say.

She smiled. "So, my best friend Shenae is the maid of honour and the bridesmaids were supposed to be my sisters, but Leslie just found out she's pregnant and her due date is *literally* three days after the wedding."

"Oh my God," Mom breathed excitedly, and I almost cried.

"So we considered moving the wedding, but Leslie said she didn't want us to. But she didn't feel right about staying in the wedding party because she doesn't know if she'll even be able to make it," Audrey continued. "I know it's super awkward because I already had my wedding party picked and I hate to make anyone feel like the second choice or whatever, but Josh and I were *really* hoping you'd be my bridesmaid, Tessa."

Fuck.

Fuck.

Fuckity fuck fuck *fucking* fuck.

"Oh, wow," I said. "I, um... I didn't ever expect to... um—"

"I know it's so much to ask," Audrey said quickly. "Leslie will still be helping with a lot and Shenae already made a ton of plans so commitment-wise, it would be super chill for you. Almost the same as being a guest. You'd just also get a cute dress and your hair done and all that."

"Oh, *Audrey*," Mom said, and she clapped her hand to her mouth as her eyes began to water. "This is... oh, I can't even stand how—"

"Only if you're okay with it, though," Audrey said, apparently concerned by my severe lack of response.

And I wasn't. I wasn't okay with it. I had no desire to be in my brother's wedding party. If I had the choice, I wouldn't even attend it, but there was that whole "inability to disappoint my parents" thing that kept me making horrible decisions.

Including, apparently, this one.

"Of course I am," I said. "I'm so honoured. I... I'll be there. In a dress."

A squeal of excitement went around the table and Mom burst into tears, so we had to take a break while she dramatically hugged everyone and dabbed at her eyes with a tissue.

I felt like crying too, but I didn't.

Once we'd settled back at the table and Mom had stopped sniffling with happy tears, Mrs. Hameed smiled conspiratorially.

"So, that covers the weddings," she said. "But will Lorelei be joining the grandma club soon?"

Audrey chuckled, her cheeks turning red. "I mean, we're hoping for a honeymoon baby."

Mom and Mrs. Hameed both wiggled in excitement. Mrs. Hameed looked at me with a playful sparkle in her eyes.

"Tessa, dear, you'll have to get a move on it yourself if you want to have the first grandbaby yourself."

I froze.

They all looked at me expectantly. Mom was smiling. Audrey looked vaguely concerned. Mrs. Hameed looked completely oblivious to how awkward she was making things.

Tell them you decided not to have kids, I thought. Tell them you're not interested in it right now. Tell them you haven't talked about it but maybe one day. Tell them you're divorced. Tell them you *can't* have kids. Tell them—

"Well, um, now that Brad is... is less busy. At work. Because he... he got promoted. He's travelling less," I said. "So... so we, um, thought we'd start trying."

Mom gasped in excitement. "*Really*?!"

"Yeah. Why would I lie about that?" I said as I tried to figure out why I lied about that. "But I mean, we could wait until after the wedding so I don't—"

"Absolutely not," Audrey said firmly. "One, do *not* put your life on hold for my wedding. Two, it's like, six months away. So even if you get pregnant right this second, you'd just be all adorably round and—oh, how *cute* would those pictures be?"

Mom teared up again. "They would be *so* cute!"

"Well, it might not happen," I said, almost hating how apologetic I sounded. "Like, we're just trying, so—"

"Of course, but even if it was after the wedding—" She stopped and gasped. "Can you *imagine* if you both end up with babies at the same time?"

I could not imagine that.

As soon as I could do so without looking suspicious, I escaped the table. It didn't take very long, luckily. Mrs. Hameed and Mom dove into the baby talk and since Audrey actually *wanted* to have a baby with someone, she seemed content to field their questions and excitement. As Mrs. Hameed not-so-subtly hinted to Audrey that inviting her in-laws into the delivery room was both completely normal and a sign of respect, I excused myself under the guise of needing the bathroom.

I doubt anyone noticed that I said anything.

That was a blessing since it meant I could linger a little longer in the bathroom than needed without anyone thinking that my fettuccine alfredo wasn't sitting well. I mean, I used the bathroom, obviously, but I mainly just had to pee. Then I checked my phone and responded to Chuck's text asking me to confirm I'd gotten to Burnsley in one piece, which he replied to almost instantly.

Chuck

And Bradley didn't pick up any serial killer hitchhikers before heroically sacrificing himself so you could run to safety?

Me

> Yeah, right. Me, run? We'd both be dead. Though given how well things are going, that might have been preferable.

Chuck

> It can't be that bad.

Me

> I just agreed to be a bridesmaid in my brother's wedding.

Chuck

> Okay, that sucks, but it's not THAT bad.

Me

> And then I may or may not have implied that Brad and I are trying to have a baby.

My phone started ringing less than thirty seconds later. I nearly dropped it in the toilet in my panic to silence it, then lunged towards the sink with my pants still around my knees so I could turn the tap on.

"You did *what*?!" Chuck screeched as soon as I answered.

"I can't talk right now, dumbass," I whispered into the phone. "I'm hiding in the bathroom."

"Tessa, I swear to God, if you come up with some ridiculous plan to bring a fake baby into your fake marriage—"

I struggled to pull my pants up with one hand. "Oh my God, Chuck. I wouldn't go that far. It just, like, wouldn't happen. That's it."

"And what about when your mom pressures you more?" he hissed. "Then what?"

I sighed and cradled my phone with my shoulder as I adjusted the waistband of my pants. "By then, Audrey should hopefully be pregnant and she can deal with her."

"Right, because that's so—" and then he said something else, but his voice was so low I couldn't hear it over the running tap.

"What?" I whispered.

"What?" Chuck whispered back.

"Why are you whispering?" I asked.

"I... oh." His voice returned to normal. "Because you were whispering, obviously."

I rubbed the bridge of my nose. "Why am I like this?"

"You are asking the wrong person. Is your brother's cute friend there for eye candy, at least?"

"I, at no point, said that Zain was *cute*."

"And yet you knew exactly who I was talking about."

"Yeah, because he's the only friend of Josh's I've told you about."

Chuck laughed. "Whatever you say, Tessa Jezabel Lane. So he's there?"

"...yes."

"And? Is he still cute?"

"No. He never has been. He's gross and stupid and—*oh my God*."

"Tessa?" Chuck asked, alarmed, but I was too busy almost having a heart attack to respond after someone turned the doorknob, making the bathroom door jostle, and I nearly dropped my phone again.

"Just a minute!" I yelped.

"Sorry," said a muffled voice from the hallway.

Thank God I'd remembered to lock the door.

"Tessa? What happened?" Chuck hissed.

"I have to go," I whispered. "Someone's trying to use the bathroom."

"Ugh. Fine. But take a sneaky pic of your brother's hot friend so I can see how delusional you're being about not liking him."

"Asshole," I muttered, then hung up without saying goodbye.

Tucking the phone into my pocket, I flushed the toilet and pried my wedding rings off so I could wash my hands before quickly fixing my hair. My hope was that whoever was out there wandered away so there wasn't that awkward moment of me opening the door and having to acknowledge that they'd almost walked in on me.

And also that they hadn't heard me talking.

Unfortunately, Zain was standing stupidly in the hallway, leaning against the wall looking like he'd walked straight out of a fashion magazine for moody guys who looked good in tight jeans and white t-shirts and dark button-up shirts hanging open with the stupid sleeves rolled up. His stupid hair was brushed back off his face as he stood there, his arms crossed and his stupid tattoos peeking out on his stupid nicely toned forearms. There was an apologetic look on his stupid attractive face as I opened the door.

"Sorry," he said again. "I didn't know you were in there."

"It's fine," I said. "Didn't mean to take so long."

He nodded as he straightened up. "Are you alright?"

I stared, blinking at his question as I tried to comprehend *why* Zain was asking me that. "Uh... yeah. Thanks. I just had to... to pee. I do that sometimes. Usually after drinking water and stuff."

Something that was almost like embarrassment flashed across his face. "Oh, not like... I mean—"

"Like, I guess the fettuccine alfredo I had for lunch was a bit heavy, but I didn't really think we have the kind of relationship where we'd talk about—"

"I meant in general," he said quickly. "Like... like, how are you doing?"

I blinked at him again. I guess it was theoretically possible that he'd heard me talking to Chuck, but if he had, he would have for *sure* said something about it, seeing as I'd been talking about him. And then there was the way he'd said hello when I first walked in, acknowledging me when everyone else was fawning over Brad...

I stared at him long enough that his thick eyebrows furrowed together in an offended glare.

"What?" he asked with a huff.

"I don't think you've asked me anything like that before in the entire time we've known each other," I said. "Why do you care now?"

His lips parted as if to protest, but nothing came out.

Because he didn't care. He never had.

"Right, well. I'm gonna go now," I said. "I think your mom has more questions about my uterus that she's just itching to ask."

I slipped past him so he could go into the bathroom. He closed the door behind him and I was just about to turn back into the kitchen when it opened again.

"Hey Teacup," he called.

I stopped and sighed as I turned to him. "What now?"

A smirk played across his lips and he held up his hand, which had my wedding rings pinched between his thumb and forefinger.

"Forgetting something?" he asked innocently.

Chapter Eighteen

Zain was being weird.

Like, super fucking weird.

Asking me awkward questions outside the bathroom and handing me my forgotten wedding rings was just the start of it. After I'd squished my finger back through the rings, I returned to my spot in the kitchen, where the other women had thankfully moved on from the marriage-and-babies conversation and to the much more intriguing topic of... Zain.

"I simply don't understand it," Mrs. Hameed was complaining in a hushed voice as I sat down at the table. "If you asked me three months ago, I would have said that he was perfectly content with everything. Almost *too* content, like he'd lost some of his drive."

"I completely agree, Nadia," Mom said, nodding along as Mrs. Hameed kept talking.

"He has a good *job*. A nice *house*. He's close to his *family*. Truly, the only thing he needed was to find a nice girl and settle down." She shook her head, putting her hand on the table gracefully. "But now he wants to *move*. Ahmed finally convinces me he should retire so we could move into Kelowna to be close to the boys and our grandbabies, and now Zain wants to transfer to Victoria. I just don't know why he would do that."

I glanced around the table, wondering if I was the only one who knew exactly why he would do that. If I wasn't, the rest did a much better job of hiding their thoughts, but thankfully no one was looking at me.

"Maybe it'll be good for him," Audrey said. "I mean, career-wise, at least? If he's trying for a promotion..."

"He can get promoted here," Mrs. Hameed said. "This whole time, he could've tried to move up with the company here and now if he just waits a year more, he can do the exact same job here that he's trying to get in Victoria. They're expanding, you know, and Vernon is so much closer than Victoria."

"Maybe he can transfer back?" Mom said. "Gary did something like that when we were first married. He worked in northern Alberta for a while selling machinery there and then when they expanded here, he was a shoo-in for the role and we moved right back home."

"Maybe." Mrs. Hameed sighed and reached for the cup of tea sitting in front of her. "Unless he's doing it because he doesn't want me and Ahmed to live so close to him."

Okay, so *all* of us were thinking the same thing.

But of course, everyone started comforting her with a rousing chorus of "Oh, no, that's not it at all" and "Of course not, Nadia, he's just focused on his career" and "I'm sure it has nothing to do with Zain feeling pressured by your presence to live a certain way when you've insinuated no less than three times since I've been here that you're unhappy he hasn't settled down and given you some grandkids, and I haven't even been here the entire time."

Well, that last one might have just been in my head.

As much as I didn't like Zain—and I didn't, because Zain was an asshole and I was already filling the asshole quota in my own life—I did feel bad for him. Not that I'd ever heard him complain directly, but over the years, Mom had felt the need to continually update me on all the gossip from Burnsley, including from the Hameeds. I remember the near-falling-out she had with Mrs. Hameed when Zain decided to go to business school like Josh instead of following in his brother and father's footsteps to become a doctor.

"He's not even willing to consider dentistry!" I remember Mrs. Hameed lamenting one day when the guys were applying for university. "I thought maybe he wanted to try law, but he's just so set on being some kind of *businessman*."

She nearly spat the word out, seemingly forgetting what my dad did for a living, and I think it was the closest they'd ever had to an argument since becoming friends when Josh and Zain were kids.

So I got it. I understood what it was like to have your parents be disappointed in all your life choices. And that meant that I had some sympathy for Zain, even though he was an asshole.

Sort of.

"Really, Lorelei, it's okay," Zain said as my mom fretted during dinner later that night.

"I am *so* sorry, sweetie," Mom said, grimacing. "Let me order another pizza. It'll be here in no time."

"Can I just sneak by and get—" I started, but Mom jostled me out of the way and nearly made me drop the entire plate of pizza I was holding. Ugh.

I was standing awkwardly between the two of them waiting for Mom to move away from the cheesy bread so I could get the end pieces. I may have hated being back in Burnsley, but there was nothing like the cheesy bread from Nico's Pizza, the local pizza joint I'd grown up on. The moment Mom said that was what we were having for dinner, my mouth had started watering at the thought of the soft, doughy pieces of heaven.

And, more specifically, of the end pieces: the perfect mix of crusty and chewy, the cheese crunchy where it had bubbled and burned just the slightest bit. Those end pieces had caused straight-up warfare in the Lane house when I'd been growing up.

But as adults, it was sort of recognized that as the person who visited Burnsley the least, the end pieces were mine. Josh could have them whenever he wanted, obviously. And Dylan had only recently moved to Kamploops, though he still was closer to Burnsley than I was.

Even still, they weren't *indefinitely* mine. If Josh or Dylan got to them before I did, those pieces of heaven were gone.

So I'd been trying to snag them. Then Zain had come up behind me and quietly asked Mom if she'd remembered to ask for no bacon on the all-dressed pizza, which she hadn't. And Dr. and Mrs. Hameed had insisted Mom only order a small vegetarian since they were the only ones who would eat the vegetarian pizza, so there wasn't any of that left, and since my family were staunch supporters of the "bacon is its own food group and should be represented at every meal" camp, every other pizza *also* had bacon or, at the very least, ham on it.

And while Zain's parents were somewhat traditional, I knew from growing up with him around all the time that he and his brother were both more culturally Muslim. But even though he drank beer with Josh sometimes, he still didn't eat pork.

"It's honestly fine," Zain repeated as Mom reached for the landline to order another pizza. "I'll pick the bacon off."

"You will?" Mrs. Hameed said from the table, a look of disgust on her face.

Zain's jaw twitched as he clenched it, as if just remembering his parents were in the room. "Or I'll just... eat later."

"Don't be silly," Mrs. Hameed said. "Have some of the vegetarian, Zain. Here. I can settle for just the one piece."

"I don't want anyone to go hungry," Mom said, her forehead creased. "I can order you something else, Zain. I feel awful. You'd think after twenty-ish years, I'd know, but—"

"It's fine," Zain said again. "Really. Don't worry about it."

"Well, you can't just not *eat*. What if I—oh!" Mom whirled around, grabbing the box of cheesy bread off the counter. "It's not a full *pizza*, but you could take the cheesy bread for yourself instead!"

"Perfect," Dad said loudly. "Now why don't you sit down, Lorelei? The rest of us would like to fill our plates."

I stared in horror as she handed the almost-full box of cheesy bread to Zain, who shrugged and turned to go back to the table.

"Tessa, can you grab me a beer from the fridge?" Josh asked from the place he was trapped at the back of the table. "Since you're right there?"

I swallowed back the grief at the loss of my end pieces and gritted my teeth together. "Certainly."

"Me too, Teacup," Dad said. "And it looks like Brad's almost empty, too. Dylan, you want one?"

"Sure," Dylan said.

"Can do," I said, putting my plate down and turning to the fridge.

"Does anyone else need anything while Tessa is up?" Josh asked.

"A water would be lovely," Mrs. Hameed said.

"Yes, that would be great," added Dr. Hameed.

"Let me help you with that, beautiful," Brad said.

"I've got it," I said stiffly.

"I'll get your plate then," he said.

"It's fine, I—"

But he'd already stood up from the table, crossed to the counter, and picked up my plate.

"Let me help you," he said, then leaned in and pressed a kiss to my cheek.

I suppressed the urge to blow chunks all over the kitchen because of the feel of Brad's lips on my skin. By the time I finished getting everyone's drinks, everyone else had filled their plates or claimed their seats at the table and were chatting loudly as they devoured their pizza. Brad had set my food next to him at the table.

And in the seat next to mine sat Zain, who was slowly picking at the cheesy bread. I tried not to stare at the single end piece still sitting on his plate as I finally sat down.

"Do you want it?" he asked after I'd pulled my chair close to the table.

I glanced at him. "Huh?"

He was looking at me, something in his dark eyes guarded at the same time it was welcoming.

"The end piece," he said in a quiet voice. "I'm probably not going to eat it."

I stared at him, my mouth half-open.

"Zain, did I just hear you say the end piece is up for grabs?" Josh asked from the other side of the table, his mouth full of half-chewed food.

Zain's eyes were still on mine. His eyebrow flicked up just slightly as the corners of his mouth curled up in the slightest approximation of a smirk. My jaw twitched, then I glanced down at his plate.

"Yeah," I grumbled. "I'll take it."

"Sorry, Josh," Zain said, finally looking away and picking up the end piece. "Tessa already dibsed it."

"Aw, come on, man," Josh groaned. "It's not like Tessa needs more cheesy bread."

And of course, everyone heard that. Everyone went silent. Everyone glanced from me to Josh, wondering if he'd said what they thought he just said, and if I'd taken it the way they thought I was going to take it. Zain paused, then lifted his head and frowned at Josh.

"Did you just—"

"Tessa can have all the cheesy bread she wants," Brad interrupted, his voice cold as he looked at my brother. "I'll order her more, if she wants it."

Josh was an asshole, like all us Lanes were, but to be fair to him, he was also very stupid. He chewed his pizza with a sense of slow confusion, his eyebrows furrowed as he looked at Brad, then seemed to realize what he said.

"Oh!" he said, looking at me. "I didn't mean because of... I mean, you know what I meant."

I did. I knew that he'd been coming up with an excuse as to why Zain should give him the end piece and not me. And I could've just graciously said that.

But it was funnier to watch him squirm.

"Know what?" I asked. "That I'm fat? I did already know that, thank you."

"No, that—"

"A piece of cheesy bread isn't going to make a difference," I continued.

"Tessa, come on," Josh said. "You know I'm not saying that."

"Why would it matter?" I asked. "Were you saying I'm fat like it's a bad thing?"

"Why would you talk about my wife like that?" Brad asked.

And that's when it stopped being funny.

Because one, I didn't need anyone to stand up for me. And two, I didn't need a reminder that everyone here thought I was Brad Schubert's fucking *wife*.

"I wasn't talking about her like that!" Josh said. "Man, I swear, it was just—"

"I'm just fucking with you, Josh." I moved my plate closer to Zain, waiting patiently for him to put the end piece on it. "I know what you meant. But I'm still taking the bread."

Awkward chuckles went around the table as Zain put the end piece on my plate. Which was fine. Laughing about my weight seemed to make other people uncomfortable, but considering how uncomfortable I was just having to be in Burnsley, I figured they deserved it.

After dinner, Mom got up and started clearing the table. As usual, Mrs. Hameed got up to help her, which meant Audrey got up to help them, and it was my duty as a uterus-haver to join them while the men sat around and lifted their glasses so the women could take the dishes off the table and wipe up their messes unhindered. I hated it, of course, but the faster we got cleaned up, the sooner I could hopefully convince Brad that we needed to leave.

Except then Zain stood up and started helping with the dishes.

Which meant Brad stood up and started helping, too.

"We've got this, Lorelei," Brad said to my mom, putting an arm around her shoulder and guiding her back to the table. "Sit and relax."

"Well, look at you boys being such gentlemen," she said like it was the epitome of chivalry for them to pitch in around the house.

But it was fine. Many hands make for getting back to the hotel and ordering overpriced bottles of wine through room service faster or however the saying goes. So I silently washed the dishes as Brad and Zain got into some kind of silent domestic pissing contest over who could dry them faster.

Once the dishes were done, I tried to catch Brad's eye so we could go, but Dad offered him another beer and he accepted, settling at the table next to Dylan.

"So how goes gamer life?" he asked my younger brother.

"Good," Dylan, man of many words that he was, replied without looking up from his phone.

"I saw you're streaming on Gaminar these days. *Moondusk Hollow* any fun? I caught the start of it but had to go to a meeting before you really got into it."

Dylan looked up from his phone, his eyes slightly wide. "You watch my channel?"

"Once in a while, when I have a chance," he replied.

"I didn't even know you gamed," Dylan said.

"I don't usually have time, but I'm trying to get back into it. Any tips on starting out when I get to it?"

"Yeah, man," Dylan said. "Okay, so when you first start out—"

Fucking Brad. He could even get *Dylan* talking. There wasn't a single person in the goddamn room who didn't like him.

Except me.

I sank down into a chair at the table and waited as he and Dylan got into a discussion about whatever fucking game they were talking about, occasionally tuning in to the conversation between Mrs. Hameed and Audrey or drifting over to the business talk Dad was having with Zain and Dr. Hameed in between trying to hint at Brad that I wanted to leave. A few minutes passed, then a few more, then an hour, and when I couldn't take it anymore, I stood up.

"Where you going, Teacup?" Dad asked brightly as he cracked another beer.

"I need sleep," I said, looking at Brad pointedly. "I think we need to head back to the hotel now."

Mrs. Hameed frowned. "The hotel?"

"Dylan's staying in the guest room," Mom said.

"And we'd rather a hotel than a blow-up mattress in the living room," Brad said, moving his chair away from the table.

Dr. Hameed looked at Dylan, a slight frown on his face. "And you don't give up the room for your sister and her husband?"

"Uh…" Dylan said blankly.

"It's alright," Brad said. "We like the privacy."

"I just bet you do," Josh said, snickering.

Brad did that dude-look where he raised his eyebrows and tilted his chin in a knowing glance. "What can I say, man? I've been away on business all week."

"I absolutely do not need to hear that about my daughter," Dad said.

"Hear what?" Brad asked innocently. "I just meant it's been a busy week. A nice, private, good night's sleep with absolutely no shenanigans whatsoever is just what I need to get ready for the party this weekend."

"And maybe get a start on those grandbabies," Mrs. Hameed murmured, making Mom cackle with laughter.

"Right," I said stiffly. "So Brad? Ready to go?"

"Of course, beautiful," he said. "You know you can just say the word."

"Well, I've said it," I muttered, but no one heard me.

"Which hotel are you staying at?" Dr. Hameed asked Brad, and I saw Zain shift uncomfortably in the chair beside me.

"The Mountainview," Brad replied.

Dr. Hameed glanced at his son. "Well, that's a wonderful coincidence."

"You can go anytime, Dad," Zain said. "I can call a taxi."

"Nonsense," Mrs. Hameed said. "I'm sure Tessa and Brad wouldn't mind giving you a ride to the hotel." She looked up at me. "Would you? It's the opposite direction from our house, so..."

I really wanted to say no.

I opened my mouth to respond and say no.

But I couldn't think of a single reason not to.

"I can't think of a single reason not to," Brad said in that pleasant way where he was covering up for the fact that he totally didn't want to.

"Unless you're wanting to hang out with Josh more," I said to Zain, hoping it didn't sound as desperate as it felt.

"Honestly, I think we need to head out, too," Audrey said.

"It's not even that late," Josh said. "You're tired, babe?"

She nodded. "I wouldn't mind a shower and an early night. We have all the decorating and stuff to do tomorrow, then the party Saturday."

Josh put his arm around her shoulders and kissed her cheek. "What she says, goes. Looks like we're headed out, too. Tess, you don't mind taking Zain? It just makes sense."

"That it does," Zain said flatly.

So that was how Zain and his suitcase ended up in our rental. He sat stiffly in the front seat after I insisted he take it so I didn't have to look at either of them while we drove and I frantically tried to figure out how Brad and I were going to check into two different rooms without Zain noticing.

Because of course he hadn't checked into his room. Of *course* he hadn't. His brother had picked Zain up in Vernon on his way from Kelowna to Burnsley, squishing him in the back seat between his niece and nephew. And Rayan was staying with his parents, of course, and the kids needed their own room, so Zain was staying at a hotel like Brad and I were. But, similar to me and Brad, they'd gotten into town too early for Zain to check in, so the intent had been for him to go from my parents' place to the hotel after his visit with Josh.

But it was fine, I told myself. We'd just check into one room and pretend to go up to it, then I'd send Brad right the hell back down to check into his room.

Easy peasy.

There were two clerks at the desk. I walked up to the one standing on the left, a thin white woman who looked to be in her late twenties and who was wearing the frumpy vest-and-dress-shirt uniform combo of the hotel in a way that actually managed to look good. She had long, blonde hair and wore heavy makeup, but had a genuinely pleasant smile on her face as I walked up.

"Here to check in?" she asked.

"Yes," I said, handing her my ID. "For Tessa Lane."

She nodded and turned to her computer, typing quickly as Brad walked up behind me with our luggage and Zain approached the other clerk.

"And are you checking into both rooms right now?" the clerk asked me.

Out of the corner of my eye, I saw Zain look over. I blinked twice at the clerk.

"What?" I said.

"Both rooms?" the clerk pressed. "It says here you called yesterday to book an adjoining room. I have it listed as one person staying in each?"

I had. I had done that. And I had forgotten that meant both rooms were going to be under my name. I opened my mouth, then closed it, frozen as I stared at the woman while Zain looked on.

"There must be a mistake," Brad said smoothly. "I initially wasn't going to be joining my wife, but a last-minute change at work meant I could. She called to update the reservation to a king-size, I believe, instead of a single queen?"

Fucking Brad. Always had to come up with a goddamn solution when I was frozen with panic.

"Right," I said. "That was what I... I did. They must have misheard me or something. We don't need two rooms. That would be weird. Sorry."

"It's okay, beautiful." Brad's arm slipped around my waist and he smiled charmingly at the clerk. "Is there any way we can make that change now?"

"Well, it shouldn't be a problem to cancel the one room," the clerk said. "But to upgrade the other room is, um..."

"Of course, we completely understand if you can't—" Brad leaned forward, resting his arm on the counter as he glanced down at the clerk's nametag before looking up at her and shooting her his trademark bullshit smile. "—Alyssa. But could you look into it for us? We'd be happy to pay an extra charge for the upgrade."

I could almost see her panties melting beneath her rigid hotel uniform. She licked her lips, two patches of pink appearing on her cheeks as she typed quickly on the computer.

"It looks like the only room left with a king-size is one of the premium suites," she said, her voice soft. "It, um, has a jacuzzi and some extra furniture with an unobstructed mountain view."

"That sounds absolutely lovely," Brad said in a soft, deep voice. "How much extra is that room?"

Alyssa cleared her throat. "Well, I can't upgrade you for free. But I can probably discount it a bit and..." She typed quickly again, then turned the monitor screen towards us. "This would be the new total."

If I hadn't eaten enough cheese and carbs that day to potentially cause an intestinal blockage, I would have shat myself. It was three times as much as the room I'd originally booked. There was no way I could afford that, not when I worked for a fucking failure of a charity and had already dropped a stupid amount of money on last-minute plane tickets and—

"Perfect," Brad said, then let go of my waist so he could dig out his wallet. "Could I also get you to change the card on file? My wife put the reservation on hers, but I was hoping to get the points on mine."

Fucking Brad.

Zain finished up around the same time we did. After another lingering smile to Alyssa, Brad put his hand on my lower back and guided me towards the elevators.

"Sounds like you got quite the deal," Zain said in his flat, even voice.

"Not too bad at all," Brad replied. "You end up in a decent room?"

He shrugged. "Just a regular one. But I don't need much more than a bed and a working TV."

The elevator came and we all got on. Brad tapped his room key on the card reader and selected the top floor, then Zain mimicked the action and selected the floor beneath ours. The doors slid closed and we stood there uncomfortably as the elevator began to rise. As it got to Zain's floor, I let out a quiet breath.

"Well, have a good night," Brad said as the elevator slowed to a stop.

"And you," Zain replied, then looked at me. "It was good to see you, Tessa. I'm glad you could make it this time."

I was still processing that when the doors opened and Zain stepped off, making his way casually down the hallway with his small suitcase rolling behind him.

"Well, that was awkward," Brad said as the doors closed again.

"Not as awkward as it's about to be for you," I said.

He looked at me, a frown on his face. "What do you mean?"

"I can't imagine you'll be able to maintain the suave, cool, Mr. Is There Anything You Can Do For Us Alyssa act when you go back downstairs and tell her you need that second room after all."

Brad sighed. "Tess, come on. I'll just sleep on the couch and—"

"You knew damn well that I said I'd never share a room with you again." The elevator dinged and the doors slid open. "Thanks for the upgrade though, dear *husband*. I'll see you in the morning."

Chapter Nineteen

HAD I KNOWN PRETENDING my fake husband was trying to fuck a baby into me would be such an effective excuse, I would've used it earlier.

I figured it out the next morning, which was approximately four years later than I wished I'd figured it out. Because sure, I knew the guys had a late morning tee-time which was coincidentally at the exact time that the hall my parents were renting opened so Mom could start decorating. And sure, I *could* have gotten out of the jacuzzi early enough to get to my parents' place for the time Brad said he'd meet the other guys there.

Though honestly, it was in everyone's best interests that I get that extra jacuzzi time in. I spent most of it masturbating and was in a far more cheerful mood when I finished than I would have been otherwise.

But it wasn't like I could tell anyone *that*.

When Brad and I rolled up to my parents' place in the SUV, my unimpressed-looking dad was standing in the driveway with Josh, Zain, and Dr. Hameed. They looked like something out of a golf magazine: Dad in his khaki golf shorts and one of his many, many, *many* polo golf shirts, a blue ball cap on his head. Josh, dressed almost identically, though his cap was a slightly darker shade of blue and his shirt was tighter around the arms. Dr. Hameed had his slacks belted tightly around his hips and his white polo was ironed so neatly that I wasn't sure it was actually made of fabric. The only one dressed differently was Zain, who had covered most of his tattoos with a white long-sleeved t-shirt that had a black zip-up vest over it as he leaned moodily against a set of golf clubs, his hair brushed back off his forehead.

"About time," Dad called as Brad and I got out of the SUV.

"I almost had to beg Audrey to DD for us," Josh added, though he was smiling good-naturedly.

"Sorry," Brad said. "We got held up."

"Let me guess," Dad said. "Tessa said she'd only need ten minutes to get ready and you believed her."

"It's not Tessa's fault," Brad said loyally as he half-jogged up the driveway to load the golf clubs into the rental. "She was ready to go."

"Sure she was," Josh said. "Tess, you knew we had a tee-time."

"Sorry," I said before Brad could stand up for me again. "As much as I'd love to, I can't control when I'm ovulating, and as I'm sure you know, when you're doing it *so* often, it can take a guy longer to finish since—"

"Okay, okay, okay," Dad said quickly, patches of red appearing on his face. "I don't need to hear it."

Zain's throat flexed as he swallowed and he looked away as a strange expression crossed his face. Disgust, maybe, or embarrassment. Brad chuckled awkwardly, his face going red. And that made the excuse even better, since anytime I could make either of them uncomfortable was a good day.

Though, it did have its downside, which was the subtle high-five Josh gave Brad as I walked past them to go inside. Like it wasn't weird enough for me to lie to my family about being late because we were fucking, Josh had to go and make it extra weird by congratulating the guy fucking his sister.

That was Josh, though. He wasn't the overprotective kind of older brother. Or the supportive kind of older brother. Or the kind of older brother who liked, cared about, or acknowledged me in any way. Aside from laughing at me, making fun of everything I ever tried to do, and actively trying to prevent me from being an artist—though, I suppose in hindsight, that could technically count as him being protective seeing as how everything in my life had fallen to shit—Josh barely interacted with me.

And yet I had to be in his stupid fucking wedding party.

The excuse worked great later that day, too, after Mom and Audrey and I finished decorating the hall. Sweaty and sore and hungry, I feigned a headache and asked Mom if she'd drop me off at the hotel on her way back home so when Brad got back from golfing, we could give it one more go.

Since, of course, the guys weren't done golfing. Well, I mean, they were. But what was a round of golf without stopping at the clubhouse afterwards for overpriced beer and swanky appetizers with names like *rollò con würstel* and *cornichons frits* like they weren't just pigs in a blanket and deep-fried pickles?

"And could we maybe stop at the drugstore?" I asked, trying to make my voice sound somewhat weak. "I just feel like a nice, relaxing bath would help my headache. And maybe one of those face mask things."

I did feel a bit guilty when Mom excitedly squealed and said that yes, of course she'd drop me off at the hotel. Maybe it was a bit of an asshole move for me to pretend we were trying to have kids knowing how much my mom wanted grandchildren, but in fairness, if my parents hadn't wanted me to be an asshole, they probably shouldn't have had children themselves.

Because I was an asshole. And I came from a family of assholes.

Which was probably why Brad fit in so well, I thought to myself as I filled up the jacuzzi again and poured in the lavender bath salts I'd bought. Brad was the biggest asshole I knew. And what was worse was that very few people believed me when I said that.

The jacuzzi was in the same part of the hotel room as the bed, tucked into a corner near the window so one could look out at the scenery or turn around and watch TV while they relaxed. The room filled with the scent of lavender and I undressed, then grabbed the sheet mask I'd bought at the drugstore and slathered the goopy material all over my face before getting in. Hot, comforting water jetted around me, soothing my muscles after the long day of decorating.

With a sigh, I relaxed, then grabbed the remote I'd put next to the tub. I put on some true crime documentary that Dottie had suggested a couple of weeks earlier when I brought Millie home after a walk. But as much as a riveting unsolved mystery about a serial killer tried to capture my attention, those thoughts I'd had a million times before began to spiral.

I'd given up so much when I left Brad. Everything from my comfortable lifestyle to my inspiration. When we'd been together, I painted constantly. I had shows lined up, high-end commissions flowing in, an actual following of people who adored my work. I'd been on the verge of my moment, of that break, my foot hovering over the line that would transition me from aspiring to acclaimed.

And then I'd tripped.

A million times, I'd blamed Brad for being the one to trip me. And a million times more, I blamed myself. I told myself if I'd just listened to him, if I'd stayed, if I'd let us work through things rather than laying so much importance on my self-respect, I would've achieved the dreams I'd had since I was a little girl staring up in awe at colours and shapes on the walls of the Vancouver Art Gallery.

Once upon a time, I'd loved him. More than anything in the world, I'd loved him. He'd been my entire heart. And as much as I hated him now, I couldn't shake the memories of a time when I didn't. When I used to wake up next to a person who was looking at me like I was the sunrise, who treated me gently when I needed it and passionately when I wanted it.

When I used to be able to paint. When my heart was full of love and inspiration and hope.

Because that was what he'd taken from me. I wouldn't go so far as to say that Brad had been my muse, but I couldn't discount how much of an effect he had on my art. How having just one person who thought I could do it made all the difference. How that girl I used to be had needed him and his unwavering belief in me.

If I'd known that girl, the one who existed in the world of once upon a time, the way I knew myself now, I would tell her to suck it up. I'd tell her to get through that first year of university, take out some student loans, and just keep trying. That she didn't need some man to believe in her, especially one who was far too old for her at the time; she was capable of it herself. That she'd have to suffer for a while, but it would be okay.

That girl had just needed someone to tell her it would all be okay.

I would tell that girl, that past version of myself who cried so many times and was one fateful night away from quitting, that she could do it. That she shouldn't have to suffer for her art, but that she didn't have to give up who she was to be the artist she knew she could be.

I'd tell her to stay away from him. Because the thing she'd needed all along was inside her. That she didn't need a man who had no business being with a twenty-year-old woman. That she hadn't lost it, not at that point.

But that she would, and it would be his fault.

Before I could spiral any further, a loud knock at the door jolted me out of my thoughts and some of the water out of the jacuzzi as I jumped.

"The fuck?" I gasped, glaring in the general direction of the door. I hadn't ordered room service or anything yet and I wasn't expecting anyone.

The person knocked again.

"Just a sec," I called as I lifted myself out of the jacuzzi and grabbed the definitely-not-one-size-fits-all robe hanging next to the tub. It closed in the front, thankfully, but I hesitated before going to the door, wondering if I should put actual clothes on so whoever it was didn't get an eyeful of cleavage.

There was another loud knock, hard enough that it rattled the door.

"I'm coming, one sec," I said indignantly.

"Tess, please open up," came a desperate plea, then another round of loud, urgent pounding. "Come *on*, open the fucking door!"

"Brad?" I said, confused as I crossed the room and peeked out the eyehole.

Sure enough, my ex-husband was there, his head blocking nearly the entire view out of the peephole. He was turned so I could only see the side of his face, but there was no mistaking the panic there.

"Tessa, *please*!"

I unlatched the chain, then barely had enough time to step back before the door flew open and Brad tumbled into the room.

He was shirtless and his hair was a mess. The slacks he'd worn golfing earlier were unbuttoned and nearly fell off as he tripped, bracing himself against the wall before scurrying past me.

"What the fuck?" I gasped.

"—gonna kill me," Brad panted, terror in his eyes.

Oh, good. A killer was on the loose. So kind of him to hide behind me before telling me as I stood next to the fucking *open door*.

Instinctively, I whirled around and tried to slam it closed, but it was too late. A hand shot out, catching the door with a loud *thunk*. My heart leapt into my throat and I stepped back, horrified that I was about to be murdered in an almost-too-small bathrobe before my sheet mask had even finished giving me a soft and dewy glow.

Then the door flew back open and Zain stepped in.

I could understand why Brad thought he was about to die. I had never seen a look like that on anyone's face, let alone on Zain's. His dark eyes were lit up with fury and his jaw was clenched, exaggerating the lines of his face. He was still wearing the long-sleeved t-shirt he'd had on when

I saw him that morning, but the sleeves were pushed up to his elbows and his forearms were tight with tension as he shoved the door open. Zain wasn't overly tall—maybe within an inch or two of Brad's height, so around five-eight or five-nine—but in that moment, he looked like he was towering over both of us.

Though, that might have just been because Brad was legitimately cowering behind me.

"Tell him," he pleaded. "You've gotta tell him because he thinks—"

"Shut the fuck up," Zain spat, his voice a low growl.

"Tessa, *tell him!*" Brad repeated. "Please, beautiful—"

"Don't you fucking call her that," Zain said. "You don't *deserve* to even speak to her, let alone—"

"That's my *wife*, I can—"

"Oh, so because she's your wife, you can do whatever you want, you fucking bastard?"

"Fuck you, Zain. She's never gonna want—"

Zain lunged forward and Brad yelped, grabbing my arm as he tucked himself behind me even tighter.

"Jesus Christ, Tessa, just tell him the truth or—"

"Will you two idiots calm down?" I snapped. "Zain, just back off for a second and—" I stopped, shaking my arm. "—let *go* of me, Brad."

"Calm down?" Zain repeated, still looking like he was about to set Brad on fire with his mind. "Dunno if you'll be saying that when you find out your husband is a fucking cheater."

My mouth dropped open enough that I could feel the sheet mask shift down on my skin. Zain stared at me, then his expression changed, softening until there was so much pain in his eyes that I almost *felt* it.

"Tessa, I'm sorry," Zain said, his voice softer. "But I just caught him in a hotel room with another woman."

Oh.

Oh, shit.

Chapter Twenty

I CONSIDERED THROWING BRAD under the bus.

Figuratively.

Well, mostly figuratively.

As Zain looked at me with yet another expression I'd never seen before—one of sympathy and grief and regret that he had to be the one to tell me that Brad was cheating on me—I figured Brad might deserve being thrown under a literal bus.

Just a little.

Unfortunately, I didn't have a bus on hand.

Still, I considered pretending it was true. It would have been an out, you know? Zain catches him with another woman and tells me, I pretend to be devastated and tell Brad right then and there that I want a divorce... all my problems are solved.

But that would have made me an accomplice to, at best, manslaughter.

I mean, they wouldn't have been able to try Zain for first-degree murder when he lunged forward and shoved Brad face-first into the jacuzzi, drowning my ex-husband in lavender-scented bathwater as retribution for dishonouring his marriage vows. That would imply it was premeditated, and Zain clearly hadn't thought this through. Second-degree murder was a distinct possibility, but with the right lawyer, he could probably get off on manslaughter charges.

The problem was that if Zain murdered Brad, there would be an investigation, since Zain and I didn't really have the type of relationship where I'd help him hide a body and people would likely notice that Brad was missing. So the whole charade would fall apart since it would probably come to light that Brad and I had been divorced for years.

And this was why. This, right here, was fucking *why*.

Because Brad was really good at pretending to be the perfect everything. The perfect husband. The perfect ex-husband. The person who would do anything to get me back, who said hurting me was the biggest regret of his life, and blah-blah-fucking-*blah*.

All that talk, all that commitment to proving to me I should take him back, and he couldn't go *one* night without fake-cheating on his fake-wife.

"I caught him answering the door of the room across from mine," Zain said, anger still evident in his soft voice. "He was in there with that girl from yesterday. The hotel clerk. Tessa, he's *cheating* on you."

"Oh," I said.

A heavy moment of tense silence fell across the room. Zain looked at me expectantly, then frowned.

"Oh?" he repeated.

"Come on, Tessa," Brad pleaded from behind me. "Tell him I'm not."

I bit my lip, still caught in Zain's gaze.

"He's not," I said, almost apologetically.

Zain's eyes grew dark and angry again as he glanced over my shoulder.

"So you just tell her what to say to protect you?" he asked Brad sarcastically.

"I didn't—"

"You just fucking told her what to say and she said it!" Zain shouted. "You're her goddamn husband. You were supposed to protect her and love her and treat her like a fucking goddess, and instead you're going around behind her back and cheating on her instead of taking care of her like she needs."

"Boy, you don't think that highly of me, do you?" I asked.

Zain stopped and looked at me. "What?"

"I can take care of my fucking self," I said, glaring at him. "Don't sit there and act like you know what I need, Zain. You don't know me."

Zain's lips were still parted, but he fell silent. Anger was still flaring through me, but when a confused sort of hurt flickered in his eyes, it faded. Nervously, I went to run my hand through my hair, only remembering I was still wearing the sheet mask when I brushed it with my hand.

Because the situation couldn't get any more awkward.

Sighing, I tugged the mask off my face, breaking eye contact with Zain as I crumpled the stupid thing in my hand.

"He's not cheating on me," I said, staring at the Converse sneakers on Zain's feet. "We've—"

"—got an open relationship?" Zain asked.

"—been divorced for five years," I said at the same time, then my eyes went wide as they shot up to meet his. "Wait—"

"*What*?!" he said.

"I mean, what you said," I said. "That. That's what's happening here."

"Is it? Because it sounded like you said you're divorced."

I swallowed hard. "You must have misheard me."

"Oh, of course," he said sarcastically. "I can see how 'we have an open relationship' could easily sound like 'we've been fucking *divorced* for'—What the *fuck*, Tessa?"

I cringed, then looked up at the ceiling. "Fine. We're divorced. He's not cheating on me. He's just a moron."

"Uh, I'm standing right here," Brad said.

I turned to face him. "Let me say it again so we're clear. You're a fucking *moron*."

He had the decency to look ashamed. "I'm sor—"

"Fuck off."

"Tessa, wait—"

"I have to explain this whole fucking situation now thanks to you," I hissed. "So why don't you get out of my fucking room and go back to your little hookup that you just couldn't *wait* to have before Zain literally drowns you in the jacuzzi?"

He looked over my shoulder at Zain, then back at me with a pained expression. "Can we talk later?"

"No. Get out."

"Tess—"

"Get out before *I* drown you in the jacuzzi."

He looked like he was about to protest, then made the much smarter decision to keep his stupid mouth shut and leave, though he made sure to keep me between himself and Zain. Zain followed him with his eyes, watching in wary silence until Brad let himself out. Then, he turned to me.

"What the fuck?" he asked.

"You can't tell anyone," I said immediately.

That didn't seem to be what he was expecting. "*What?*"

"You can't tell anyone we're divorced," I said.

"Oh, sure, no problem," he said, his voice flat. "That's completely understandable. It's so incredibly common to find out that someone's been divorced for years but is here pretending to still be married and—Tessa, you told everyone you're trying to have a fucking *kid*."

I glared at him. "Yeah, well... I have my reasons."

"You better start sharing those fucking reasons," he said. "Because I just scared the shit out of some hotel clerk and almost beat the shit out of your—" He made exaggerated air quotes. "—'husband' trying to defend you only to find out you're fucking lying about everything."

"I never asked you to defend me," I said. "And why would you bother, anyway? You've never given a shit before."

He raised his eyebrows. "Excuse me?"

"Don't pretend you're doing this for *me* when it's just about this hate-on you've always had for Brad. You might think I'm stupid, but I'm not."

"Setting aside the fact that I was completely right in not liking that fucking rat, I've never thought you were stupid," he replied. "But that doesn't mean I can figure out why the fuck you're lying about this to your entire family."

I scoffed. "Like you'd understand."

He laughed, though the sound was dry. "Try me."

"Try *what*?" I said. "Try to explain to you what it's like to be the fourth favourite child in a family with three kids, and two of them are tied for first? So you spend your whole entire life feeling like no one in your family wants you, believes in you, or cares about you, and then you bring someone home that they adore and get along with and you just... you just want to hold onto that? How the fuck am I going to explain to you what that's like, huh?"

"That's not—"

"And how do you want me to explain that if I tell everyone my marriage failed, then I'm going to have to tell them everything else I failed at, too? Because, oh yeah, I'm lying about that too, okay? I'm a fucking failed artist, just like all of you thought I would be. Do you remember my dad losing his shit because I wanted to go to art school, Zain? Do you remember everyone thinking I was a fucking joke? You should, because you were one of them."

"I wasn't—"

"So yeah, I haven't told them I'm divorced because Brad knows he fucked up and is willing to play the game with me so I can pretend to my family that I'm successful at *something* because I have some inherent need to impress them." I folded my arms across my chest, which I probably should have done earlier because the robe was just *barely* staying closed. "I know he's a cheater, okay? Now I do, anyway. If I'd known—"

I stopped, clenching my jaw and staring at a spot on the wall just past Zain's head as that familiar anger surged through me. Not shame. Not humiliation. Just anger.

Because sure, I was standing there in a bathrobe with goopy mask residue all over my face and lavender bathwater still dripping down my legs as I told the man I'd had a crush on growing up that my marriage failed because my husband was a pathological cheater.

But I didn't have much shame to begin with, and once a person is humiliated the way Brad had humiliated me, everything else seems pretty small in comparison. So all that was left was anger.

"If you'd known what, Tess?" Zain asked. "Tell me what happened."

But I wasn't ready to have that conversation. Not with *him*.

"What do I need to do for you not to tell anyone?" I asked.

He blinked. "Excuse me?"

I took my eyes off the random spot on the wall I'd been staring at. "You're a businessman, right?"

"I mean, that's not..." He stopped and sighed. "Where are you going with this?"

"I need this to say between you and me," I said, my voice as neutral as I could make it. "And Brad, technically, I guess, but it's not like he's going to say shit. I don't want my family to know, so let's make a deal."

"A deal," he repeated, then paused. "You want to make a deal for me to keep quiet?"

His voice was still flat and even, but there was something deeper to it than there had been before. Something as intrigued as it was intriguing.

Something as terrifying as it was thrilling.

"It's only fair," I said. "Tell me what I can do to keep this between us."

Zain crossed his arms and leaned back against the wall, his stance far too casual for the dark look in his eyes. "That depends."

"On what?"

"What you're willing to give me, Tessa," he asked.

And oh, fuck.

I didn't know if the tension in the room had been there the entire time or if it flared up as he spoke. Regardless, it was there, thick and dizzying and all-encompassing. And suddenly the man standing there wasn't Zain as I knew him.

No, the man standing there didn't have Zain's typically guarded expression or neutral eyes. The man standing there was the grown-up version of how thirteen-year-old me had pictured him. My brother's best friend, the older boy, the quiet one, who was intriguing and mysterious and didn't want anything to do with me.

Until now, apparently.

Because now there was a look in his eyes that hadn't been there before. One that I couldn't quite interpret. Now, his lips were curled into something that wasn't quite a smirk and wasn't at all a smile. Now, his arms were folded and he was leaning against the wall, studying me.

Challenging me.

It wasn't like I was stupid. I could hear the implications under his words. I was very aware of what that meant—what I was willing to *give* him—and that I was barely clad in an almost-too-small terry-cloth robe and nothing else as we stood in the crowded entrance of the hotel room.

I just didn't know when Zain became the kind of person to make those implications towards me, of all people.

"You seem to have some suggestions in mind already," I replied.

He shrugged nonchalantly. "That's neither here nor there."

I sighed. "Just tell me what you want, Zain."

"Why should I?" he asked. "You're the one who needs something out of this negotiation. So it's up to you to put the cards on the table. It's just business, *beautiful*."

I glared at him. "Don't you *ever* fucking call me that."

He half-laughed. "Why not?"

"I don't like it."

"Brad gets to call you that."

"Since when do you want to do the things Brad does?"

He opened his mouth, then hesitated and shut it before shaking his head.

"Just answer the question, Zain," I said. "Give me your suggestions, since I know you have them."

He studied me for another moment, head tilted to the side.

"What if I suggested something horrible, huh?" he asked, his voice low.

"What do you mean?"

"I mean…" He shifted on the wall, bending his knee so he could rest his foot against the wall as he leaned on it. "How important is this to you, Tess?"

"I wouldn't be offering this if it wasn't important," I said.

"What if I asked you to go down on me, right here, right now?"

I drew in a breath as he finally stopped talking in insinuations, but kept my face as neutral as I could.

"Is it important enough that you'd do it?" he continued. "If I told you to get on your knees and suck me off, would you do it? To keep your family from finding out about this? Or what if I asked you to go over to that bed and lie down and let me do whatever I wanted to your body for as long as I wanted? How much is keeping this secret worth to you?"

And maybe I should've been nervous. Or disgusted. Or angry with him for suggesting it. I definitely shouldn't have had a traitorous little part of me that was slightly intrigued by the thought of it all.

But I didn't have time to unpack that last bit right then. Especially because, as much as I couldn't stand him, I'd known Zain long enough to know he was full of shit.

"As disgusting of an asshole as even pretending to suggest that makes you, you wouldn't actually," I said. "You're not the kind of sick fuck who would get off on that."

"You don't think so?" he asked.

I rolled my eyes. "Do it, then. You want me to suck your dick? Ask for it, Zain."

"That's not the point," he said. "I want to know if—"

"If what?" I stepped forward and Zain raised his eyebrows, then his jaw dropped open as I fell to my knees in front of him. "Ask me for it, then. Hope you're looking forward to the toothiest blowjob you've ever gotten in your life and the disgust of thinking about the time you made your best friend's little sister suck your cock. Won't that be fun to think of every time you look at Josh from now until forever? God, that'll make his wedding interesting, won't it?"

He was silent.

That wasn't unusual, seeing as it was Zain. What was unusual was that he was staring down at me, his lips still parted, completely unable to mask the shock on his face.

"Well?" I pressed. "Go on. Ask for it."

He sighed. "Stand up, Tessa."

"So that's a no? No toothy blowjob on the menu tonight?"

"I just wanted to know how fucking delusional you are about this."

I rolled my eyes as I carefully got to my feet, pinching the front of the robe closed so I didn't accidentally flash him. "You don't have to understand it to respect it."

"There is no reason I have to respect this. *None.*"

"Which is why I'm very politely asking you to forget everything you saw tonight, and in return, what kind of favour I can do to thank you for continuing to make this none of your fucking business."

He regarded me for a moment, pulling his lower lip between his teeth absentmindedly as he studied me. Then, he nodded slowly.

"I'm sure my mom's already bitched about it to you," he said. "But I'm trying to get a promotion at work that'll get me transferred to Victoria. There's a convention coming up and one of our biggest potential clients will be there. Fucked as it might be, a single guy in his thirties doesn't inspire as much confidence as a guy in his thirties with a wife or girlfriend. And that's something that's hurting my chances of this promotion."

He stopped, a slow smirk spreading across his face before he continued. "So since you already have plenty of experience faking a relationship, you can be my date to the closing night dinner I have to go to."

Ugh.

I mean, it wasn't the *worst* thing he could have asked for, but it wasn't great, either. Still, I needed him to stay quiet, so…

"Fine," I said.

"It's on a Saturday," he said. "You'll have to stay there overnight."

"Let me guess," I said. "We have to share a hotel room and there's only one bed."

He snorted. "Yeah, probably. Don't worry. If I can't get a suite with a pull-out couch or something, I'll tell them you're gassy and ask to have a cot brought up for you."

"How chivalrous."

"You're welcome."

He unfolded his arms and stood up straight. I expected him to turn and leave, but instead, he caught my gaze again and took a step forward.

"By the way," he said casually, then took another step, which brought him directly in front of me. "There's one more thing."

Apparently, I'd spent all my snarky defiance on making Zain uncomfortable by kneeling in front of him, because a sudden shiver ran over me and my breath caught in my throat.

"What?" I asked.

A smile curled across Zain's lips.

"I just want you to know," he said. "I would've kept it a secret regardless."

"Huh?"

"What I saw tonight." His voice was a low, almost seductive rumble. "I wouldn't have told anyone, Tessa. All you had to do was ask. But I guess you don't think that *highly* of me."

Without meaning to, I let my eyes flick down to his lips. As soon as I realized it, I looked back up at him, but he'd caught the momentary slip and the corners of his eyes were crinkling as he smirked at me.

"So you're saying I don't have to go to your stupid work event?" I asked, fighting to keep my voice steady.

"Oh, you do," he said. "But not because of that."

"But—"

"Because you think I'm the kind of *asshole* who would make you do something like that as payment for keeping a secret."

He was going to kiss me.

I was sure of it.

I was terrified of it.

I wanted it.

He was so close. Dangerously close. Everything in me was screaming. Some of it was screaming for me to push him away, to tell him no, that I hated his stupid scrawny ass and he was an absolute dickhead. Some of it was telling me this was a joke, a prank, that he was teasing me and mocking me because that's just what Zain did. He was friends with Josh, after all.

And the rest of it was telling me to kiss him. That I wanted it. That the only reason I didn't still have a childhood crush on him was because I wasn't a child and I'd convinced myself that I hated him because he made fun of me. And that I should kiss him because he was talking in that low growl of a voice and he looks so hot with his tattoos and long-ish hair and he'd tried to *defend* me, like I was some damsel in distress who needed that and even though I absolutely didn't, wasn't it just so nice that someone cared enough to fucking *try*?

I couldn't speak. Couldn't breathe. Couldn't do anything but look up at Zain, trapped between him and the wall, a piece of dark hair falling across his forehead and his eyes holding mine and his lips right *there*, parted and ready and waiting and—

He brought his hand up to my face and my breath hitched, but instead of leaning in, he rubbed his thumb across my cheek.

"You had some goo left from the mask," he said casually, then wiped his hand on the shoulder of my robe before straightening up and stepping back. Before I'd so much as managed a breath to recover, then turned to the door.

"I'll grab your number before the weekend's over so I can give you the details for the event," he said. "And don't worry, Teacup. I'm not some sick fuck who's gonna ask you for *it* just because he can. Your secret's safe with me."

Then he left, and I stood there in the entry of the hotel room, not sure if I was feeling unsteady because someone had found out my secret...

Or because I had secretly wanted Zain to ask me for it.

Chapter Twenty-One

"Tessa! Is that you?"

Despite recognizing her voice instantly, I kept my glass raised to my lips, hoping with the entirety of my ass—which was far larger than my heart—that Mrs. Katz would think she'd mistaken me for some other gorgeous fat woman with wavy brown hair.

However, that would have required luck, and the only luck on my side that weekend was the kind of luck where everything goes the complete opposite way of how you want things to go. And I guess the mother of my childhood best friend who had no idea we'd had a falling out a few years earlier would have recognized me anyway, given that I'd spent as much time at her house as a child as I'd spent at my own.

"Tessa," Mrs. Katz repeated, her voice warm as she walked up to me.

"Oh!" I said, pretending to be surprised. "Sorry, I didn't hear you!"

She smiled and opened her arms. "That's okay, sweet pea. Come here, it's been *far* too long. Kira said you were out of town last time we went up to visit her and Jackson."

"Oh, yeah," I said as I hugged her back. "I was at, um, an art retreat that weekend."

She frowned as she let go. "We were there for a week, though."

"Right," I said, forcing a laugh. "But right after the retreat I was doing this business trip thing for the charity I work at."

"Look at you," she said fondly. "You must be doing so, so well."

"So well," I lied. "How are *you*, though?"

"Oh, good." She was beaming. "Just waiting for the call, you know."

I did not know. "Right, of course."

"From Kira? To let us know they... I mean, you know she and Jackson are trying to adopt."

"Oh," I said. "That call. I thought you meant another call."

Mrs. Katz frowned again. "She told you, didn't she? It's all she's been talking about for months."

"Yeah, of course." I tried to laugh. "Sorry, my brain is a little scattered today."

She pressed her lips together conspiratorially. "Well, hormones will do that to you."

I stared at her. "Hormones?"

"Your mom may have mentioned you and Brad are working on baking a little bun yourselves." She nudged me playfully. "Best friends do everything together, right? I'm sure you and Kira planned this out."

Fuck.

As expected, the anniversary party was turning out to be the worst part of the weekend. At least, that's what I expected before Zain had burst into my hotel room the previous night. After that, I thought maybe the anniversary party wouldn't seem so bad, but as usual, I was wrong.

Things had been awkward from the moment Brad and I had arrived to help finish setting up. Mom and Dad had gone all out, planning an event that was like if a wedding and a high school reunion had a very tacky, very extravagant-on-a-budget baby. There was a DJ and a dance floor, dinner tables but no dinner, and an open bar that had any type of alcohol you could have wanted, as long as all you wanted was cheap beer, cheap wine, or cheap vodka.

They were already there when we walked in, along with Dylan, Josh, Audrey, and a few assorted extended family members who lived under the impression that "Party starts at seven" meant "Show up by six-thirty."

Oh, and of course, Zain.

"About time, Teacup," Dad said when I walked in, then frowned. "Jeez, who died?"

"What?" I asked, shrugging off my leather jacket.

He raised his eyebrows and looked pointedly at my outfit. "You look like you're on the way to a funeral."

It was my trademark fancy-ish-event outfit. Though I'd upgraded it from basics to designer pieces over the years, it had started when I was in university and couldn't afford to buy a new outfit for every showcase or gallery opening I went to. Since I had an aversion to dresses in general, I'd put together a pants-based version of a little black dress: a low cut satin-y black top that skimmed off my curves and was loosely tucked into black leather pants. On my feet were black pumps, of course, and I had a small black clutch purse that I used to carry around the basics: wallet, phone, keys, and a tube of killer red lipstick.

If that looked like a funeral outfit, then it was the sluttiest funeral I'd ever been to.

Which was what I wanted to respond with. But it was my dad, and my family, and the words stuck in my throat as all of them chuckled at my dad's quip. Which was fine. My main purpose in this family was to be an easy laugh.

And then Zain spoke up.

"I think she looks great," he said as I put my jacket and clutch on the table reserved for family.

And since Zain rarely spoke up, everyone looked at him, almost shocked.

And since it was *Zain*, Brad couldn't just stand there and let him compliment me. A protective hand slipped around my waist.

"She always looks phenomenal," he said, his voice smooth.

Then Zain flicked an eyebrow up at him before glancing at me, and Brad's face turned red, and I was so certain Zain was going to open his stupid mouth and ruin everything that I braced myself.

But he just shrugged and turned to Mom. "What else did you need us to set up?"

If anyone noticed the higher-than-usual tension between Zain and Brad, no one said anything. Still, I tried to keep them on separate sides of the room as much as possible, which got easier when what felt like three-quarters of the population of Burnsley arrived for the party.

Except then I had to deal with catching up with what felt like three-quarters of the population of Burnsley all night.

Including Kira's mom.

"Tessa?" Mrs. Katz asked when I didn't respond. "What's wrong?"

"Nothing," I said too quickly. "Everything's fine with me and Kira."

Her eyebrows went up on her forehead. "Is it?"

"Of course. Why wouldn't it be?"

She looked concerned. "Well, I don't know, but when you bring it up out of nowhere like that—"

"Well holy shit, look at what the cat dragged in!" my dad bellowed from a short distance away.

"Oh, excuse me," I said to Mrs. Katz, jumping on any chance to walk away from the conversation I could. "I need to go meet... that person."

Before she could say anything, I turned and walked over to the table where my dad had looked up from his conversation with my brothers, Audrey, and Zain. There was a huge grin on his face as he looked at a short man clad in khakis and a dress shirt with the top three buttons undone striding confidently across the room.

"Who's that old fucker?" Dad said loudly.

"Damn, that's sad!" the man replied just as boisterously. "I knew you'd gotten old, Gary, but I hadn't heard about the memory loss! It's me, the man who stood up with you while you married that angel of a wife of yours? Though, maybe I should pretend it was the opposite and I was the one who married Lorelei, if you don't remember anyway."

Dad guffawed and extended his hand to the man as he walked up, but he shoved it out of the way.

"Not a fuckin' chance are you getting away without a hug," he said, and then threw his arms around my dad. "It's been years, buddy!"

"And whose fault is that?" Dad said. When they parted, he turned back to the table, grinning broadly. "You guys probably don't recognize this bastard, but it's your Uncle Mike."

"We have an Uncle Mike?" Dylan said.

Mike laughed. "Ah, well, you wouldn't remember me, kiddo. You weren't even out of your dad's nutsack last time I was in Burnsley."

Dylan might have been oblivious enough not to know who Mike was, but both Josh and I recognized him. I couldn't remember ever meeting Mike in person, but we'd heard stories of him over the years. He'd been my dad's best man and closest friend. I knew they still kept in touch, mostly when Dad was travelling for conferences and stuff. Mike was a complete workaholic who had never gotten married, retired early, and then bought a private island somewhere in the Caribbean.

At least, according to Dad, who occasionally mentioned it while lamenting his life choices when Josh or I pissed him off growing up. I'd always thought he was exaggerating, but given Mike's tan and carefree attitude, it seemed like he might have been telling the truth.

"Uncle Mike!" Josh said, laughing as he stood up to shake his hand. "Dad's told us all about you."

"Nothing good, I hope," Mike said, shoving Josh's hand out of the way and hugging him with the same vigor he'd hugged Dad. "I'd hate to think your dad was a fuckin' liar."

Dad roared with laughter. "This is my oldest, Josh."

"Josh," Mike said. "I remember when your mom popped you out. Sorry that you ended up looking just like this ugly son-of-a-bitch. Damn, it's like staring into a very unfortunate time machine."

Josh's roar of laughter sounded just like Dad's, proving Mike's point.

"He's following my footsteps, too," Dad said. "Climbing the ladder at Fiore. He'll outrank me soon enough." He motioned to Audrey, who was sitting at the table with an amused expression on her face. "And he's getting married this fall to this lovely woman."

"My fiancée," Josh said, genuine adoration on his face as he looked at her. "Audrey."

"Pleasure to meet you," Audrey said.

"Well, damn!" Mike said, and kissed her cheek. "Congratulations, kids. Remind me to give you a wedding gift before I go."

Audrey looked stunned. "Oh, no, that's not—"

"Ah, you're right," Mike said, cutting her off. "I'll be too fuckin' drunk to remember. Here."

He took a ratty leather wallet from his back pocket, opened it, and pulled out a wad of cash that he promptly stuffed into Audrey's hand.

"This should cover, what, about half of Gary's bar tab?" he asked.

Josh stared down at the cash in Audrey's hand. "This is like... a thousand dollars."

"Hmm, good point." Mike took another stack of cash from his wallet. "Here ya go. Congrats, you two!"

"Oh my God," Audrey said. "This really isn't necessary, but thank you."

Mike waved it off. "Consider it thirty-odd years of birthday gifts or whatever."

Before they could keep protesting, Dad motioned at Dylan.

"My other son, Dylan," he said. "He's a video game nerd."

"I'm a Gaminar streamer, Dad," Dylan muttered, his face turning red.

"No shit?!" Mike said. "You play any Heylo Games?"

"Uh... yeah," Dylan said, looking surprised.

"I've got a stake or two in that company." He pulled a phone out of another one of his pockets. "What's your Gaminar tag? I'll get them to add you to our influencer list. Free games and swag and all that shit."

"Fuck, for real?" Dylan said, gaping at him. "I... I mean, yeah. It's DillyBomb45."

Mike tapped on his phone. "Done."

"You're spoiling my kids rotten," Dad said.

"Eh, they were already rotten," Mike said. "They're *your* kids, after all."

Dad snorted and jerked his thumb at Zain. "Well, this one's Zain."

Zain looked at Mike uncomfortably. "I'm not one of his kids."

"He's Josh's version of you," Dad said.

Mike, clearly sensing that Zain didn't want anything from him, clapped him on the shoulder. "Well, we all know that means you're the best off here! Nice to meet ya, buddy."

Then Mike looked at me. There was a beat of silence where no one spoke.

"Hi," I finally said. "I'm Tessa."

"My daughter," Dad added. "And her husband is Brad—" He motioned towards the dance floor. "—the one over there dancing with Lorelei."

"Well, I'll have to cut in to get my dance with Lorelei in a bit," Mike said, but he was still looking at me. "Jesus, Tessa. Last time I saw you, I'm pretty sure you were in diapers, and now look at you. Did you..."

He frowned as he trailed off.

"Did I what?" I asked, but he turned to Dad.

"Did your mom pass before you had the kids?" he asked.

Dad's throat flexed as he swallowed, the smile on his face fading a bit. "She did."

"Damn. Sorry, man." Mike patted him on the back, then looked back at me. "You wouldn't've known Gary's mom but you know, you look *just* like her."

I blinked. "I do?"

"Oh, absolutely fuckin' gorgeous. You're a spitting image." Mike burst out laughing. "There was a reason we always wanted to hang out at Gar's place growing up, if you know what I mean."

It was flattering in a creepy, cringey kind of way. I didn't feel like Mike was leering at me, though, and tried to smile. "I, uh… thanks."

"And what is it you do?" Mike asked.

"I'm an artist," I replied.

He let out a loud noise of disbelief. "No shit. No *shit*? Gar, she's your mom reincarnated."

Dad half-laughed, but his jaw twitched. "Don't need to tell me twice."

Well, maybe he didn't need to be told twice, but I sure did, because this was the first I was hearing of it.

"Grandma was an artist?" I asked.

"Oh yeah," Mike said. "Always had some hobby on the go. She did these beautiful landscapes and flowers and stuff."

"The worst was the pottery phase," Dad said. "I think there was clay in every damn meal for months."

"What happened to all her stuff?" I asked. "Her… her paintings?"

Dad shrugged. "We threw most of it out after my dad died, I think. Some of it went to thrift stores. I don't know for sure. There was a lot of garbage to sort through, Teacup."

"I think I still have a painting or two," Mike said. "Floating around somewhere. I'll take a look when I'm back on the island, if you want."

"I would really, really like that," I said.

He smiled, though there was an almost sympathetic look to them. "And you know, I'm always looking for new pieces to add to my collection. You got a portfolio or some paintings I could see?"

Before I could answer, Dad did.

"Oh, don't bother, Mike," Dad said. "I'm sure we've got some of her stuff hanging around our place you can get out of my garage."

For a moment, no one spoke. Mike looked at my dad semi-incredulously while Josh looked anywhere but at me and Dylan stared down at his phone.

But I could still feel eyes on me, and without even choosing to, I glanced in the direction the sensation was coming from to see Zain watching me.

Because of course he was. Because of course he wanted to see me be humiliated yet again.

"So, you do commissions, Tessa?" Mike finally said, breaking the silence.

I snapped my eyes away from Zain's. "Sometimes, yes."

"Perfect. You got a business card? I'll contact you for something one of these days, okay?"

"Sure." I grabbed my clutch off the table and took a card out, handing it to him. "It was very nice to meet you, Mike."

"And you, darling." He elbowed Dad. "Now, let me go get my hands on Lorelei. It's been *far* too long."

The two of them started to cross the room towards Mom, who was still dancing with Brad. All of us watched silently for a moment. Out of the corner of my eye, I saw Audrey nudge Josh.

"Ow! What was that for?" I heard him mutter.

She hissed something back, which I guessed was probably "Say something to your sister," because a moment later he cleared his throat.

"Uh, Tessa, are you—"

"Excuse me," I said. "I need to go to the bathroom."

Then, before Mike and Dad could reach Mom and end my blissfully Brad-free time, I turned on my heel and walked towards the exit.

Chapter Twenty-Two

March in Burnsley was not exactly warm.

But I didn't think of that before dashing out of the hall. It wasn't until I opened the door to the parking lot and a blast of chilly air hit me that I remembered how cold it was. Despite satin not being known for insulative properties, I decided suffering outside for a bit was a better option than returning to the party to get my leather jacket.

Which was dumb, because I was definitely suffering.

But I couldn't bring myself to go back inside. Instead, I sat on a bench, which was also a bad choice, since the thin material of my top felt colder than the air around it and it got even worse when I leaned against the back of the bench.

Mike's presence had been a whirlwind. There was his personality in general—as over-the-top loud as he was over-the-top generous—as well as the revelation that, once upon a time, there actually *had* been someone in my family that I would've fit in with.

Then there was the way Dad had acted, which wasn't all that unusual. I mean, introducing his sons, his son's friend, and his son-in-law who was across the room while leaving his daughter to introduce herself was typical of him.

But there was the blasé way he'd said they had thrown all his mom's paintings away. It would've been one thing for them to have been destroyed in the fire or something. But to throw them away... fuck.

My heart ached enough that it almost distracted me from the weather.

But not enough to distract me when I heard the door open and a few moments later, someone silently sat down on the bench next to me. I stiffened, ready to turn to my ex-husband and tell him to fuck off, but it wasn't Brad.

Which I should have figured out earlier. Brad would never be quiet for that long. So instead, I sat in my confusion, silent in return as I stared out at the parking lot.

"Cold?" Zain finally asked.

"Like you care," I said.

"I don't, obviously. But I found this jacket that looks about your size and figured I'd bring it out for unrelated reasons." He held up his hand, dangling my leather jacket from a single finger. "But if you don't want it, I can bring it back inside."

Ugh. He was *intolerable*.

Glaring at the ground in front of me, I hesitated, then snatched my jacket from him and put it on.

"Thanks," I muttered.

"Don't mention it," he said.

So I didn't.

Leaning against the back of the bench again, I folded my arms across my chest, waiting for him to leave. I mean, he was out there in his tailored suit jacket with nothing else overtop of it. It couldn't have been *that* warm, even though every single tattoo he had was covered up by what he was wearing. And it was hanging open to show off the green shirt he had on underneath. And his pants couldn't have been much warmer than my leather ones because... I mean, they were dress pants.

But apparently I was upset enough that I forgot Zain was the king of silently brooding. After waiting for a bit and still getting no indication that he was going to leave, I sighed. "What do you want, Zain?"

"I wanted to check on you."

I looked at him, my face twisted in doubt. "Excuse me?"

"Well, if you freeze to death, you won't be able to hold up your end of our little deal. So I wanted to make sure you didn't."

I snorted and turned away, glaring out at the parking lot. "Right. Of course."

He was quiet for another moment.

"Also, about last night—"

"I don't want to talk to you about last night."

He ignored me. "I wanted to say I understand what you mean now."

"About what?"

"About not... you know. Fitting in. Feeling like you don't belong. I... I get that."

"Well, yippee for you. Anything else?"

"Yeah. What does that actually have to do with pretending to be married to your asshole 'husband'?"

"Fuck off, Zain."

"Nah." He leaned against the back of the bench. "It's a fair question. You said a lot of shit to me last night that didn't make any sense."

"And let me guess, you stayed up all night pondering it."

"Of course not," he said. "Just until around three or so."

I rolled my eyes but didn't respond.

"Here's what doesn't make sense," he finally said. "You think your family doesn't accept you or care about you—"

"You *just* fucking said you got it."

"And if you'd let me finish, you'd realize there was a 'but' in there," he said.

Fucking stupid snarky Zain. "Fine. But what?"

"But I don't get what Brad has to do with that."

"Then you're an idiot."

He chuckled softly. "Don't I know it. Is it seriously just because it looks like you have a good marriage or something?"

"Yes."

"Hmm." Zain leaned back against the bench. "See, I dunno about that, Teacup. I know you too well to think that's *it*."

"You don't know me at all."

"I've known you for twenty-five years."

I wrinkled my nose. "Don't say it like that. It makes you sound old."

That earned me another soft laugh and I hated it. I *hated* making people I didn't like laugh because some intrinsic part of me felt warm and fuzzy and pleased when someone thought I said something funny.

"Come on," he said. "Tell me the real reason."

"You really wanna know?" I asked.

"Of course I do, Tessa."

"Too bad," I said. "It's none of your fucking business."

That laugh came out more like a derisive snort, probably because it wasn't a laugh and it was definitely a derisive snort. "Fine. Let's try something easier, then. What'd you mean when you said you were the fourth favourite child?"

I looked at him. "What?"

"Last night. You said you're the fourth favourite child. Last I checked, Dylan and Josh were two people. Who's the other one?"

"You can't be serious."

"I am."

I scoffed, then shook my head. "You're an idiot."

"So I've heard. Twice."

I held up one finger. "Dylan and Josh. Tied for first. Then—" I held up a second finger. "—You."

That seemed to surprise him. "What? No, that's—"

"—accurate, I know." I put up a third finger. "Then Brad." My fourth finger went up. "Then me. For now, anyway. I'm assuming once Josh and Audrey are actually married, I'll be bumped down, but for now I'm claiming the spot on the technicality."

"That's not true at all."

"It's always been true. I've been disappointing them since the moment they found out I was going to be born without a penis." I half-laughed. "You heard how my dad talked about me. Someone *else* was trying to be nice to me and he had to shoot it down. So don't tell me it's not fucking true."

I heard him draw in a breath as if he was going to respond, but nothing came out. Instead, he sat back against the bench.

Silent.

It was awkward. Not because it was an awkward silence, but because it was almost... well, comfortable. I was still sad, still frustrated, still angry that Zain was sitting there instead of walking away.

But at the same time, I was glad he didn't.

"It was because they were right," I said a few minutes later.

"Who?" he asked.

"My family. My dad. About the art and stuff."

He sighed. "They weren't, Tessa. They just don't understand what—"

"No, I mean, they were. I almost flunked out of university."

"What?"

Cold as I was, heat was rising up my cheeks. "My first year. I was trying to figure out how to get away with not going back. The only reason I did was because of Brad."

"Because of Brad," he repeated, unimpressed. "Why?"

"I hooked up with him the first night we met."

"Not exactly information I'm thrilled to learn," he said dryly.

I turned my head to glare at him. "Do you want to hear what happened or not? Because you keep asking me all these fucking questions and now that I'm trying to tell you, you're acting like an asshole."

He held my gaze for a moment, then shrugged. "Fine. Tell me."

"Well, now maybe I don't want to."

"Alright. Then don't."

Annoyed, I turned back to the parking lot, folding my arms across my chest. Zain sat there, saying nothing but not leaving, like he was expecting me to start telling him the whole story.

Well, I wasn't going to. He could sit there and freeze all he wanted while he pretended to give a shit about me. Because we both knew he didn't. We both knew he was out there just to... to something.

Okay, maybe I didn't know why he was out there. But I still wasn't going to talk to him, I told myself firmly. It was none of his fucking business.

But my mouth apparently didn't get the memo.

"Do you remember the first time he came to Burnsley with me?" I asked. "For my birthday? When I turned twenty."

"How could I forget?" Zain said, his voice disinterested and cold.

"That was the second time I saw him in person."

That got his attention. "What?"

"We hooked up the first night we met, which was near the end of the semester. I met him at this art showcase that had some students featured in it."

"Let me guess. He told you he was floored by your talent and tenacity right from the start, just like he told everyone," Zain said. "Despite the fact that he was trying to hook up with fucking students."

"It wasn't all students. And I wasn't in the show. Kira was. And a bunch of my classmates. But my stuff wasn't good enough to be featured."

"Oh," Zain said.

"We hooked up, whether you like it or not," I said. "The next day he found this... this sketchbook I had left out. An old one that was half-full. I only had it out because I had one last assignment to do and didn't want to buy a new book to do it. He asked me about it and I said it was garbage and I wasn't going to go back to school in the fall. And he freaked out."

"Because you wanted to drop out?"

"Because he didn't realize I was nineteen." I smiled in spite of myself. "All those things you and probably everyone else thought about him being too old for me? He really did have those thoughts first. Yeah, he's an asshole, but there were... He did have some... I don't know. Morals. Ethics. Whatever. But like, it was a fancy event. I was dressed up and not obviously one of the students. He thought I was in my mid-twenties and I thought he was in his mid-twenties. So it wasn't like... He is an asshole. But he wasn't trying to pick up a girl ten years younger than him."

"Considering that didn't stop him from staying with a girl ten years younger than him, I don't think he deserves that much credit," Zain said dryly.

I ignored him. "In the middle of him panicking that he slept with a 'literal teenager' despite the fact that I was almost twenty, he realized what I'd said about not coming back to school and started telling me that I had to. That my stuff was good and that I was being too hard on myself because I'd scratched out the drawing in the sketchbook when it was a good drawing. So then I had to tell him it was an old sketchbook and that I hadn't scratched it out, that my stupid ass brother had grabbed it from me while I was drawing and I'd gouged a line across the page. And he starts telling me that brothers can be stupid and that it didn't mean I wasn't any good and I had to tell him, you know? That I was failing at my classes and that my family had all said I wasn't good enough and that I had to go home and tell my dad I wasted his money on art school, just like he'd said I was going to."

I stopped, closing my eyes for a second as something painful lumped in my throat. Zain didn't say anything and I swallowed it back before continuing.

"He didn't like that. Because he... he thought my stuff was good. So he told me to go home to Burnsley, turn twenty, and come back to Vancouver in the fall. And that if I still wanted him after I'd been away for a while, then we'd figure something out." I stared down at my hands. "He believed in me, Zain. Not a single other person did."

"But he came to Burnsley," Zain said. "He didn't wait for you to go back to Vancouver."

I pressed my lips together. "Yeah, well... it was an interesting summer."

"Interesting?"

"If you didn't want to hear me say I hooked up with him the first night we met, you're not gonna want to hear about the summer."

He made a disgusted noise. "You're right. I don't. Because he was fucking twenty-nine and you were nineteen."

"I was and am very aware of your feelings on the matter of our ages," I said stiffly. "Remember? You called him out at my birthday dinner?"

"For good reason," he muttered.

"It was my birthday, Zain. You were a dick about it."

"You were twenty."

"And he sat there at that table of people who all thought I was a fucking joke and told them I was special. That I was good at what I did." I blinked hard to stop my eyes from stinging. "Everyone at that table—well, except you, I guess—liked him. My dad thought he was awesome. He and Josh got along. Mom was proud of me for finding this very put together, very polite man that fit into our family like he was meant to be there. And he told them all I was worth believing in."

Zain was silent as I blinked again, taking a shaky breath and letting it out slowly before I could continue.

"My twentieth birthday," I said. "And because of him, it was the first time anyone in my family looked at me like I fit in. And then *you* had to go and call him out for being older than me."

"Pretty sure he agreed with me," he said. "And there was a whole fucking speech about how him being older than you was at the forefront of his mind but you still wanted him and he was never gonna hurt you or hold you back and blah-blah-blah."

"Because I deserved the best in the world," I said, smiling bitterly. "And he refused to let me settle for any less. And then you asked him if he thought he was the best and he said he had to be so he wouldn't lose me. Pretty convincing, right?"

"Uh... I guess."

I shrugged. "I mean, I believed it. Everyone else there believed it. Everyone other than you and me still believe it."

"I suppose that's true."

"Yeah." I laughed softly. "Too bad he was sleeping with three other women at the same time."

"*What*?!"

"Yep."

"He was cheating right from the start?"

I nodded. "He had a girlfriend the night we met. Broke up with her two weeks later. Found another one, then was dating her and this other girl at the same time. I *think* he tried to be faithful once in a while after it was clear we were like, serious-serious. Like, in hindsight, he went through periods where he was moody and withdrawn for no reason."

"That was when he was cheating?"

"No. That would've been the few times he didn't have a side chick."

"Jesus. You sure know how to pick them."

"And you sure know how to be an asshole."

He shrugged in agreement. "So that's it. After all that, even though he's a complete shitstain, you're still pretending to be married to him because of your family."

"Yep."

"What happens when you meet someone else?"

I frowned. "What do you mean?"

He shrugged. "You know. You meet someone else, fall in love, wanna be with that person forever. Do you hope they put up with this batshit crazy situation or...?"

I shrugged. "Hasn't been an issue yet."

"Hmm," he said. "Sounds lonely."

"Lonely?"

"Yeah. Not being with someone because you're pretending to be married to your ex. I imagine that's pretty lonely."

Laughing, I shook my head. "I'm not lonely. Trust me."

"You just said you're not with anyone. What happens when you... I dunno." He shrugged. "When you want to go out? When you want to be around someone? When you want to get laid?"

"Who says I'm not getting laid?"

From the corner of my eye, I saw him turn towards me. "What?"

I looked over, blinking innocently at him. "What?"

"What are you—" He stopped and shook his head. "Never mind. We should, uh... probably get back inside."

"That's it?" I asked. "We're done talking?"

"What else would you want to talk about?"

I shrugged, glancing down at my hands. "I thought maybe you were going to apologize."

"Apologize for what?"

"Last night."

"You want me to apologize for trying to tell you he's a cheater?"

"Not that." I looked up at him. "The other thing. Before you left."

He stared at me, then realized what I meant. His tongue poked out as he wetted his lips, which was just... just fucking *sinful* of him.

"Nah," he said. "I was well within my rights to get back at you for that little stunt you pulled."

"What stunt?" I asked.

His eyes flicked down. "You think I was going to let you get away with kneeling down and teasing me like that?"

"Like you would've wanted anything."

A slow smirk spread across his face, the corners of his dark brown eyes crinkling as he looked at me.

"When you were sitting there acting like it was payback or something you owed me? No. But any other situation where I had you on your knees in front of me with your tits hanging out of that robe? I would've wanted something, Teacup." He flicked his eyes down again, then back up. "In the most disrespectful way."

I stared at him, frozen in place as his dark eyes bored into mine. My mouth was dry, as was my throat.

But other parts of me... well.

Other parts were not dry at all.

"What are you saying?" I whispered, and my voice shook.

He smiled, but didn't respond to my question.

"I'll see you inside," he said, then in one fluid motion, he stood up and walked away, leaving me shaken on that bench with my eyes wide and my panties damp.

Part 4

Confession: If no one else loves you right, do it yourself.

Chapter
Twenty-Three

MILLIE WAS BEING A complete bitch.

Which was fair, seeing as she was a dog and all.

"Girl," I said as I trudged across the beach towards the tennis ball lying abandoned in the sand. "You're supposed to be doing this part. Not me."

The little white dog looked up at me with her big brown eyes and boofed, then emphatically wiggled her butt.

"Don't distract me with those butt wiggles."

"That's what Mr. Leopard Print said this weekend," Chuck said on the other end of the phone.

"And I bet you listened just as well as Millie is," I muttered. "Just a sec. I need to grab her ball before someone else does."

Millie picked that moment to rush ahead of me towards her ball. I stopped, raising my eyebrows as I waited to see if she'd fucking *fetch* it.

"That's closer," I said as she veered off-course and picked up an abandoned stick ten feet away from the ball before turning around and beelining back towards me. She bounded up, bumped her head against my shin, then dropped the stick and looked up at me expectantly. I twisted my mouth to the side.

"If I bend down to pick this up, are you going to snatch it away and take off again?" I asked.

Millie boofed, then wagged her tail.

"Okay, but if you do, I'm going to be annoyed," I said.

She boofed again.

I bent down.

She snatched the stick and took off. Sighing, I started trudging again, making my way towards the tennis ball she'd abandoned to play with a fucking stick.

I hadn't intended to walk Millie after getting back from Burnsley. My intent had been to go home, throw all my stuff in the laundry, then lie on the couch with a beer while I alternated between napping and watching something mindlessly entertaining enough to distract me from the weekend I'd had. It had been something I'd been looking forward to from the moment I'd woken up that morning.

So of course, Zain ruined it.

At least, I blamed Zain for the unremitting wave of restlessness that washed over me. It was his fault I was on edge, obviously. I could have blamed Brad, of course, but I blamed Brad for most things that went wrong in my life, so I figured I'd change it up. Live a little. Blame Zain fucking Hameed for my inability to turn my mind off or sit still.

I'd tried everything to get over the restlessness. Eating. Showering. Eating again. Scrolling through eight thousand movies on three different streaming services trying to find something that would capture my attention. But nothing got rid of that crawling sensation of agitation.

So I figured maybe a walk with Millie would help.

"The fuck you doing here so early?" Dottie asked when she opened her door.

"I'm bored," I said.

"You know, when my kids said they were bored, that was when the mop bucket and toothbrushes came out."

"Thank God I'm not your kid."

"You sure? Sparkling grout can do wonders for boredom." She started to turn around, leaning heavily on her cane. "If you're quick about it, you can get both bathrooms done."

"Trust me, I don't like you enough to scrub your bathrooms, Mrs. Price," I said. "Does Millie need a walk or not?"

Dottie cackled and slapped a dark brown hand against the wall. "Damn, Tessa. Something's got you being an extra crispy bitch today."

I laughed. Or at least, I tried to laugh. Apparently, my laugh was not very convincing and she frowned.

"Of all the things I've said about you over the years, I didn't think that would be the thing that went too far," she said.

"It wasn't," I said. "It was fine. I laughed. See?"

And I forced another laugh.

"Mmm," Dottie said, the sound coming out in a low, unimpressed grunt. "What's got you down, Tessa?"

"Nothing," I said, probably a bit too quickly. "It's just one of those days. I thought a walk might help."

"Work stuff?" she guessed. "A paint shortage? Too many people recycling so not enough trash left for your garbage art?"

I chuckled and shook my head. "Really, nothing's wrong."

"Ahh," she said. "So it's boy troubles."

I rolled my eyes. "I'm thirty. I don't have *boy* troubles."

She snorted. "Whatever. Man troubles, then."

"I... no."

"Liar."

Laughing, I shook my head. "Fine. It's sort of that, but sort of not."

She tapped her cane twice on the ground. "I knew it. See, Tessa, this is why you gotta date women. Can't have man troubles with a woman."

"You get dating troubles regardless of who you date," I said. "And anyway, I don't date."

The corners of her lips turned down as she turned away from me again so she could call Millie to the door. "Well, whatever you kids are calling it these days. Here, take a ball with you so you can go to the dog beach. Mills could use a good romp in the sand."

Millie seemed to know where we were going, so instead of her usual meandering stroll, she trotted along in front of me, wagging her tail the whole way and glancing back whenever she felt like I was walking too slow for her. Which she did a few times that day, since Chuck started texting me asking if I was back yet and how the rest of the weekend had been. The third time, she'd boofed and sat down pointedly, refusing to move until I promised her I'd stop texting and would just call Chuck when we got to the dog park.

Which was why I was now being treated to a play-by-play story of Chuck spending his Saturday night cage dancing, because apparently it just couldn't wait until after the Monday morning staff meeting the next day.

"Okay, so, Mr. Leopard Print," he said as I kept walking towards Millie's ball. "He's standing there, right? And I'm wiggling my butt because like… I mean, I'm naked in a cage. Of *course* I'm wiggling my butt."

"I still don't understand why you were naked in the cage in the first place," I said.

"Oh, for old times' sake," he said. "Modelling at Brenda's studio gave me one of those nostalgic itches I couldn't help but scratch."

"As long as you weren't scratching it while you were in the cage," I said.

"Oh, absolutely not," Chuck said, his voice low and serious. "They have very strict rules about touching yourself in the cages. Like, this one guy in the one across from me got kicked out because—well, I mean, you can guess. But he didn't know. He was young, right? Most of them are.

Like, I was the oldest guy in there by a few years, but you know what, Tessa? I was one of the most popular ones. I still got it."

"I just bet you do."

"And you think Mr. Leopard Print would have recognized that," he continued. "But no. He was perfectly content to flirt and flirt and flirt and when I finally got *out* of the cage so we could touch without one of us having to stick a limb through the bars, he took off!"

"Maybe he had a fetish or something. Like he needed the cage to be into it."

Chuck scoffed. "He could've just said that. But like, whatever. His loss. I mean, he probably wouldn't have made me eggs in the morning, you know? Good riddance."

"Yeah." I bent down to pick up Millie's tennis ball, though I had to pause when she shoved her head into my palm and demanded scritchies. "You deserve better."

"Okay, Tessa Michelle Lane," Chuck said sharply. "What are you not telling me?"

I finished scritching Millie's ears and frowned as I straightened up. "What?"

"You're not telling me something," he repeated.

"That's an unfair standard to hold me to. Of course I wasn't telling you something. I wasn't the one talking."

"And you also just agreed that I was too good for Mr. Leopard Print instead of telling me to take what I can get, which means something is *very* wrong. So what is it?"

"Nothing."

"Tessa."

"Nothing's wrong, Chuck."

"Did you murder someone?"

I burst out laughing. "What?"

"Come on. You're acting weird and being defensive after spending three days in a remote mountain location... Who was it, Tessa? Did he have it coming? Was he to blame? Would I have done the same? Was it Lipschitz?"

"Okay, Chicago," I said. "Burnsley's not that remote. I mean, the town sort of is, but there's a bunch of people that live there."

"I'm not hearing a no."

"No, but I wouldn't admit it to you if I had, now, would I?"

"Well, no, but—You know what, not the point. What happened?"

I sighed. "There's nothing to—"

"Tell me right now or I swear I'll call Brad myself."

"Excuse me? What makes you think Brad has anything to do with this?"

"Let's see," Chuck said, unimpressed. "Well, first, Brad is the thing that has the most negative impact on your life. He's also approximately the only person in the world who would make me go from 'you're on your own and I'll miss you while you're in prison' to 'I'll help you bury the body.' And the last meaningful thing I heard from you was that you agreed to be a bridesmaid in your brother's wedding and then immediately told your family you and Brad were trying to have a baby."

I snapped to get Millie's attention. The little white dog looked up at me. I waved her ball around, then hurled it forward with all my strength. Millie, unable to resist her canine instincts any longer, zipped after it, floppy ears flailing on either side of her head.

"Oh yeah," I said. "I forgot about that."

"How could you *forget* that?"

"A lot happened this weekend."

"Exactly!" he snapped. "And you're not telling me about it."

"Well, there's not much to—"

"Was it Zain?"

I let out a hollow laugh. "What makes you think it's Zain?"

He gasped suddenly. "You fucked Zain, didn't you?"

"Oh my God," I groaned. "No. I didn't fuck Zain. I just…"

"What?"

"Nothing. It's not important."

"Tessa Lynn Marie Elizabeth Anne Rose Lane, I swear to God if you don't tell me what's going on, I will allow Dinah to fire you tomorrow. Don't think I won't."

Millie was rushing back towards me with her tennis ball. I didn't say anything as she reached me, watching as she abandoned the ball at my feet before running off to sniff a pile of leaves or something near the edge of the water. Sighing, I bent down and picked up the tennis ball.

"Zain knows," I said quietly.

"Zain *knows*?!" he gasped. "I can't believe that—wait. What does he know?"

"About the divorce. He knows I've been lying."

Chuck's dramatic snark faded instantly. "Oh my God. What… how… are you okay?"

"Sort of. I guess if anyone was going to find out, I'm glad it was him. He barely ever speaks so at least there's a fighting chance of it staying secret. Except I think he… well… there might have been this whole kneeling-in-front-of-him thing that I did…"

"Tessa," Chuck said, his voice steady. "Let me be clear. If you don't start giving me details immediately, I am going to drive down to the dog park and use Millie's leash to tie you up until you start talking."

"Sounds kinky."

"*Tessa—*"

"Okay, alright." I wandered over to Millie only for her to take off to sniff something else further down the beach. Resigned, I began reliving the whole shitshow to Chuck.

The hotel check-in debacle.

Brad's inability to keep his dick in his pants for *one* fucking weekend.

Zain asking me how far I'd go to keep my divorce a secret.

Me proving to Zain how far I'd go to keep it a secret.

Long lost Uncle Mike doling out cash and gifts and the knowledge of the grandmother I was apparently so similar to.

My dad's comments about me.

And, of course, Zain coming outside to find me. Bringing me my jacket. Telling him the whole story. And his joke about wanting me *disrespectfully*.

"You think he was joking?" Chuck asked.

"He wasn't serious."

"I beg to disagree."

"Then beg."

"Look who's getting kinky now. Want me to lick your boots while I do it?"

I laughed. "Look, that's just Zain, okay? Like, he's only keeping it secret because I promised him I'd go to some work dinner thing he has so he'd keep his mouth shut."

"What?" Chuck's voice was bewildered. "Why?"

"Because he needs a fake girlfriend to help him get a promotion."

Chuck laughed so loudly that Millie looked up at me, alarm in her round brown eyes. Or maybe she just happened to look up at that exact moment and I was projecting. Either way, I pulled the phone away from my ear.

"This is like a fucking movie, Tessa!" Chuck said when he finally started using words again. "He's obviously into you, otherwise he wouldn't have asked you to be his fake date when he could have asked for *literally* anything else—"

"Not *anything*."

"You got to your knees in front of him and offered to suck his dick," he said. "And he picked a fake date."

"So if he was into me, wouldn't he have picked the blowjob?"

"You told him you were going to use teeth. So no." He let out a soft, sighing whine. "Look at you, living out a romcom in real time right in front of me. Miss 'So Many Threesomes She Doesn't Even Fuck The Same Couples Twice. Miss Fake Dating My Brother's Best Friend. Why does all the cool shit happen to you?"

"This is not *cool shit*." I tried to stop it, but my voice wavered. "This sucks, okay? I'm freaking out. Someone who is far closer to the rest of my family than they are to me knows about the thing I've been trying to keep secret for years. He's fucking with my head and even though he said he would've kept it secret, I can't just *trust* that. People don't keep secrets like that without expecting something in return, so that's why I'm going to his stupid fucking work dinner."

A tense silence travelled through the line.

"Okay," Chuck said. "You're right. I'm sorry."

I swallowed back my burning misery and watched as Millie shoved her face into another dog's butt to say hello.

"It's fine." I cleared my throat, trying not to sniffle into the phone. "So anyway. I gave Zain my number after the party because we, yet again, had to drive him back to the hotel since it would just be *so* convenient, according to his mom. Brad got on my case about what I was doing and Zain kindly reminded him he had no place to say anything. I kindly reminded Zain to shut the fuck up and we all went off to our respective rooms. Other than a text from him to make sure he had the right number, I haven't heard anything. So now I just have to trust that my asshole brother's asshole best friend won't tell the rest of the assholes in my life about my asshole ex so I can keep pretending I'm the asshole who has my shit together until Brad dies and/or agrees to fake his death."

"That is a lot," Chuck said. "Are you going to be okay?"

"Yeah," I muttered. "I'll survive. I'm just restless and annoyed. Like yeah, all the Zain stuff sucked, but being around Brad always does this to me. I haven't had to deal with it in a while and it's not like I can get over it the same way I did last time."

"Why not?"

Millie had made friends with the dog she'd been sniffing and they were playing a game of chase or something. I watched for a moment, my lips pressed together.

"Tess?" Chuck asked.

"I was with Nathan and Mel last time," I said.

"*Oooh*," he said, his voice low and knowing.

"Yeah. It was the beginning of the end, actually." I laughed dryly. "And somehow walking a dog isn't taking the edge off in quite the same way."

"Well, I mean, they might not be an option, but that doesn't mean you have *no* options."

I frowned. "What do you mean?"

"What about Finn Mc-Nice-Dick and Julie-The-Not-So-Virgin?"

"No."

"Yeah, but you said you had a great time with them."

I rolled my eyes. "One and done, Chuck. That's the rule."

"Right, but like, you developed the rules *after* the last time you saw Brad," he argued. "So maybe there's some kind of rule exception for situations where you have to deal with an asshole ex-husband and an asshole brother's-best-friend. Especially since it would help you get all cheerful and on track for a wonderfully successful week back at the office where everything is horrible and on fire."

Millie and her new dog friend picked that moment to jump at each other, then tumbled into the sand as they wrestled.

He made a good point.

Getting laid would help immensely. Not just because of the reasons I'd given Chuck, but because of the ones I hadn't given him, too. Like how part of the reason I couldn't sit still was that I kept picturing Zain wetting his lips with his tongue.

Or remembering the rasp of his voice as he lowered it to speak with me.

And the way his eyes flicked up and down.

The heat of his thumb as he wiped it across my cheek, sending sparks shivering through me.

The fact that I now knew what his face looked like from an angle I should never have seen it from, kneeling in front of him naked save for a too-small robe.

I couldn't sit still because stupid fucking Zain Hameed had wormed his way into my head and was living there rent-free, making me horny as fuck even though I knew he would never, ever do anything about it.

But someone else might.

A slow smirk spread across my face. "That's a great idea, actually."

"It is?" Chuck said, obviously surprised.

"Millie!" I called, snapping my fingers to get her attention. "Come on! Time to go!"

"You're going to call them?" he asked hopefully.

"Nope," I said as Millie gave me a look of betrayal before sulking across the beach towards me. "I have something better in mind."

Chapter Twenty-Four

"I don't think I've ever seen you get stood up before."

I looked up at the sound of the familiar voice, letting my eyes trail up the familiar hands and forearms before landing on that familiarly delectable face. There was an apologetic look on it, but beneath that was something hesitant and nervous.

"Well, it was bound to happen eventually," I replied, trying to look as put out as I could for someone who was faking being stood up. "Just my time, I guess."

"Maybe it's kind of like the playoffs," he said.

I raised an eyebrow. "How so?"

He shrugged, an embarrassed smile flickering across his lips. "You know. When you win a playoff game, you're supposed to do the same things you did before the game so you win the next one. It's, like, lucky and stuff. So... maybe because you didn't sit at your lucky booth in my section tonight..."

I laughed. Genuinely, even. "That might be it."

The hot Bar One server—who I guess had a name that I knew now, which was Charles—looked slightly relieved. Not completely relieved, but enough that the embarrassed smile went from a flicker to an actual smirk before his throat flexed as he swallowed nervously.

"Although, uh, not to be pushy or anything..." he said, glancing down at his hands. "Just, uh, was there a reason for that? 'Cause if you were avoiding me after Wednesday, that's cool and all, I get it. I know it's kind of weird that I was at the class and I thought, like, maybe I should just leave or something, but I just, um—"

"Charles," I said.

"—thought it would look weird if I got up and left after seeing you and I didn't want you to think it was because of you or anything, and if I hadn't been late, I would've been able to ask you first but—"

"Charles," I said again, trying not to laugh.

"—then your friend said you were in the bathroom and I thought, like, 'Oh shit, what if I'd made you uncomfortable,' so if you decided not to sit in my section because of that, I get it and I'll leave you alone right now, I just—"

"Aren't you wondering how I know your name?" I asked.

He stopped, his mouth still half-open, and looked at me. "Uh... I thought because you'd seen it on a receipt or something."

"Your name is on the receipt?" I repeated.

"Yeah," he said, laughing. "Right at the top."

"Oh," I said. "I never look at the receipt. My friend who was modelling with me told me you introduced yourself."

"Yeah," he said. "Chuck, right? Chuck, um, David?"

"That's the one."

"It wasn't to tell you that I was, like, a creep or something hanging around the hallway waiting for you, right?" he asked.

I burst out laughing. "Charles. I'm the one who hinted you should come say hi after the class."

Another one of those sweet, embarrassed smiles spread across his face. "Yeah, but maybe it was because you wanted to be like, 'Never bring this up again' or something."

"Even after you've seen and heard me meet with multiple different couples on a regular basis over the past couple of years and seem to know *exactly* what I'm meeting them for?"

"I mean, there's a difference between that and seeing you naked. I didn't want to presume or something."

"And I appreciate how very respectful you are," I said. "But I promise, I legitimately had to take a phone call that couldn't wait. I wasn't trying to avoid you."

"Okay," he said. "And tonight?"

I smiled and lifted my beer to my lips. "I wanted to make sure you weren't trying to avoid me. And anyway, it all worked out, since now you can sit and have a drink with me. But if getting a tip out of me was more important..."

He burst out laughing, though the sound was relieved. "No, that's... it's fine. Okay."

I waited, but he didn't make a move. I raised my eyebrows at him. "So?"

"So...?"

"Will you sit and have a drink with me?" I asked. "I mean, if it's not too weird?"

"Why would it be weird?"

I shrugged. "I don't know. I've never worked at a bar or anything before so maybe it's weird to drink where you work. Or maybe because the last time I saw you, you stared at my naked ass for a few hours, but I'm cool with it if you are, so..."

He started laughing. "No, it's fine. That's... I mean, sure. Except I don't, um, drink. But I'd love to sit with you anyway."

Ugh. Well, I thought, everyone has flaws. Even perfect guys with nice asses and fuckable hands.

"As long as you don't mind that I do," I said.

He smiled and shook his head, then slid into the booth across from me. "Not at all."

Thank God.

This was going easier than I'd thought it would be. Which was good, because there were a *lot* of variables that meant it might not even work at all. Charles might not have been working at Bar One that night, for example. So when I got on the bus to head downtown and finally put Plan B into action, it was a bit of a risk. And since Plan B was usually... well, Plan *B*, I didn't have a new Plan B now that Plan B was actually Plan A.

He'd looked hopeful when I first walked into the bar, then worried when I purposely avoided my usual booth and sat in one on the other side of the bar, where I knew he usually didn't work. That worry had turned into something almost confused when I smiled at him brightly after the other server working brought me my beer, and even more confused when I heard the manager tell him to clock off for the night and raised an eyebrow questioningly at him.

But here he was, sitting across from me. Plan B seemed to be working perfectly.

"So," I said. "I'm Tessa, by the way."

He laughed softly. "Yeah, Chuck mentioned that. But nice to officially meet you."

"I didn't know you were an artist," I said.

"Oh, I'm not, really," he said. "It's just a hobby."

"That doesn't mean you're not an artist," I said. "How long have you been taking classes with Brenda?"

He sucked his lower lip into his mouth thoughtfully. "I guess about six months now? I used to love drawing as a kid but I'd gotten out of it. When I saw her classes, I just thought why not? So I took her beginner's program and had a blast, then when she sent out the email about the figure drawing class I thought it might be fun."

"And wasn't it?"

"It was. I just didn't know... you know. What the protocol was when you sort-of-kind-of know one of the models."

"It was your first figure drawing class?"

He nodded. "Was it yours?"

"First one modelling, yeah." I licked my lips, then leaned forward. "Can I tell you a secret?"

He mirrored my action, leaning across the table. "Yes, please."

"We thought we were there to draw."

His eyes went round. "Seriously? And you...?"

"Chuck fucked up," I said. "He signed us up to model by mistake. But we figured, you know... I have nothing to be ashamed of and he's a bit of an exhibitionist."

"He is?"

"Completely. He was dancing naked in a cage this weekend. Not something I'd ever expect to know about a coworker, but here we are."

"Oh, God," he said, laughing. "You *work* together? What do you guys do?"

"We work for a shitty art charity," I said. "Brenda does some work with us sometimes."

"Really? You're both artists?"

"I... sort of am," I said. "I don't do much of it anymore. Chuck is more of an art appreciator. But I wanted to brush up on my skills a bit, so he said he'd come to a class with me."

"That's sweet of him," Charles said.

I shrugged. "He's an alright guy. Sometimes. When he's not accidentally signing me up to be a nude model. But to his credit, he got right up there with me, so that helped a lot."

Charles nodded slowly, a faraway, thoughtful sort of look on his face. "I feel like you have the strangest life I've ever heard of."

"You have no idea," I said. "But why do you say that?"

"I mean, you have a cool job," he said. "And somehow accidentally became a nude model. And then—" He gestured vaguely "—the, uh…"

"Threesomes?"

"So that is what it is?" he asked.

I raised my eyebrows at him. "It's not obvious?"

"Well, yeah," he said. "But maybe there was some unlikely explanation that I hadn't thought of or something."

"Nope," I said, sipping my beer. "I meet couples here with the intent of having sex with them. You guessed right."

"Just couples?" he asked.

And damn if my heart didn't do a little victory dance at the implication.

"Usually," I said. "I like that things are no-strings-attached and casual. But that doesn't mean I'm *never* interested in hooking up with one person."

"What about, like, connecting people?" he asked. "Like, would you bring a couple of single people together, or…?"

"I haven't before," I said. "Not to say I wouldn't, but couples are usually easier to hook up with. Why do you ask?"

He shrugged. "Just curious. You're one of the most interesting regulars we have. No one who works here knows what the whole story is, so…"

"You all talk about me?" I asked, amused.

"Not bad things," he said, his face turning red. "Not bad things at all. Molly constantly talks about how jealous she is of you. That's, um, the bartender. Not the one working tonight, but she's usually here when you… well. I shouldn't have said that."

"Charles," I said. "Trust me. I'm not embarrassed about it. If I was, I wouldn't be meeting couples in the same public place on a regular basis."

He smiled. "Okay. Cool. 'Cause, um… Molly… she might be interested. If you were ever looking for, like, a solo person."

I pressed my lips together, amused. "Well, tell *Molly* that I'll keep that in mind."

"I will." He cleared his throat, glancing around again before looking at me. "Um, and also... I was wondering if, um..."

Damn. This was going *way* smoother than I thought it would. I wasn't even going to have to be the one to ask him to fuck me.

"... if you don't mind, and I totally... like, I don't want to be pushy, but can I ask you one more thing?" he said.

"Of course," I said, keeping my voice low.

He bit his lip nervously and looked down at his hands. "Okay. I, um... I was just wondering if you might, um... Like, if there was a way that, maybe—" He stopped and sighed, his eyebrows furrowing almost painfully. "Fuck. I'm so bad at this."

"Just spit it out," I said as encouragingly as I could. "I won't be upset or anything. I promise."

"Right. Okay." He took a deep breath, though his face was still turning red. "I was wondering if your friend... Chuck... is he single?"

I blinked. "Chuck?"

Charles nodded, not quite looking at me. "I... Like, *clearly*, since I can barely ask you and he's not even here, but I'm not good at... you know. Like... asking. People. Things. And when we were talking in the hallway after the class, I just wanted to... to see if he... but then I was like, it would probably be so inappropriate for me to ask after drawing him. But he... and I just don't know... *how*."

"You're into Chuck but were too nervous to ask for his number after the art class?"

His throat flexed as he swallowed. "Yeah. Yeah, I... I haven't... Wait." He finally looked back at me, alarm in his eyes. "He's... he is into guys, right?"

His expression was so genuinely concerned that all I could do was laugh. "Well, anyone, really, including guys. And... so are you?"

Charles's jaw twitched, but he nodded before looking back down at the table. "I... yeah."

There was something sad in his voice and I studied him for a moment.

"Is that something you've discovered recently?" I asked.

When he nodded, even my cold, dark little heart felt sympathetic for him.

"Like, last year, but it's all still pretty new," he admitted quietly. "And I haven't, um... really dated. Or anything. I was trying to ask him for his number when we were in the hallway, but I got nervous and just..." He trailed off, shaking his head. "He was so funny and confident and I started thinking, like, what would he want with someone who can barely tell him my name?"

Well, Plan-B-turned-Plan-A was a failure. And sure, I was a self-professed asshole, but I wasn't the kind of asshole who was going to punish someone for not being interested in fucking me.

"Chuck thinks you're hot as fuck," I said. "He literally interrupted the class more than once so he could check you out and made me position us so he had a better view of you while we were posing."

Charles's eyes flicked up. "Really?"

I nodded, trying not to smile. "Give me your number. I'll send it to him."

The way he tried to cover how ecstatic he felt was an abysmal failure, but it made my stupid disappointed little heart swell with happiness by proxy.

After he gave me his number, we chatted for a few more minutes, probably because Charles figured it would be rude to get me to do him a favour and then immediately leave. Which I wouldn't have minded, since the disappointment of finding out he was into my friend and not me was still smarting, but Charles was a sweet and funny guy. We talked art a bit more and he told me how he'd wanted to be a tattoo artist at one point, but had been talked out of it because he'd been told people like him weren't *artists*. When I asked what that meant, he talked about how he was into all sorts of sports and outdoorsy things and how people said that guys who did stuff like that couldn't also be tattoo artists.

Which was, of course, bullshit.

But even though Charles was the kind of sick fuck who enjoyed things like jogging and weight-lifting, I could see us becoming friends. By the time he said goodbye so he could go home and chill after his shift, I was really hoping he and Chuck would hit it off. After he left, I took another sip of my beer, then sent a message to Chuck with Charles's phone number and nothing else. His response came seconds later.

Chuck sent an eyeroll emoji.

Chuck

…what?

Me

Charles. The hot server with fuckable hands? The one I was gonna go pick up tonight to fuck? Stared at you naked for a few hours on Wednesday and decided 'Hey, I'd totally be into that?' That Charles?

Chuck

That's your hot server, though.

Me

And he's into you. So text him. He was too nervous to ask you for your number himself.

Chuck

Oh my God.

You're joking.

Seriously? He is? Like, hot server fuckable hands Charles with the tattoos??? We're talking about the same guy, right?

I let him freak out for approximately five more messages before telling him to stop messaging me and start messaging Charles, who I was picturing lying in bed on his stomach with his chin propped up in his hands, hearts in his eyes, and pink-stained cheeks as he waited breathlessly for his first message from Chuck.

Me

And I expect full explicit details of all Charles-related information, seeing as I'm the matchmaker here.

Chuck

I'll take detailed notes. Texting him now. Byeeee.

I put my phone down, taking a casual sip of my beer. I didn't have much left, but I figured I had to stall for a little so it didn't look like I'd been hoping Charles would come home with me only to get rejected.

Let no one say I wasn't committed to a charade.

So I sat, nursing the last quarter of my beer as the bar bustled around me, tapping my fingers to the soundtrack of mindless chatter that underscored my still-restless agitation that now had no outlet.

Was it bad that I couldn't figure out how to shake this mood without sex? I stared at my beer, vaguely concerned. Maybe that was saying something about me that I didn't want to think about. Maybe it was a sign that I needed to develop healthier coping skills and not rely on sex to reset my psyche.

Or maybe that was bullshit. Maybe sex was just awesome and fuck anyone who was going to judge me for indulging in pleasure when I wanted to feel good.

But not really, because I wouldn't fuck people who judged me like that.

Or, more realistically, maybe it was Mel and Nathan's fault. Maybe the last time I'd been in Burnsley dealing with the disaster of a human that was my ex-husband, they'd Pavloved me into associating getting through a weekend with Brad to epic, mind-blowing, wonderful sex when I returned to Vancouver. Like the wheels of the plane touching down was a bell ringing and fucking was my reward.

Yeah, I decided. It was definitely their fault.

Of course, their fault or not, it made me think of them, which did the exact opposite of making me feel better. I mean, I tried to avoid thinking about them at least as much, if not more, than I avoided thinking about Brad. How there could be worse people than Brad in the world, I didn't know. And how I managed to find them, fuck them, and be ruined by them, I didn't know either.

I had a type, I guess, and that type was assholes.

Mel and Nathan had been my second threesome, but the first one that had mattered. They were the ones that made me think a relationship like that could work. That my mind and my body and my soul had more to give than one person could handle, and that no single person could meet the needs I had.

That it was okay.

That I belonged.

That I could be happy with them.

And then they'd shat all over that and given me a Pavlovian response of horniness to spending the weekend with people I hated.

The fucking bastards.

Sighing, I forced myself to take a slow sip of beer before picking up my phone again in an attempt to stop thinking of *them*. No new messages, of course, since Chuck was busy, so I distracted myself by opening MatchMi.

> *Howdy, TessTheUnicorn! You have 24 unread messages. Your last login was 3 days ago.*

I raised my eyebrows. Sure, I was popular, but twenty-four messages seemed excessive.

At least, until I did the math. Usually I checked MatchMi a couple of times a day and cleared out my inbox, but I'd turned notifications off on Thursday morning and hadn't so much as glanced at the app since.

Still, even with twenty-four messages, there wasn't much potential there. I didn't bother sending back dick pics to the six I'd received, just reported and blocked the senders. There were a few I didn't bother reading before deleting. A woman looking for a unicorn who was willing to be tied up, blindfolded, and left abandoned in their bedroom for her husband to discover as part of his birthday present.

I pressed my lips together and screenshotted that one before blocking her, figuring if I ever heard about a serial killer murdering bisexual women by luring them into super red-flag-laden threesomes, I could pass it on to the police.

And then, right at the end of my new messages, the one from Finn and Julie.

I went to open it, then hesitated, my finger hovering over the screen. Opening it was a bad idea. It didn't take a genius to figure that out. Not when I left that threesome feeling light and happy and a bit regretful that I was walking away at all. Not when they asked to be friends and reminded me they were open to a repeat session. That would go against all the rules I set for myself.

Rules that were in place for a reason.

Rules that were in place because of the only time I'd spent the night with a couple more than once.

Rules that proved they still had a hold over my life.

I frowned, then without another thought, tapped the screen.

Julie's been stressing about whether or not to send a thank you message or whatever and keeps talking about socio-economic protocol or something and I keep saying you're cool enough that if this doesn't follow whatever protocol she's talking about, it'll be okay, but you know how Julie is. She's so fuckin hot and smart and that brain works too hard sometimes, you know?

So I'm gonna type this and send it for her (don't worry I'm gonna tell her first).

And since she likes lists I'm gonna make it a list.

Reasons why Tessa fucking rocks:

1. Julie woke up Wednesday morning and hasn't stopped smiling since. The girls at work keep asking her what's got her in such a good mood but she can't tell them

2. She feels like a bunch of shit clicked into place for her and that was because of you

3. She hasn't stopped talking about how hilarious and smart and confident you are and wants to be like that, too

4. You were super sweet in how you reminded her it was a one-time thing (even though we both would do it again in a heartbeat if you asked us to) (also I think this is what she's so stressed about cuz she didn't want to make you feel uncomfortable or pressured or whatever. I keep saying you weren't because you would've said something but like, Julie. Thinking too much. You know how it is. Anyway the point is if you wanted to be, like, fuck buddies or whatever, we'd be down. But also we'd be down to be buddies in general)

5. (okay now we're on my additions to the list) You're funny

6. You're hot

7. You give an amazing blowjob

8. Seriously it was such a good blowjob

9. You got Julie to sit on your face which I've wanted her to do for so long and now she's cool with it and she did it last night again and like if they invented a way for me to be a chair but also still be able to have a tongue and taste stuff, I would do it

10. You got a blue Gatorade and everyone knows blue is the best Gatorade

So from both of us, THANK YOU you rock don't ever change you're amazing.

Like yeah we were looking for a threesome but it wouldn't have been as awesome with anyone but you.

Oh and also I was thinking about what you said about how if you could be any animal you'd be a raccoon and you know what? I think you'd be a unicorn cuz you're the whole package and also kinda horny.

K that's it. THANKS AGAIN.

Finn

I stared at the message for a bit.

Partly because it always took a few minutes to follow Finn's way of thinking. But mostly because... well.

I'd never gotten a message like that before.

A thank you message? Yeah. Messages sneakily hinting people wanted a second round? Regularly.

But a message saying that *I* was the reason it was so good? That I was funny and hot and had good taste in Gatorade? It was... well, sweet. And like, yeah, being with them had been awesome. It had been one of the best threesomes I'd ever had. And maybe that meant—

No.

I put my phone down and took a sip of beer.

One and done. I didn't do second threesomes. I didn't take that risk. But on the other hand, Finn's mouth.

Finn's dick.

Julie's tits.

The enticing thought of helping Julie fine-tune her skills and teaching her how to lick my pussy the way I liked it.

I licked my lips and picked up my phone, looking at the message again. If anyone was going to keep this casual, it would be them. Julie was in the process of finding herself. She was just starting to navigate her sexuality. There was no way she was looking for a third person to complicate things. And Finn was just happy to be there, regardless of where "there" was.

Grabbing my beer, I downed the rest of it in one gulp, then tapped the screen to open a new chat box.

TessTheUnicorn

> Hey. Are either of you around?

I got a response just moments later.

Finn&Julie

> OMG. Hi Tessa! Yes, I'm around. It's Julie.

> I'm so happy to hear from you. I thought maybe the message was too forward when we didn't hear back and I was hoping we didn't offend you or anything. I tried to explain to Finn why the unicorn thing wasn't quite accurate, but he wanted to leave it in.

TessTheUnicorn

> No, it was fine. I was out of town and had my phone off. Thanks for the message and I had a great time on Tuesday, too.

> So glad to hear that. I have definitely been thinking about it non-stop jkiuw

I frowned, trying to figure out what her typo meant, but my phone started buzzing again before I could.

> Wouldn't it be awesome if there was a way to like, take your memories and then make them into movies so you could watch them whenever you wanted without forgetting anything?

> And then also you could be in the movie too

> Cuz I would for sure do that

> I've already been thinkin about it every day so I don't forget any part of it

> It's Finn BTW I took Julie's phone sorry

It took everything in me not to laugh out loud.

> Hi Finn. And yes, that would totally be awesome. Especially if they had sound.

> OMG. Sorry Tessa. He said he was just going to say thank you!

> It's okay. Actually, I have something that might help Finn maintain those memories.

I had no idea which of them responded next. My guess was Finn on account of the barrage of single-line texts, but I guess it could have been Julie for one or two of them before he stole her phone again.

> REALLY?

> That's so cool

> Is it like a journal or something?

> Because that's cool too but not quite like what I was thinking

> But if you think it's a good idea I'd try it

> How do you spell meange a tres?

> Uh.. not like that I guess

My phone kept vibrating with new messages while I typed, but I managed to get another message sent.

> Well, I meant more like… maybe we could do it again.

Silence.

I stared at the phone, half-wishing I hadn't finished my beer on account of how dry my mouth went. A minute passed, then two.

Well, I thought, that answers that.

Except then Julie messaged back.

Finn&Julie

> For real? Because yes, Finn and I would love that. Like so, so much. We weren't joking about that. But as much as I'd love to do it again and again, I don't want you to feel like we're using you. I'm just worried because you said it was a one-time thing.

TessTheUnicorn

> I did say that. But I also said we weren't going to fuck Tuesday night. And you were both so fun and hot and like Finn said, I'm a horny unicorn. So maybe it could be like a two-time thing?

I sent it, then quickly typed another message.

TessTheUnicorn

> But ONLY two times. This would be it. If you're down for it.

Finn&Julie

> Yes. Absolutely yes. We're down. When?

TessTheUnicorn

> What are you up to right now

Finn&Julie

> Like… right now? Like tonight?

TessTheUnicorn

> If you're game.

There was another pause before Julie messaged again.

Finn&Julie

> We are. Yes. It's just that… okay, I know you said hotels were one of the rules, too. But I'm on call right now. It's super unlikely that anything would happen tonight, but it's way, way easier for me to leave from our apartment than pack everything up and go to a hotel in case someone goes into labour.

> Would you be willing to come to our place?

Fuck.

That was absolutely one of the rules. And an important one. What I'd said about not feeling like I was invading their space was true, but it was also a safety thing.

Then again, it wasn't like this was the first time. I knew them both. I knew where they worked, even. Maybe that rule was more important for people I was fucking for the first time.

Another message came through just then.

Finn&Julie

> That was dumb, wasn't it? I'm so sorry. Another night? If you're willing?

I should have said yes, another night. And then blocked them because a second threesome was a bad idea.

TessTheUnicorn

> What's the address?

Chapter Twenty-Five

I SECOND GUESSED MYSELF the entire way there.

An Uber was too expensive, I told myself. I'd spent a shit ton of money this weekend on flights and food and car rentals.

Then I clicked the "book" button.

I should just cancel, I thought, then waved to the server as I got up and walked outside when the driver was a minute away.

If I give him an extra good tip, he might be willing to take me to my place instead, I mused as he wove in and out of traffic on the way to some generic apartment building in Mount Pleasant.

I can get out, run the other direction, then order another Uber to take me home, I decided when he parked the car.

But we all knew I didn't *run*.

And even if I did, I wouldn't have had a chance. The driver pulled right up to the entrance of the building. I thanked him, got out, and paused to leave a tip. In the time it took me to rate the driver five stars, the door to the building flew open.

"Tessa!"

I looked up to see Finn standing there, waving and grinning. Or, well, *standing* was the wrong word. He was balanced on one foot, his body lunged forward to hold the outer door open with one hand while he kept the inner door open with his other foot.

God, he was fucking tall.

And God, he was fucking... *fuck*.

That fucking smile was on his face, bright and cheerful and excited. He was wearing a white t-shirt that clung to his biceps and had some kind of logo on the front. I couldn't have said what logo, since he was also wearing grey sweatpants.

Grey fucking sweatpants.

Fuck.

"Hey," I said. "I guess I have the right building."

"Probably. Unless you weren't coming to see us. Then you may have the wrong building," he said.

I laughed as I walked towards him. "Were you waiting for me?"

"Well, yeah," he said. "Julie said you were coming. But while we were waiting, she asked me to drop Alfie off at our downstairs neighbour's so he doesn't bug us, you know? Then I saw you get out of the car and figured I'd let you in, but I don't have my keys, so..."

He gestured towards his foot.

"So I don't get to meet your dog?" I asked as I walked into the building.

He shrugged, smiling apologetically. "Maybe in the morning?"

"I don't stay overnight," I said gently.

"Oh, yeah. Another time then!" He let the door swing shut behind us, then turned to me and made a move forward before pausing and frowning. "Do I, uh, hug you to say hello? Or like, do we kiss, or...?"

"I don't know," I said. "I don't usually do this twice. What do you think we should do?"

His lower lip curled between his teeth as his gaze flicked down to my mouth. "Can I kiss you?"

"Do you think Julie will mind?"

"I mean, she got to kiss you by herself last time, so it's only fair."

I couldn't stop myself from laughing. "Sure, Finn."

"Oh, thank God," he breathed, then grabbed me.

And *fuck*.

It was another one of those reality-shattering kisses. My head spun as Finn captured my mouth, electricity sparking between us. The world faded away, as did my breath. And my thoughts. And gravity. All that mattered was his lips and his tongue and the way he wrapped his arms around me and—

He pulled back, a faint line appearing between his eyes. "Is everything okay, Tess?"

I blinked. "What? Yes. Of course. Why?"

He studied me for a moment, head tilting to the side. "You seem... down."

"I do? How?"

His lips parted, but after a silent moment, he shook his head as though he couldn't explain. "Just something about how you kissed was different."

A shiver rushed through me. The fact that he could tell through a *kiss*, apparently...

"I had a crazy weekend," I said. "A lot of, uh, family drama, I guess you could say. But now I'm here and seeing you has made me feel better already."

Finn licked his lips, the concern fading off his face and replaced by a wicked, flirtatious look.

"Bet we can make that even better," he said, then threw an arm around my shoulders and led me up a flight of stairs.

And damn if he wasn't completely right about that.

Julie and Finn lived in a small but modern apartment on the second floor. The moment the door opened, I was hit with a fresh, clean scent, a mix of lemons and linen and something crisp I couldn't put my finger on. From what I could see from the front hallway, the place was impeccably clean, with sparkling floors in the kitchen and a sink empty of all dishes.

I could hear a vacuum running from another room, though as soon as the door closed behind me and Finn, it switched off.

"Finn?" Julie called out, then her voice started getting progressively closer. "Are you back? There's dog hair all over the top of the washing machine. Can you please go wipe it down before she gets here and thinks we live in some kind of—oh."

She cut herself off as she stepped into the hallway and saw me standing just in front of Finn. Her blondish-brown hair was tied up in a lopsided ponytail and there was a flush of red crossing her cheeks. In one hand was a vacuum and a microfiber cloth was tucked into the waistband of her leggings, which clung enticingly to her curves.

"I promise I won't look on top of your washing machine," I said.

Julie let out a nervous laugh. "I'm so sorry. I just, I—" She looked down at the vacuum and then up at me. "—My mom was super intense about our house being clean whenever we had guests over and now I can't shake the habit."

I smiled in what I hoped was a reassuring way as I slipped my shoes off. "Your place is cleaner than mine and I don't even have a dog. I have a bin of recycling near the front door that I keep forgetting to empty and a hook that has, like, four bras hanging off it. It's just a part of the decor now."

She tilted her head to the side. "Why do you have bras next to the front door?"

"I take them off as soon as I get home," I said. "And I only put them on when I'm going to leave again. Why would I wear those stupid harnesses a second longer than I have to?"

"That's a great point," Finn said, then put a hand on my upper back. "Have we mentioned that you don't have to wear a bra here? Or a shirt. Actually, it's clothing optional at all times. Except when, like, my mom is over or something."

I turned my head to look at him. "And is your mom over right now?"

Solemnly, he shook his head.

"Well then," I said, bringing my hands to the hem of my shirt and lifting it. "That's excellent news."

There was a bang as Julie dropped the vacuum. As she moved into the hallway with me and Finn, she tugged the cleaning rag out of her pants and tossed it to the side, then helped me with the onerous task of lifting my shirt over my head.

"I don't even get a kiss hello before you start getting naked?" she teased.

Grinning, I dropped my shirt to the floor, then put a finger beneath her chin and pulled her face to mine.

"Hello," I said, then kissed her. "How was the rest of your week?"

I felt her smile as she kissed me back before trailing her hands up my sides to my bra.

"Good," she said, unhooking my bra. "Busy. Lots to do at work, visited some new moms and their babies, couldn't stop picturing the look on your face when you're coming. You know." She slipped her tongue into my mouth and I moaned. "The usual. How was your weekend?"

"Better now," I murmured as her hands trailed down to my jeans and worked the button loose.

"Why wasn't it good before?" she asked.

I nipped at her lower lip before shoving my jeans down and letting them fall to the floor. "Just some personal bullshit. It doesn't matter."

There was concern on her face when she pulled back, but she didn't say anything. Instead, she brushed my hair off my face, then hooked her fingers into the waistband of my panties and guided them down my legs. Once they were off, I reached for her, intent on pulling her clothes off as fast as she'd removed mine, but she stopped and shook her head.

"Let me go freshen up quick," she said. "Finn, why don't you take her to the bedroom and get started?"

Finn was leaning against the wall in the entryway with his arms crossed across his chest and his eyes glued to the two of us. There was heat in his eyes as he straightened up and unfolded his arms.

"Yes, ma'am," he said, then took my arm and chivalrously led me naked through the seriously-way-too-clean-for-two-busy-people-with-a-dog apartment while Julie scurried to the bathroom.

The bedroom was as clean as the rest of the place, the king-sized bed pristinely made until Finn guided me onto it. I propped myself up on my elbows, intent on watching him take off those wonderfully lewd grey sweatpants, but he made to follow me onto the bed instead.

"You're not undressing?" I asked.

A lopsided smirk spread across his face. "Yeah."

I waited for him to start, but he got onto the bed still fully clothed. "Um... now?"

"Oh," he said. "No. I've been thinking about how good you taste all week, so I'm gonna eat you out first."

Then all at once, he grabbed my hips, yanked me forward, and buried his face in my pussy.

I fell back against the bed, too shocked to even say anything before a moan was making its way out of my lips. His tongue slid between my folds, dipping just the slightest bit into my entrance. A hot sigh of relief brushed against my skin, then his tongue delved deeper before he pulled back and licked from the base of my slit all the way up to my clit.

"Jesus," I whispered as I looked down at the mop of blonde hair between my legs. "That feels good."

Blue eyes flicked up to mine, the corners crinkled as he grinned, and then he curled his tongue in a slow circle around my clit.

I watched Finn lick my pussy for a while longer, transfixed by the sight of someone so unwavering in his dedication to my clit. A strong hand on each of my inner thighs kept me spread wide for him, his fingers digging in as he ate my pussy in the most selflessly greedy way I'd ever experienced.

Quivering, I closed my eyes, tilting my head back and losing myself to the indulgence of his mouth as he licked away all the stress and worries and restlessness of the weekend without even realizing what he was doing.

The slow ministrations of his tongue weren't intended to make me come. No, he was doing it to warm me up, to tease me a bit, to spoil me and get me ready for the intensity of what was coming next. It was calming, in a way. Relaxing. Exactly what I needed and hadn't known I wanted.

It wasn't until I felt someone watching me that I opened my eyes again. When I did, Julie was standing in the doorway, her lip sandwiched between her teeth and the oddest, most beautiful expression on her face. She was naked, her gorgeous pink nipples already hard and the little triangle of hair between her legs already begging me to kiss it. She watched Finn eat me out, desire and excitement written across her face and mixed with something soft. Something sweet and pure and exhilarated. That look only grew as our eyes met and she smiled, then stepped forward and climbed onto the bed beside her boyfriend.

"Is there room for me in there?" she asked.

Finn paused what he was doing, his chin already shining with wetness as he grinned at her.

"Always, babe," he said.

She leaned in and kissed him, her tongue snaking out to lick my juices from his lips. Finn moaned against her, the sound soft and needy and excited, his cheeks turning pink. Julie's mouth twitched and she brought her hand between my legs, running a fingertip up my slit before dipping it inside of me. I let out a soft breath, unable to stop my pussy from clenching around her, and her mouth twitched into a wider smile as she parted from Finn and nodded.

In unison, they brought their heads down. Finn pushed my legs open as wide as he could so they could both fit. For a while, they took turns, each of them tasting me with the occasional pause to kiss each other, but after a while, he let Julie take what she wanted. He turned his head, kissing my thigh before sinking his teeth into it and making me gasp.

The gasp turned into a moan as Julie pushed her fingers inside me again, fingering me slowly as she lapped at my clit. I tried not to squirm, but it was impossible, and I felt Finn smile against my thigh. He placed a final kiss against the tender skin before surrendering completely to Julie and moving out from between my legs.

"Time to undress?" I asked breathlessly.

He shook his head, wiping a hand across his mouth before moving up next to me on the bed. "Not yet."

I fake-pouted, but reached for him anyway, intending to at least get a hand into the waistband of those salacious sweatpants of his, but he was too fast. A large hand caught my wrist, his fingers circling around it as he brought my hand to his lips instead.

"I want to touch," I whined.

"Not yet," he repeated, kissing my hand again.

I licked my lips. "You two are spoiling me. I should at least return the favour."

Finn raised his eyebrows, his eyes sparkling with amusement.

"You think we're doing *you* a favour?" he asked, his voice low and husky. "This isn't a favour, Tess. This is fucking heaven. And as for spoiling, well—" He let go of my hand and leaned forward until he was hovering over me, his mouth close enough that I could feel his words but too far to kiss. "—I think you need to be spoiled a little right now."

"You think so?" I asked.

"Yes, ma'am." His tongue poked out, wetting his lips. "I think you need to see how fucking greedy we are for your body."

Then his lips were on mine, absorbing the little noise of pleasure I made as Julie sucked on my clit like he had no idea, no *fucking* idea, what those words were doing to me. Electricity shivered through me, sparking where each of them had their mouths and dancing along my skin.

"And if I'm greedy for your body, too?" I asked against his mouth.

Finn smiled and sucked on my lip before replying.

"Tell you what," he said. "You can get me naked... *after* you come on my girlfriend's face. How does that sound?"

That sounded good.

It sounded really good.

Although, it did mean that I needed to guide Julie a bit, on account of it being her second time eating pussy. Which should have been easy, except then Finn started sucking on my nipples and I could barely think, let alone speak.

Biting my lip, I wrapped one arm around Finn, feeling the silkiness of his hair as he sucked on my breasts. I brought the other down to Julie's head, winding my fingers through her hair and pulling gently until she was forced to look up at me, her eyes wide with curiosity.

"Need you to suck on my clit," I said as steadily as I could. "Softly at first, then harder as you go. Then you're going to kind of hold it in place while you use your tongue to flick it as you're sucking. Does that make—"

But I didn't finish the sentence. I couldn't. It trailed off into a throaty moan as Julie grinned and shoved her head back down and did *exactly* what I'd told her.

Fuck, was she a quick learner.

She'd said that, hadn't she? At some point. I couldn't remember. Not with the way she was making out with my pussy, making soft noises of appreciation as she licked. And she was so eager, so fucking *desperate* to make me feel good.

As was Finn.

It was beyond bliss. Every instruction I gave them, they followed instantly.

"Put your fingers inside me. Fuck me with them. Suck on my nipple. Don't stop sucking on my clit. Harder, Finn. Another finger, Jules. Fuck, another one. And—yes, just like that. Finn, faster. Julie, harder. Yes. Don't stop. Don't stop. D-Don't stop, don't stop, don't—"

And then I was coming, screaming out my release as I gripped a fistful of Finn's hair with one hand and a fistful of Julie's with the other. My body tensed, muscles tightening and releasing, my back arching and my feet pressed against Julie's upper back while I clung to Finn as though I was going to fall off the edge of the world, or at least the bed. White edges and dark centers flashed across my vision, stars in my eyes and shooting through my nerves, only disappearing when I thought I was going to pass out.

When my hands loosened and I slumped against the bed, they took over again. Julie didn't move, soothing my overwhelmed pussy with her tongue as Finn carefully untangled himself from my arm and sat back on his knees. Still half-breathless, I looked over at him, noting the straining bulge in his grey sweatpants.

"You okay?" he asked.

"Take off your clothes," I gasped. "*Now.*"

He grinned. "Yes, ma'am."

It wasn't like he stripped down slowly, but by the time he was naked, I'd recovered enough to pull Julie away from my pussy. He pulled off his boxers just as I pushed Julie onto her back and buried my face between her legs, inhaling her scent and lapping at the significant wetness coating her lips.

"You know what we never did the other night?" Finn asked, his voice slightly muffled by Julie's thighs cradling my head.

"Hmm?" I grunted against her pussy.

A hand trailed along the curve of my ass, caressing it before warm fingertips dragged along my lower back.

"I never got to fuck you like this," he said. "From behind while you ate her out."

Surprisingly, he was right. It was a quintessential threesome set up, and honestly, one of the things I loved the most. A cock in my pussy and a pussy in my face, large hands gripping my hips and pounding me hard and smaller hands tangled in my hair, thighs pressed to my ears and holding me in place. How we had an entire threesome without doing it was impressive, but I agreed with Finn that it needed to be rectified immediately.

Except, for some reason, it was like nothing I'd experienced before.

Part of the reason I loved being in the middle like that was that it gave me control at the same time that it didn't. It was personal and impersonal. I had my face pressed into the most intimate place imaginable, but I couldn't see her face. I had someone inside me as deep as he could go, but I couldn't look at him. Their pleasures were taken in my body and my mouth, but I could time my orgasm the way I wanted to. I could come as quickly as I wanted, or I could draw things out, pay attention to the cues, listen to her getting closer and closer and feel his thrusts get harder and harder so I could speed up or slow down and make us all explode at the same time.

That's what I was going to do. I was going to let the energy the three of us made fill their bedroom all at once. I was going to wait until Finn was about to finish and shatter all over his cock before taking Julie over the edge.

But Finn... Finn fucked me up.

Because he didn't just fuck me from behind. He got the condom on, positioned himself behind me, and then revered me. Admired me. Yeah, sure, you could call the fact that his cock was inside me "fucking," but it just... it wasn't.

He wasn't trying to get off. He wasn't losing control. He was caressing me, touching me, slipping one hand around my hips so he could put it between my legs and finger my clit while he steadied himself on my lower back with the other.

And just... *fuck*.

When he kissed me in the lobby, I felt like I was falling. When he kissed me on the street on Tuesday, the world had disappeared. But neither of those things compared to that moment, to the way that suddenly all I could think about was that feeling of fullness, of pleasure, of being *his*. Neither of those moments compared my attention being torn away from Julie's pussy, to not being able to focus on the woman in front of me because I had to turn away, gripping her thigh as I braced myself.

"Finn," I whimpered. "Oh my *God*."

From somewhere above me, Julie giggled.

"He's so good, isn't he?" she said. "He's so good at this."

All I could do was moan a response.

"You both make it easy to be good," Finn said. "I want to be good for you."

"You are," I gasped. "You're fucking me so good, Finn. You're so good."

His next thrust came harder, slightly off rhythm from his previous ones as he groaned.

"Say it," he pleaded. "Say it again, please. Say..."

"You're good," I repeated, squeezing my eyes shut as I rested my head on Julie's thigh. "You're a good boy, Finn."

The noise he made just then was the last thing I understood for a while. That big cock of his started slamming inside me, deep and hard and demanding, and every thrust pushed a puff of breath out of my lungs. It was all I could do to hold on, balling the sheets up in one hand and gripping a soft thigh with the other.

"So good," someone said, and I was pretty sure it wasn't me, but I couldn't fully tell.

Finn made another noise and then my body was being moved. An arm wrapped around my ribs and a large hand cupped my breast. Suddenly I was no longer bracing myself against the bed or her thigh because

Finn was holding me up as he pounded me, fingering my clit as his hips slapped against my ass. I blinked, suddenly aware of Julie sitting in front of me, excitement on her face as she fingered herself because I wasn't, because I'd forgotten, because Finn was fucking me like I'd never been fucked before and I was going to come again.

I hadn't even made her come yet.

My orgasm hit with an intensity I couldn't control, making me writhe in Finn's arms. I needed to hold something, to clutch something, but there was nothing in my hands, nothing within reach, and so all my body could do was clench my pussy around his cock as I wailed in his arms.

"Fuck, Tessa," he moaned. "That's right, babe, come on it, show me how good I make you feel. Let me feel it…"

God, the only thing better would have been if he could've come inside me. Normally I didn't think that way, but with how intense that was… I wanted to feel him.

And that. That should have made me worry.

But I was distracted. I was coming, all sensation and pressure, electric release that shattered every bit of me as Finn fucked his way through his orgasm. And it wasn't until he stilled, panting, his body resting heavily against mine as he held me in his arms, that my thoughts returned to Julie.

"Fuck," I gasped, wriggling away from Finn. "I'm sorry. Come here, let me—"

But even as I tried to capture her pussy with my mouth again, a soft hand cupped my chin and stopped me.

"You can take a second to recover," she said, her eyes crinkled with amusement. "Trust me. I know what it's like when he fucks me like that. It's a lot."

"Yeah, but you—"

"—would love for you to come up here and kiss me," she finished.

I didn't have it in me to argue, so I flopped down beside her and took her in my arms. As I caught my breath, we kissed, gentle, unhurried things that didn't quite seem real. On the other side of her, Finn curled up behind her, burying his face against her neck so he could press kisses to it. I touched every inch of her I could reach, caressing her and kneading her breasts and gliding my fingertips along the softness of her skin, then brought my hand between her legs and fingered her until she shook in my arms and came all over my fingers.

When she finished, we lay there for a while, catching our breaths and laughing as we talked about what we'd just done. I waited, like I always did, for the inevitable moment when Julie would curl up in Finn's arms and I'd feel like an intruder, which was my cue to get up and go to the bathroom and leave.

But it never came.

"Is anyone else thirsty?" Finn asked.

"Super thirsty," Julie said, then grimaced. "We didn't even think of getting Gatorade this time."

"Oh, I could go for a Gatorade," Finn said wistfully, then looked over at me. "Blue?"

"Huh?" I asked.

He grinned. "You want a blue one? I'll run to the store."

"Oh," I said. "I mean, you don't have to. I can just—"

But he was already climbing out of bed.

"Hang out here," he said. "I shouldn't be too long."

"You can cuddle with me," Julie said, scooting closer.

And for some fucking reason, I couldn't say no to that.

Chapter Twenty-Six

"WHY IS IT ONE and done?" Julie asked.

There was something angelic about her post-sex. Something about the way the light from the nightstand caught her mussed-up hair, turning it more of a reddish-gold than a brownish-blonde. The rasp of her quiet voice. The sheets loose around her body, a bare arm crooked to hold the blankets under her chin as she lay on her side looking at me.

A gorgeous little angel, who had to go and ask the cruelest of questions.

Worse, I knew I was going to answer it, even as I tried to laugh it off. "Well, I guess with you and Finn it was more like two and done."

Julie didn't laugh. A small line appeared between her eyebrows. "Yeah, but why, though?"

I opened my mouth to respond. I mean, I had a prepared answer. It wasn't like that was the first time I'd been asked that exact question. I told people it was because I was looking for something casual. Because I liked fucking two people at once. Because I didn't have time to date one person, let alone two at the same time.

But none of those prepared answers came out.

Sighing, I looked at a spot over Julie's head. "It's too easy for people to get hurt."

"People as in you? Or the couple you're with?"

"I mean, both, technically. If a couple breaks up because of me, that's their problem. I don't hide anything going into this. But if I was with them more than once and *then* they broke up, it gets... harder. More personal."

She nodded slowly. "Has that ever happened?"

"No. Because it's one-and-done."

A laugh escaped her lips. "I mean, has anyone you've been with broken up after?"

I shrugged. "If they have, I don't know about it. But I would say it's unlikely that it was related to us fucking. I screen people before doing this. If they can't handle a threesome, they generally won't make it into bed with me."

"So it's because you don't want to get hurt, then."

Fuck.

I'd walked right into that one, hadn't I?

I tried to laugh, still looking at the spot over her head instead of meeting her eye. "Well, obviously I'm more concerned with myself. No one wants to get hurt."

Julie didn't say anything. Which was fine. She didn't have to say anything. And I didn't have to look at her. I'd never signed up for this kind of conversation and had no obligation to continue it. Once I got my lazy ass out of their bed and went home, I wasn't even going to see her again.

The silence stretched on until, without even asking me permission, my eyes trailed down and met Julie's. There was something deep in them. Something perceptive.

Something I would have called pity in anyone else's eyes, but in Julie's, it was just sympathy.

"So someone hurt you before?" she asked. "You can tell me what happened, Tess."

Except I couldn't.

Because the truthful answer was no.

It wasn't some*one*.

It was multiple someones.

Brad was the obvious one, of course. He was the ex-husband. We'd been married. I'd loved him with everything I had.

Or at least, I thought I did.

It was hard to remember how it felt to love him before I'd walked in on him with not one, but two other women. That kind of thing tainted people, made the memories of them twist and warp until you couldn't remember why you loved them in the first place.

And nothing prepares you for that. Nothing fucking prepares you for finding out your husband is a serial cheater.

Nothing prepares you for going to a work conference with him because it's taking place near this art retreat you've *always* wanted to go to, and you beg and plead for him to take you with him until he caves.

And nothing prepares you for the crushing disappointment of going to that retreat, only for the cabin you're supposed to be staying in for the next three days to flood and ruin thousands of dollars of your art supplies.

And you decide you're not going to tell your husband about it until you're back at the hotel because you know he's working hard at the conference and you don't want to distract him. So you go back to the hotel and drag your water-sodden suitcase up to the fourth floor and let yourself in the room just in time to see some sporty-looking brunette lick your husband's balls while a thin blonde woman sits on top of him, stuffing his cock up her ass.

That kind of thing fucks you up.

Especially when you find out that this isn't the first, or second, or eighth, or twentieth time he's done this.

Because he's lost count of all the women he's fucked while he's supposed to have been with just you.

It fucks you up that he thinks he deserves some credit for being honest with you about it, finally. And for always using a condom when he cheated on you.

But the real thing that fucks you up is realizing you're so fucking stupid that you missed the signs for years.

That he's not addicted to sex, but to cheating. He always has been. And you've never been worth trying to change that for.

So yeah, Brad fucked me up, but the reason he might not have been the one to fuck me up the worst was because at least with him, I had the moment of revenge. I had the moment of standing in the hallway of that same hotel just as he came out of the room. The look on his face as we made eye contact. The disbelieving "No" that slipped from his lips as I turned to go into a room that wasn't ours, flanked on either side by the husbands of the women he'd fucked.

Because I was an asshole, too.

The sound of him banging on that closed door as I indulged in those two men, channeling our betrayed anger and heartbreak into each other, was burned in my memory. It had seared away the memories of our wedding day and the first time he'd told me he loved me and the certainty I'd had that he was my forever.

When I looked at him now, I heard that sound all over again.

"*No.*"

Bang. Bang. Bang.

And yeah, that was fucked up.

But he deserved it.

But then there was Nathan and Mel. And they... well.

They weren't people I wanted to think about when I was lying in bed with someone as sweet and wonderful as Julie. I didn't want to associate her with thoughts of them, but I couldn't help it.

Because they were the reason for the rules.

Nothing prepares you for having not one but two people who convinced you that they cared about you. Who made you feel like you mattered. Like you *were* worth something. Like being with them was worth the look of disgust in your best friend's eyes when you try to convince her you can love two people at once.

And when Kira asks you if it's just some weird sex thing because she doesn't get it, you think you can put up with it. When she tries to tell you that you need help because this is *clearly* just some psychological problem stemming from catching your ex-husband in the middle of a threesome, you think Nathan and Mel are worth fighting with her.

Until they're not.

But that...

My heart couldn't handle thinking about that.

And sure, that means being cheated on still seems worse, except Kira can't even muster up enough sympathy to stop herself from saying she told you so before you can even tell her what happened, and that she hopes you can move on and settle down now because normal people don't have more than one partner. And when you get upset because you never felt more right in your life than when you were with two people instead of one, she asks you what you thought was going to happen.

"You couldn't have possibly thought they would love you forever."

And you know she regrets it the moment she says it, but things are never the same again. They can never be the same again.

So you decide that the only person who needs to love you is you. Because no one else fucking does it right. And you *deserve* to be loved right, even if you have to do it yourself.

So that was when I made the rules.

No threesomes with people I knew personally, because it would ruin everything.

One and done, because it's too easy to complicate things.

Never stay the night, because when you wake up in the morning, everything will be different.

Always at a hotel, because you'll never feel as lonely as you do when you see their wedding portrait on the wall while you're getting dressed by yourself.

And never, ever, *ever* let anyone fall in love with you.

But I couldn't bring myself to say that, even as Julie stared at me, waiting patiently for a story I wasn't going to tell.

I couldn't bring myself to relive it.

So did what I always seemed to do.

I lied.

"I'm just not built for serious relationships," I finally said. "Being with people like this gives me a… a moment. I'm part of something without having to commit to anything else."

"It sounds lonely," she said softly.

Her words mixed with Zain's in my mind, so similar and so recent, and I couldn't quite think of a response. When I didn't say anything, Julie shifted, bringing herself close to me and curling up like she had before. She was still naked and so warm, so soft, so…

"You deserve to be happy, Tessa," she whispered. "Seeing each other doesn't have to be serious. It just needs to make you happy."

And fuck.

Fuck.

Her face was next to mine. Close. Her eyes were on mine for one moment, then flicked down to my lips. Her breath was hot against my skin and her nipples were brushing against my breasts and her arms were around me and—

And her boyfriend wasn't home.

"Julie, we can't," I whispered, forcing myself to say three of the hardest words I'd ever said.

Her eyes shot back up to mine, shocked. "Huh?"

"Finn's not here," I said. "It's one thing to kiss, but we didn't talk about... about *this* with him. It's not fair to him to not know."

"He'll say yes," she said.

Anger flared up in me, sudden and intense. "You do *not* know that. You can't just assume because we all had sex that he'd be okay with—"

Without a word, Julie let go of me and sat straight up. My heart hammered as she turned, certain she was going to bolt out of the bed and the room and my life, but she just reached for the nightstand and grabbed her phone.

"What are you doing?" I asked, sitting up.

She didn't respond, just tapped the screen, then turned back to me and held the phone between us, Finn's name appearing at the top and the speakerphone icon highlighted.

"Julie," I said. "That isn't—"

"Hey babe," Finn answered, the sound of a store bustling in the background. "There's a line up, sorry. I won't be much longer."

"Can Tessa and I have sex?" Julie asked.

"Uh, yeah," Finn said. "When?"

My jaw fell open.

"Right now?" she said.

"Oh, absolutely," he said.

"You... you're comfortable with it?" I asked.

"Well, no," he said.

I sighed. "Then we aren't going to—"

"I mean, picturing what's going on is going to make the rest of this trip uncomfortable," he continued, lowering his voice so much that we almost couldn't hear it. "But I can hold the bag in front of me until things, uh, calm down a bit. Have fun!"

So that settled that.

Julie had barely hit the end button on her phone before she'd tossed it off the bed and threw herself into my arms, bringing both of us down on the bed again. A puff of breath slipped past my lips as her tits pushed up against mine, then her tongue was in my mouth and she was shifting so her leg was hooked around mine and I could feel the heat radiating off her pussy with my thigh.

Fuck.

Fuck.

I let her capture my mouth as her hands slid down my body. After a moment, I cupped her ass, tracing my fingers along her hips, caressing her stomach and making her shiver as I found a ticklish spot on the curve of her belly. She explored just as eagerly, her fingers moving with a sense of wild freedom she hadn't had before.

And God, I should have walked away when I had the chance.

But I was so, so fucking glad I didn't.

I was playing with her breasts when her hand slipped between my legs and a single finger pushed between my folds. I let out a soft moan, unable to stop myself from squeezing her breast as she gathered wetness on her finger before rubbing my clit the way I liked it.

The way she *knew* I liked it.

Closing my eyes, I surrendered to the sensation, letting the surge of pleasure overtake the nerves, the uncertainty, the knowledge that I'd broken the rules and didn't even care.

"You're so wet for me," she whispered. "I love knowing I do this to you."

I laughed, though it came out as more of a groan as she stroked my clit a little harder. "Are you wet for me?"

"Soaked," she replied.

"Want a hand with that?"

She giggled and nipped at my lip. "I mean, if you're offering."

I kissed her back, then let go of her breast and pulled away. "Let me show you something."

Excitement sparked in her eyes. "Yes please."

"Lie on your back."

"Yes, ma'am," she said.

I shoved the sheets and blankets away as she got into place, her head nestled on the pillow. Once she was done, I put a hand on each of her legs, feeling the smoothness of her skin beneath my palm before parting her thighs. Bringing myself over her, I straddled her left leg, then moved up until the spot just above my knee was pressed to her hot, dripping slit.

"I... I thought you were giving me a hand," she said, laughing nervously.

"Well, it wouldn't have made sense if I said I was giving you a leg," I replied.

"You're... kneeing me. In the pussy."

It took everything in me not to laugh at the concern on her face. Reaching up, I brushed her hair back, then leaned in and kissed her.

"It's like sexy kneeing. It'll feel good. I promise."

"Okay," she breathed. "I trust you."

Fuck.

I didn't acknowledge how happy that made me. Instead, I kissed her, then started pushing my knee up until she *got* it.

"Oh!" she gasped, and then her hips moved forward, like they instinctively knew what to do.

The kissing continued; the exploring continued; the squirming woman beneath me continued to soak my leg with her pussy as she used my thigh to get off. My own pussy ached, desperate for attention, but I couldn't bring myself to stop grinding my knee between her legs. Not when she was making little noises that gave me goosebumps because they were so fucking hot.

Not when her breathing was getting harder because she was getting closer, because I was going to make this woman come with my thigh.

I was going to feel her legs clamp around mine and kiss her when she cried out and pin her to the bed with my body as she writhed beneath me. And only then was I going to pay attention to my own dripping pussy, to let her finger me or lick me or hell, try the fucking knee thing on me in return.

Because I wanted her to come.

I wanted her ecstasy.

And I was really close to getting it when the door to the apartment opened with a bang.

Chapter Twenty-Seven

"I'm back!" Finn yelled from the entrance.

Julie responded with a loud moan.

"Fuck," I heard him say, and moments later the bedroom door opened and he walked in, not bothering to hide the eagerness in his eyes as he took in the sight of me straddling his naked girlfriend's leg. I turned my head and bit back a grin.

"Come here and undress," I said, beckoning him over.

An excited smile flashed across his face and I turned my attention back to Julie. She reached up to touch me, but before she could, I grabbed her wrists and pinned her arms back down on the bed, eliciting a startled gasp from her lips. Licking my lips, I leaned down to whisper to her.

"You're going to come before he's naked."

Holding her down, I rubbed my leg between hers, dipping my head to kiss the tender spot I'd found on her neck as I did. She squirmed, not fighting against the buildup of her orgasm but revelling in it, the sounds layering and rising as I brought her back to the moment she'd been in before Finn had come back.

I don't know if he was still undressing when she came a few moments later. Theoretically, it was possible that he finished taking off his clothes and then just stood there, not touching his swollen cock as I absorbed

"

Julie's cries with my mouth and felt each and every twitch and struggle as her pleasure exploded beneath me.

But it was also possible that I was just that good.

Because I was. I fucking *was*, and I knew it.

After Julie's orgasm faded and she heaved a huge breath as she relaxed against the headboard, I moved off of her. Finn was standing at the edge of the bed to my right, his thick cock jutting out and so hard it was almost purple. Clearly, he hadn't been lying about getting hard when Julie asked if she and I could fuck. It looked like he'd been stiff for a while.

I brought my lips to his cock, kissing the head before running my tongue along the sensitive spot underneath it. He made another noise, his hips shifting forward, and a moment later a drop of pre-cum leaked out of his tip. I licked it up, relishing the now-familiar taste of him, then took him into my mouth and started sucking.

"Oh my God," he murmured, and a shaking hand made its way to the back of my head.

He didn't push it down or pull my hair, just let his hand rest there as I took more of his cock in my mouth. The bed shifted beside me and I felt Julie move, crawling forward until she was beside me, then sat back on her knees.

"I came home at the right time," Finn said with a strangled chuckle.

"Mmm," Julie said, and I heard them kiss. "You did."

They kissed for a while longer, Finn keeping his hand on my head while he touched Julie's body with the other. Then I heard Julie mumble something indecipherable and he groaned.

Moments later, he put his hand on my back. His fingers traced a pattern down my spine as he curled his tall body forward, reaching further and further until his hand was cupping my ass.

Then, he stopped.

"Tess?" he asked.

"Hmph?" I replied through a mouthful of cock.

"Can I touch your, uh..."

I raised my eyebrows, not that anyone could see it. "Hmm?"

He cleared his throat.

"Your, um, butt... hole," he whispered.

I had to take his cock out of my mouth because if I didn't, I would have choked as I started giggling.

"Sorry," he said. "I didn't mean—"

"Finn, it's okay. It's just the way you said it. You can play with my ass all you want," I said, then shifted my hips from side to side in what I hoped was an enticing wiggle before taking his cock back in my mouth and attempting to swallow it.

He had to pause when I did, groaning and resting his palm flat against my ass for a moment before he recovered. Then I felt a strong finger slide down my ass crack, slow and careful as he sought out the tight little ring of muscle.

After finding it, he dipped his fingers a bit lower, collecting some of the wetness on my pussy lips and thighs. Then he brought it back to my hole and began working his finger inside of me.

And fuck, did that feel good.

Especially when, moments after my asshole clenched around the tip of his finger, a different hand reached underneath me and pushed a finger inside my pussy.

There was no resistance; I was so wet that even Finn's thick cock could have slipped inside me with no trouble. It was enough that Julie added a second finger almost instantly, making me moan around Finn's cock as I tightened around her. That made Finn moan, and I heard Julie laugh as she fingered me with a slow but intense rhythm.

"You're so fucking sexy," Finn said from above me.

I didn't know who it was directed to until Julie's lips pressed against my shoulder.

"I think she is, too," she whispered, and those words... fuck.

They made me tremble.

They made that place deep in my core, the one that had been aching with need that was now being satisfied, start to sing. That spot I'd finally given in to, that place that had craved Finn's finger in my ass and Julie's fingers in my pussy. It was already threatening to burst, already starting to overwhelm me with pleasure, and no one was even touching my fucking *clit*.

Until Julie twisted her wrist and ground the base of her thumb into it as she curled her fingers into my G-spot.

That was it for me. The dam that had been holding back those waves of pleasure cracked, giving me barely enough time to pull my mouth off of Finn's cock and replace it with my hand. Because I had to, I fucking *had* to, I couldn't lose complete control with his cock in my mouth.

But I couldn't bring myself to stop touching him.

"Tessa, wait—" he said, his voice desperate.

"I'm coming," I tried to explain, but it came out in a jumbled gurgle of a moan as I stroked his cock.

"Fuck, I can't hold back, I—" He cried out and thank God my eyes were squeezed shut, because a rope of cum hit me in the face just as my orgasm started.

My body shook, nerves firing all at once and sending bolts of euphoria through me. I forced my hand to keep moving, only capable of focusing on my pleasure and his, determined to stroke every drop of cum out of Finn's cock and onto my face. Another spurt landed on my cheek and a third across my lips and half-open mouth as Finn moaned, his cock throbbing in my hand.

It was fucking awesome.

After the last of his load hit my chin and started dripping off, I put his cock in my mouth and sucked the last few drops off the tip before releasing it. He pulled his finger out of my ass and Julie moved her hand away from my pussy so I could sit back. Before I could even speak, Finn was on the bed in front of me, cradling my face in his hands and wiping cum off of it with his thumbs.

"Fuck," he said. "Fuck, I'm so sorry. I couldn't—"

"It's okay," I said, blinking my eyes carefully at first, then opening them completely when I was certain I wouldn't get any cum in them.

Finn's forehead was creased with worried lines. "I didn't mean to come on your face."

"I liked it," I said.

He blinked at me. "Really?"

His expression was so stunned that all I could do was laugh. "Really. Besides—" I lifted my hand to my cheek, wiping a spot I could feel he'd missed. "—Julie can come help me clean it all up."

"I'd love to," Julie said, and then she was pressed against me, turning my head to capture my lips before focusing her attention to my cheeks and chin.

She did a thorough job, making sure she checked every inch of skin for cum. As she dipped her head to clean up a drop of cum that had fallen onto my chest, Finn leaned in and kissed me, his smile warm against my still-wet lips.

"I am so glad you came back," he whispered.

He let go of me and kissed Julie, then went to grab the Gatorade he'd left near the door. There was a tired, comfortable silence as we all drank, chugging back the sugary liquid and barely stopping to breathe. And after we finished, I closed my eyes, intending to just rest for a moment before I got out of bed and cleaned myself up to go home.

When I opened them what was almost certainly just a few seconds later, there was a blanket overtop of me and the room was dark. Julie was nestled in my arms and Finn was curled up behind me, his breath warm against my neck.

It took me a moment, but I swallowed hard when I realized what happened. Suppressing the sudden rush of anxious fear, I shifted carefully, hoping against all sense that I could slip out of bed without either of them noticing.

Of course, Julie's eyes flickered open the second I moved.

"Stay?" she murmured.

"I... I can't," I said.

"You can. I say you can."

"Me too," Finn said sleepily from behind me.

My heart thudded hard. "I, uh, need to pee."

"But then come back?" Julie asked.

"Um... sure," I lied.

Because I knew I shouldn't.

I knew I *couldn't*.

I shouldn't have even been there. Not in their home. Not for a second round. There were fucking *rules*. And I'd broken enough of them. Staying the night... no.

No.

It couldn't happen.

When I was done in the bathroom, I tiptoed out as quietly as I could, still naked since all my clothes were next to the front door.

And I looked towards it. I did. I stood in the hallway, my head turned towards the exit, knowing that was where I had to go.

Where I should go.

Then I turned the other direction, walked back into the bedroom, and curled up between Julie and Finn again.

Just as a one-time thing.

Epilogue

One Week Later

WE WERE THIRTY SECONDS away from calling a Code Oh Shit.

"Dinah," Chuck said patiently. "All we have to do is *tell* Loni it's reclaimed rainwater and—"

"*SHE WILL KNOW!*"

"I'm going back to my office," I said.

"To what? Waste more company funds?" Dinah spat.

"To start researching if there's a way to decontaminate rainwater to make it safe for consumption," Chuck said. "That way Loni gets what she wants and we don't poison all of our esteemed donors."

"Yeah," I said. "That."

After leaving the boardroom, I meandered to the break room, grabbed another coffee, then went back to my and Chuck's office to play on my phone until he was done. He was still working on calming Dinah down when my phone went off with a message from an unknown contact that I totally knew and just hadn't saved in my phone.

Unknown Number

> Hey Teacup. Got the details of the convention. First Saturday in May. Let me know if you want to fly into Victoria or take the ferry and I'll get it booked for you.

Fuck.

The first Saturday in May was two days after the Recycl-Ball. I was going to be in for a busy fucking week. Sighing, I tapped on Zain's number and saved it in my contacts as *Z Asshole* before texting back begrudgingly.

Me

Ferry is fine. What am I supposed to wear to this

Z Asshole

Something that shows off enough skin to make everyone jealous of me but covers enough to be classy.

Me

You're disgusting. So you want my tits out but not too much?

Z Asshole

Yeah. Slightly less than when you were wearing that robe and a little more than what you wore for your parents' party.

Though if you want to bring something like the robe to wear around the hotel room, I'm not going to complain.

Glaring at my phone, I clicked on his contact name again and changed it.

Me

So I could wear what I wore to my parents' party and pop my tits out a bit more?

Z Biggest Asshole

It's more semi-formal. A dress would probably be best.

Fuck. Now I had to go out and buy a dress I'd never wear again. This was getting worse by the minute.

"Ooo, who's texting that's making you clench your teeth like that?" Chuck asked as he bounded into our office. "Finn? Is it a dick pic? Are you going to share?"

I rolled my eyes. "No. We don't text."

"Right, of course," he said flatly. "Because of your stupid rules."

"They're not stupid," I muttered. "They're necessary."

Because they were.

My old rules weren't working with Finn and Julie. I mean, I'd known that for a while, but waking up next to them a week earlier had solidified just how horrible I was at following said rules.

Which had been obvious when I pulled up to work last Monday morning in a reasonably recent Honda Civic driven by the human equivalent of a particularly energetic otter.

I'd grimaced when I saw Chuck standing there, but there was no avoiding it. He had already seen me, and his jaw had already dropped so far that I was worried it might be dislocated. After thanking Finn for driving me to work, I'd gotten out of the car, a mostly full iced flat white clutched in one hand.

"Not a word," I said to Chuck.

"Oh, there will be plenty of words," Chuck said.

"It's not what it looks like."

"Really? Because it looks like a walking talking Greek god just dropped you off... after a sleepover, if the raggedy outfit and Starbucks run is any indication."

"We're just friends," I said.

Then, of course, Finn had to go and roll down the window.

"See ya later, Cinnamon Spice!" Finn called out the window. "Thanks for a great night!"

I took a deep breath, then let it out before turning around. "Bye... Pumpkin Spice."

He grinned and waved, then pulled out of the parking lot. I swallowed, then turned back around, where Chuck's eyebrows had annexed the majority of his forehead.

"Pumpkin—"

"Shut up. It's an inside joke."

"Inside joke?!"

"Shut *up*."

"*Pumpkin Spice*?!"

I sighed. "We were playing a stupid question game."

"A what?"

"It's his... thing. He asks weird questions. Like 'What would your Spice Girl name be?'"

"And he went with Pumpkin Spice?"

"Because it's his favourite drink," I muttered as we started walking into the office.

"Of course. But how did you end up as Cinnamon Spice?"

"I don't want to talk about it."

"Tessa Cinnamon Spice Lane, you tell me right now or I—"

"I wanted to be Salty Spice but Finn said I couldn't because I'm comforting and soft and I make people smile like the inside part of a cinnamon bun," I said grumpily.

Chuck stopped and stared at me. "That might be the nicest thing anyone's ever said about you."

"Right? Who the fuck thinks that about *me*?"

"Okay, so... you're... together? Now?"

"Of course not," I said. "He has a girlfriend."

"But you slept with them twice. That's against the rules."

He had a point. It was a point I'd already been aware of, but it was a point all the same. So after that morning's staff meeting while

Chuck was convincing Dinah that we weren't all going to be arrested for embezzlement just because Loni didn't know how taxes worked, I'd started making a new list of rules.

First, we were only going to chat through MatchMi. I didn't want their phone numbers. Their emails. Their socials. I didn't even want to know where they lived, but that ship had sailed. Chuck was appalled when I told him, but it made sense.

"It reminds all of us that this isn't serious," I said. "I'm still on MatchMi. So are they. I'm still looking for other couples to fuck. They can continue to unicorn hunt. And when they inevitably fuck me over, I can block them and move on with my life."

"So optimistic," he said in a monotonous voice, but I'd ignored him.

The second rule was what I called the zombie rule, which I told Finn and Julie about the following Thursday.

"What in the fuck is a zombie rule?" Chuck asked when I told him Friday morning.

"If someone gets bit, they have to tell everyone," I said.

"...by a zombie?" he repeated.

"The zombie is a metaphor."

"For what? How brainless these rules are?"

"For feelings, Chuck. The zombie is feelings."

He stared at me, then made a knowing noise. "So if one of you starts having feelings for the other, you have to tell the others."

"Exactly."

"And what's stopping them from just not saying anything? There's always that one guy who hides the zombie bite from everyone."

I couldn't look him in the eyes when I answered. "Yeah, well... we pinky promised."

"*You pinky promised*?! What are you, twelve?"

"Finn said you can't go back on a pinky promise," I muttered. "Anyway, that's not the only rule we came up with."

"Oh God. What else?"

"Whenever we're together, if someone bends over, the other two have to slap their butt."

He stared at me silently.

"That was also Finn's contribution," I said.

A stupid look crossed Chuck's face and he sighed. "Oh, Finn."

"Stop sighing about Finn. What about Charles?"

If there was one thing that could get Chuck to shut up, it was Charles.

"Ugh," Chuck groaned. "He's amazing. So amazing. And so *horrible*. He wants to go hiking tomorrow."

"That's... normal," I said. "Especially for him. You knew he liked hiking."

"Yeah, but he wants *me* to go with him. Hiking! Outdoors! It's like, ten degrees outside."

"So don't go."

"Oh, I'm going," he said. "He said the view will look even better when he's giving me a blowjob on top of a mountain. And then I'm taking him to that pho place near my apartment."

"You two are moving fast," I said.

"I know, right?" Chuck sighed. "Too fast. But I know a good thing when I see it, and Charles's thing is *very* good."

I snorted and we got to work, which meant Chuck got a lot done and I changed the background colour of some cells in Excel. He hadn't bothered me about the rules again until that Monday morning, a week and a day after everything had changed.

"The rules work," I said to Chuck. "No one gets hurt. I get laid. Life is good."

"If you say so," he said. "So who's texting you, if not Pumpkin Spice?"

"Stop calling him that." I sighed. "It was Zain, finally. About the work event I have to go to. I have to go shopping for a stupid dress."

"Mmm. Have fun. I hate shopping."

"I wasn't going to ask you to come."

"Good. Because I hate it."

I rolled my eyes and texted Zain back, a simple *Fine* to acknowledge I knew I had to wear a fucking dress. Just as I put my phone down, the office phone on Chuck's desk rang.

"Hello," he answered, like he always did. "Mm-hmm... Yep, I'll send her up." He hung up. "Jia says there's a package for you at the front desk."

I stared at him. "What? For me?"

"Mm-hmm. And you need to sign for it."

Sighing, I got up and walked to the front of the office. I heard Jia giggling from down the hallway, which meant I knew exactly who was going to be standing there when I turned the corner.

Sure enough, standing at the reception desk looking like a dirty dream come to life was Finn, chatting with our blushing receptionist as he held a small box with a big *FRAGILE* label on it.

"...Georgina's back tomorrow," he was saying. "So I won't see you for a while."

"Aw," Jia said, twirling a piece of hair around her finger. "That's sad. I'm going to miss you."

Ugh. She was flirting so blatantly that it was annoying. I definitely wasn't jealous or anything. Just annoyed at how annoying it was.

"There's a package for me?" I said loudly.

Finn turned, a bright smile on his face. "Tessa! Yeah, special delivery. Needs a signature and everything."

He passed me a clipboard and a pen. I looked down, raising my eyebrows as I saw a blank piece of computer paper with the handwritten words *Just pretend to sign here* on it. Trying not to laugh, I scribbled my name, then passed it back to him.

"Perfect," he said, his voice low and husky in what I knew was an entirely unintentional way. "This is all yours."

Carefully, he passed me the small box. There was no label, just the words *Cinnamon Spice* written in Sharpie.

"Just, uh, don't tilt that," he said. "Or, like, tip it over or anything."

"I won't," I said. "Pinky promise."

"Perfect." He looked at Jia, then back at me, and failed at trying to wink subtly. "Great working with you."

"What is it?" Chuck asked as soon as I got back to our office.

"I don't know yet," I said. "I haven't opened it."

"Why not?"

I rolled my eyes. "Lend me your box cutter."

"Why don't you have your own?"

"I can't be trusted." I held my hand out. "Knife, please."

When I finally convinced Chuck to lend me his box cutter and managed to carefully slice the box open, I had to laugh.

"What *is* it?" Chuck demanded.

I pulled out a Starbucks cup, the ice cubes still frozen and my name misspelled as Tezza on the side. "A coffee."

He raised his eyebrows. "Mm-hmm. Looks like it's an iced flat white with two pumps of vanilla to me."

"It's just a coffee, Chuck. Nothing serious."

"Right. That's why he knows your Starbucks order and brings it to you at work."

"It was his last day on the route. He's just being nice."

"Mm-hmm. *So* not serious."

"It's not."

"I believe you."

"You better. Asshole," I muttered, but as I turned back to my desk, I couldn't stop smiling. Pulling out my phone, I opened MatchMi.

> ***Howdy, TessTheUnicorn! You have 82 unread messages. Your last login was 30 minutes ago.***

Thanks for the coffee, I sent to my chat with Julie and Finn, then closed the app and got back to work.

The Story Continues

She's still putting the "hot" in "hot mess."

Get your copy of Unicorn for Sale, the twice-as-chaotic sequel, here:
geni.us/ufsct

Acknowledgments

THE UNICORN CONFESSIONS is a project that's been near to my heart
for a long time.

The story itself has been through numerous iterations and ideas, but
Tessa has been a constant. Writing a fat woman who is unapologetic,
believes in her own hotness, and prevails through difficulties even
though she recognizes she's a bit of a disaster of a human being was both
difficult and cathartic. Sharing her story with you is an honour – thank
you for joining this journey and I hope you'll be there for book 2 of the
series!

There are a lot of people to thank for their help with this project.
To Jason Caldwell, thank you for being so supportive, for sharing your
information and knowledge, and for being a constant friend. To Nora
Fares, thank you for pushing me to do better, for being my sounding
board, and for all your love and support. To RR, thank you for reading
numerous drafts of this book and providing your feedback – your help
was invaluable and I appreciate your insight so much.

My beta readers and proof readers: Peyton, Charlie, Lisa, Dragan,
Adam, and Sipho- thank you. Your feedback was so helpful and your
excitement for this book helped push me through the harder parts of it.
Each and every one of you contributed to making this story what it is
and I owe you so much gratitude.

Paul M, Kevin Matheny, centralsquareguy, KW, AG, PM, N, ED, KJ,
MidNyt, RP, Alex, GW, and all my incredible supporters on Patreon and

in my Cheryl's Terrors group - you are amazing. Thank you for being readers, cheerleaders, and overall awesome people. I can't express how much your support means to me.

I am lucky enough to be surrounded by friends and family who have read, supported, and encouraged my writing. Thank you to all of you. I am so grateful for the special people in my life. Mom, thanks for helping me with my taxes and for dedicating yourself to reading my books even with my multiple warnings that they get dirty. Becca and Rachel, the day you got really excited because you saw my book featured on an Instagram account and celebrated with me only to realize it was my own Instagram account made me so, so happy because it shows just how amazing of friends you are. Thank you for being the awesome people you are.

And finally, to my husband, who I love more every single day: These books wouldn't be possible without your love and support. You're my everything. Thank you for standing with me, encouraging me to follow my dreams, and being my happily ever after. I love you, and I am so honoured to spend my life with you.

Xoxo, Cheryl

Join The Chaos

Every hot mess deserves a happy ending.

Get exclusive bonus scenes, short stories, novellas, and more by joining my newsletter: **cherylterra.com/newsletter**

Find even more bonus content, early access to new work, and weekly updates that I sometimes actually do post every week on my Patreon (free tier available!): **patreon.com/cherylterra**

Also By Cheryl Terra

Also By Cheryl Terra

Find all of Cheryl's books at cherylterra.com/stories

Aurora Flats Series

Fate and Fried Chicken

If You Can Series

The Boy Next Door
Kiss Me If You Can
Hold Me If You Can
Keep Me If You Can
Sleigh Me If You Can

Unicorn Confessions Series

The Unicorn Confessions
Unicorn For Sale
Death of a Unicorn

Love Across Canada Series

Get Over It
The Devil Made Me
Runaway
Finding Home

Standalones

When It Rains
Hearts at Play: Special Edition
One Little Question
What Happens In Vegas
Selfish Love
Another Last Call